INFINITY

An Anonymous Biography

NICO LAESER

Copyright © 2015 by Jennifer Laeser
All rights reserved. This book or any portion thereof may not be reproduced or used in any manner whatsoever without the express written permission of the publisher except for the use of brief quotations in a book review.

Cover design by Nico Laeser

Editing by Kelly Hartigan (XterraWeb)
editing.xterraweb.com

NicoLaeser@gmail.com

ISBN-10: 1511442042
ISBN-13: 978-1511442046

For Thomas

I

CHAPTER 1

The car

I was seven years old the first time I died. I was riding a small red bike at the end of my street. Some of the older kids laughed and poked fun at the fact that I still had training wheels attached, and one of the group gave a subtle shove as I tried to ride around them.

The training wheels served their purpose in keeping the bike upright as I wobbled over the curb and down into the road, but the major relief from avoiding such a minor fall was soon interrupted by the sound of a car horn and screeching tires. All I could do was flinch and close my eyes.

I stood perpendicular to my motionless copy, stretched out across the road like a surrogate shadow. The driver got out of the car, ran, and dropped to his knees in front of me, while the kids took off running in the opposite direction. He shook the lifeless boy and pushed rhythmically on the small frame of his chest. I stood helpless, watching his failing attempts to revive the child, and in my periphery, the small red bike lay on its side with one of the training wheels still spinning and staring up at the sky.

The world began to dissolve, becoming something else. It couldn't have been more than a couple minutes, from the time I was hit by the car, until my eyes reopened, but it seemed like forever.

***

When I opened my eyes, I was already choking, sputtering and gasping desperate breaths of glass. I scrambled to my feet, and clutching the handle bar of my bike with one hand and my chest with the other, I stumbled into a run. The sounds of dragging metal and a loose, rattling bike chain dulled the man's panicked words before they were absorbed by the ground behind me.

Coughing, wheezing, and with tears streaming down my face, I kept on running until I arrived at the front gate to my house. I dropped my bike just inside the gate and stumbled around to the back door, where I collapsed to my knees with my arms crossed over my chest. With every stifled whooping inhalation of jagged air and saliva came a flurry of stabbing pains, followed by a burning ache as the last thin shard of air was scratched and clawed back out.

This is how my parents found me, wheezing, gasping, and crying on all fours. My father carried me inside and sat me in a chair at the kitchen table while my mother ran to the cupboard to fetch my inhaler.

My frantic pleas came in desperate half-words, sputtered and wheezed out of sackcloth lungs while the blue blur of my inhaler slowed in my mother's shaking hand. She lowered it to my mouth, plunging the button as I dragged breath and spittle through it, triggering my gag reflex and resulting in a throat coated with acidic bile to be sucked and wheezed back into my lungs during the coughing fit that followed.

After twenty minutes or so, the respiratory convulsions slowed as my body gave in to the effects of physical exhaustion. Once convinced that I was okay and that the asthma attack was over, my parents let me go to my room, where I lay on my bed, replaying the events of the day over and over again in my mind.

I tried to make sense of what I had seen in those few minutes after the car hit me, not only the scene observed initially, but everything else that transpired during this time, which to me had seemed like an eternity.

CHAPTER 2

The mud men

The amber glow from a street lamp outside, diffused by partially drawn curtains, served as a fairly adequate nightlight on the nights that I was awoken by nightmares.

The old cast iron radiator next to my bed stayed hot throughout the night and into the early morning, and yet upon waking, I could see my warm breath dissipate into the cold air around me. I scrambled through the darkness and headed toward my parent's room, seeking protection from the lingering images from my nightmare.

As soon as I stepped beyond the threshold of my bedroom, the door slammed shut behind me, and the floor and walls began to move and breathe. I could feel the darkness watching me, and as I tried to move forward, the carpet squelched under my feet. The wet, cold liquid crept up between my toes as the hallway carpet dissolved into an oily black mud from which *they* emerged from every direction, screaming, clawing at my every movement.

Slick, muscular creatures with gnashing silver teeth and long talon-tipped fingers climbed from the mud, pinstriped by blue light from the small window at the top of the stairs. Thick greasy limbs thrust through the black liquid sending a highlighted spray into the air. They thrashed at my legs, trying desperately to grab hold and pull me into the black, from which they came, as more of them closed in on me from the walls, dripping oil and snapping their jaws.

I awoke, shaking and wrapped in damp sheets. To my right, the old, white cast iron radiator, painted so long ago that the paint was flaking off, was still hot to the touch, and yet I could still see my breath.

To my left, in the shadows, there stood two dark figures, motionless, featureless, and seemingly lifeless, the same three-dimensional shadows that I had seen almost every day since the incident with the car.

I clambered from my bed and dashed across the room, only glancing back as I reached the door to see that they were no longer there. I pulled open the door and attempted to run. The floor again turned to mud and the creatures began to stir.

Thick black arms reached out from the darkness, slapping wet against my legs and grabbing at my ankles, causing me to fall forward into the mud. I tried to inhale and muster a scream but managed only a garbled choke as the oily liquid flooded over my teeth and was sucked into my throat.

I flailed beneath the surface, convulsing with every gulping inhalation of putrid oil. With only an arm's length of visible light, there wasn't time to flinch as the creatures jutted out from the black and began to thrash at my skin, ripping and tearing the flesh from my body.

I awoke gasping for air, shaking and wrapped in sweat-drenched sheets. I turned my attention to the shadows to my left and froze as the two dark figures stood motionless in the corner of my room.

Even after the daylight came, the three-dimensional shadows remained, watching and waiting. Sleep from that day forth came not without protest and only as a result of medication or pure exhaustion. Instead, I would face away from the shadows and waste away the hours, picking at the remaining flakes and patches of white paint on the old cast iron radiator next to my bed.

CHAPTER 3

Insomnia

Over a long enough period of time, sleep deprivation will cause the world of the afflicted to change. Reality shifts and life begins to take on characteristics similar to that of a dream.

The twilight hours spent awake accustomed my body to endure longer periods between meals, subsequently dissolving my appetite entirely. Within just a couple weeks, all puppy fat was eaten away, revealing the gaunt, fragile scaffold beneath my skin. My eyes were dry, bloodshot, and bruised, and they would ache, but I refused to sleep, knowing that the mud men would be waiting.

In spite of my parent's warranted concern over my appearance, I managed to lie successfully about the cause, keeping the self-perpetuated insomnia, my only defense against the mud men, a closely guarded secret. This secret led to frequent momentary blackouts and actual physical collapse, owing to mental exhaustion.

My eighth birthday was spent in a hospital bed following a blackout at the bathroom sink, collapsing me defenseless to the floor, slowed only by the toilet bowl as my head bounced off the rim. I had lain there semiconscious until my father found me and called for an ambulance. Later, in the hospital, when my parents asked what happened, I lied, telling them that I had slipped.

CHAPTER 4

Sticks and stones

I sat on one of the park swings facing the church clock, watching the minute hand tick slowly closer to the dreaded start of a new school year.

The school bell rang in the distance, and I got up from the swing, tossed my bag over the park's tall fence, and squeezed through a gap in the broken mesh. I made my way around the church and through the small adjoining cemetery.

Across the road, the playground of my school was empty. I crossed the road and walked through the school gate with my heart in my stomach, anticipating the reaction of the other kids at my frail, sickly appearance.

***

I crept into the classroom and took a seat at the back. The teacher stood facing away, appearing small and slender against the large blackboard, her blonde hair, cut to just above the shoulders, swayed with every movement as she wrote her name in white chalk.

She turned to the class and said, "Hello, class, my name is Miss Harper."

All of the children replied in unison, "Good morning, Miss Harper."

Miss Harper explained that she would be our teacher for that year and that she hoped to get to know us all very well. She continued by asking all of the class to introduce themselves in turn, starting with the children sitting at the front of the room.

"Hello, Miss Harper, my name is Stacey," a redheaded girl said without waiting a beat.

"Hello, Stacey," Miss Harper said with a smile and turned her attention to the tall mousy-haired boy sitting at the next desk.

"Hello, Miss Harper, I'm Joseph," said the boy.

This continued from left to right across the front row and then the second. About halfway through the third row, I found myself staring out the window, daydreaming about the day that I was hit by the car.

It was as though the force of the impact had not only separated me from myself but also this world as it slowly melted away, degrading the scene. Beneath the blistering landscape, a dark mass was revealed, an organic muscle-tissue-like substance that stretched and twisted. It had the slippery wet look of a serpent, and the world I knew was being enveloped by it, as though turning inside out.

I heard a voice in the distance, faint and muffled as though from inside a cardboard box. I struggled to locate the voice, and as it became louder and clearer, I realized that it was Miss Harper. All of the kids were turned over the backs of their chairs and staring at me.

Miss Harper tilted her head to one side. "Hello. Are you back with us?"

Amidst the giggling of the other children, I mumbled, "Yes. Sorry."

"Well," she said, "what is your name?"

"Zombie," muttered a boy sitting to my left, just loud enough for the kids around him to hear. They sniggered and laughed.

"And what's your name, Dick?" I snapped.

"Excuse me?" Miss Harper said sternly, "I think that you should leave the classroom and wait outside until I have time to deal with you."

I stood up, my eyes transfixed for a second on the smirking face of the blond kid at the neighboring desk, before walking out of the room with my head down. I thought about running for the exit but knew that it would only get me into more trouble.

I stood fidgeting with a loose thread on my shirt and kicking my heel against the base of the wall until Miss Harper came out of the classroom, letting the door close behind her. I could feel her eyes on me as I kept my own locked on the dirt-ingrained, blue and white checkered floor.

"Look at me, please," she said.

I breathed a sigh and looked up.

"You were late this morning, and then you disrupt my class with a vulgar outburst. Can you explain why?" she asked, loud enough to instigate giggling from inside the classroom.

For me, this was one of those times where the only response that came to mind was, "I don't know."

"Not good enough," she replied.

"He called me a zombie," I said and found myself looking away before she could confirm the description.

"Who did?" she asked and peered in to see my face.

"It doesn't matter," I replied in a defeated manner and with tears beginning to well up in my eyes.

Miss Harper's tone softened. "Hey, look at me," she said and reached out to touch my arm.

I looked down to see a black oily hand with long talon-tipped fingers closing around my arm. I spun and fell backward to the floor with an involuntary yelp. When I refocused my attention, there was no demonic creature, only Miss Harper standing at my feet with a bewildered expression.

Another teacher had seen me fall and came to ask what was going on. For Miss Harper, this was one of those times where the only response that came to mind was, "I don't know."

"Can I talk to you for a minute?" she said and ushered him down the hallway.

They stopped just out of audible range and turned to face each other, trading hand gestures and shooting the occasional glance back my way. The male teacher was tall and robust with dark hair receding to almost behind his ears. He removed his glasses and turned to me with a concerned expression as he continued to nod in apparent agreement of what Miss Harper was saying.

I got up from the floor and dusted myself off. As I turned, I noticed that they had ended their conversation and were walking back toward me. The male teacher that I would later get to know as Mr. Copeland said, "Are you alright?"

I nodded and said, "Yes, sir."

"Claire, I have to get back to my class. We'll speak more about it at coffee," he said quietly.

"Alright," Miss Harper said and turned back to me with a pitying smile.

"Are you ready to go back into class?" she asked.

"They're all going to laugh at me," I said and returned my gaze to the floor.

"I'll deal with them. You just come in and sit down," Miss Harper replied.

I followed her into the classroom and took my seat. The only sound was that of shuffling chairs. It was only after Miss Harper had reached the front of the classroom that the children around me began to stare and snigger once again.

"That's enough," Miss Harper said.

There was an awkward silence for a few seconds and then she continued, "Alright, let's get on with today's class. You each have a textbook on your desk. Please open it to page one."

She continued by explaining the morning's exercises and that we would be doing them in complete silence. For the rest of first period, I paid attention to what Miss Harper had to say and got on with the work in the textbook. Several times throughout the rest of the morning, I caught Miss Harper looking over at me, wearing the same troubled expression she wore out in the hallway.

CHAPTER 5

Peg thirteen

The bell rang at the end of the period, and twenty or so chairs screeched in unison as they were pushed back on the linoleum floor. I glanced over at Miss Harper as I stood from my desk. She formed a smile with her mouth but not with her eyes, and I offered the same in response. The last of us to exit the room were me and the boy that had introduced himself to Miss Harper as Joseph.

As we walked toward the cloakrooms to get our coats he turned to me and asked, "Did you get into trouble for what happened earlier?"

I shook my head. "Not really. She seems nice," I said as I put my bag down in the cloakroom and pulled my coat from the peg, revealing the small rectangular brass plaque with a number etched into it.

"Ooh, peg number thirteen," Joseph said in a mocking, ghoulish tone.

"It was the only peg left when I got here. I don't know if you heard, but I was late this morning," I said with a hint of sarcasm that inspired a smile from Joseph.

"My house number is thirteen too," I added through a smirk.

"Really?" he replied, "you must have a lot of bad luck."

I followed him out to the playground, and we stood telling each other stories as other kids raced by, shouting and playing.

***

"I live with my grandparents just a couple blocks down from the—" Joseph started.

"Why are you talking to the zombie?" the blond kid sneered, cutting Joseph off.

Joseph replied with a smirk, "It's better than talking to a dick."

I chuckled, and at once, the blond kid yelled, "What are you laughing at, skeleton?"

He spat in my face and turned to walk away. I lunged forward and shoved him hard. He stumbled, fell to the ground, and then sat staring at the small bloody graze through the new hole in the knee of his jeans.

He stood up with tears welling up in his eyes, turned, and ran to the opposite end of the playground to one of the teachers. Joseph and I hid behind a large group of kids and peered around to see him stamping his feet and pointing over to where we had been. We giggled and watched as the teacher led him into the school by his hand.

"He's gone to the school nurse so she can kiss it better," Joseph said, and we laughed.

***

The bell rang, and the kids filed back into the building. Joseph and I stood on the benches in the cloakroom, talking over the dividing panel as our coat pegs were almost back to back.

Joseph glanced over my shoulder; his eyes grew wide as he opened his mouth to speak. I felt something wrap around my legs right before they were pulled from under me, driving my chin down into the coat peg with a loud clack as my teeth slammed shut. The boiling heat became screaming pain, radiating through my jaw and stabbing its way past my ears. The darkening scene blurred upward as I collapsed to the blue and white checkered floor for the second time that morning. I cupped my hand to my wet chin, and it came away, a red blur. I heard shouting and crying.

I opened my eyes to Miss Harpers face. "Can you hear us?" she asked.

I tried to talk, but the searing pain throughout my head smothered my attempts.

"It's okay. We are going to get you to the hospital," the school nurse said, and I tried not to cry.

"You're going to get to ride in an ambulance." Miss Harper put her hand on my head to stroke the hair away from my face, and I closed my eyes.

I think that the nurse was asking me to try to stay awake as her voice rounded out to a dull hum, then nothing.

CHAPTER 6

Zombie

My parents were standing next to the hospital bed. I brought my hands up to rub the sleep from my eyes and brushed past the bandage and gauze now secured underneath my chin. I winced and let out an involuntary whimper as the pain climbed my face.

My mother turned to me and nudged my father. "He's awake, John."

"Your first day back at school was so bad that you had to almost break your jaw to get out of being there?" he said.

I didn't attempt a reply.

My father's smile dissolved and he asked, "How are you feeling; are you alright?"

I shrugged my shoulders in response.

My mother said, "You bumped your head in the fall, and they want to keep you here tonight. Just to make sure you are okay."

I breathed a sigh through my nose and scribbled at the air.

She frowned and then asked, "You want a pen?"

I nodded, and she fished a pen and a plain white envelope from her bag. I scrawled a message and handed it back.

She read aloud, "Can you call my school and let Miss Harper know that I am okay?" My mother smiled. "Yes, dear, we'll call in the morning. Now you get some rest."

I closed my eyes with no intention of sleeping, but when I opened them again, it was nine o'clock in the morning, and my mother was leaning over me, telling me to get dressed and that we were going home.

The car ride home was silent.

***

After we arrived home, my father sat me down in the living room and asked, "Do you remember what happened?"

I shook my head and winced at the scattered pain, agitated like stinging glitter in a shaken snow globe.

"Did you blackout?" he asked.

I shrugged my shoulders.

"The people at the hospital said that you seem okay right now, but we have to take you back to see Doctor Rodgers," my mother added.

Doctor Rodgers was the neurologist that I had seen after several blackouts that had occurred after my collapse in the bathroom. The circumstances of which had left no option for excuse or accidental cause, and it was assumed that the blackouts were due to the previous head injury sustained on impact with the toilet bowl.

The thought of having to undergo more tests, examinations, scans, treatments, and so on, made me feel like crying. I couldn't shake the thought of being once again confined to my bedroom or a hospital bed like so many times before.

I shook my head in painful protest, but my father replied, "What would happen if you blacked out when no one was around to help? What then?"

I sat and stared at the floor.

"I thought that you liked Doctor Rodgers?" my mother added.

It is hard to put across your side of an argument when your responses are limited to shrugs, subtle head movements, and sighs. I glanced over at my mother and with very little enthusiasm, shrugged my shoulders.

"I'm sorry, dear, I know that you're probably sick of hospitals and doctors, but we love you and we're worried about you," she said.

It was pointless to argue. My parents had already made up their minds and had already made an appointment with Doctor Rodgers.

"You should probably stay home tomorrow so that you are well rested when you see Doctor Rodgers on Thursday," my mother said.

On the coffee table in front of me, yesterday's newspaper was left open with the crossword half-done and a pen sitting next to it. I wrote in the corner, I am going to wash up and go to bed.

My father leaned over the table, peered at the message then sat back, and said, "Alright, I'll come up and see how you're doing in a few minutes, okay?"

I nodded, stood up, and dragged my feet to the door. As I was walking out of the room, my mother said, "Don't be sad; everything will be just fine."

I didn't acknowledge my mother's attempt to comfort me. I just carried on and trudged up the stairs. I washed my hands in the bathroom sink and stood in front of the mirror, staring at the thick white bandage and gauze taped to the underside of my chin. I scrubbed at the dried blood on my neck and behind my ears, watching the water in the sink turn yellow then pink as I squeezed out the sponge. I held my head over the sink, cupped my hands in the water and then ran them through my hair, flinching as I came to the small tender lump at the back of my head.

I grabbed a towel and patted my hair, checking with morbid curiosity for new pink stains each time I brought it away from my head and then carefully began to pull at the congealed bloody clumps of matted hair.

As I lifted my face to meet my reflection, watered down blood streaked down my cheeks and forehead. I brought my hands away from my face with clumps of hair between my fingers and began to sob. I did look like a zombie.

CHAPTER 7

Boy in a bubble

The meeting with Doctor Rodgers had gone as well as any other in the past, multiple tests and examinations that would neither prove, nor fix anything.

Afterward, I was made to wait in the child-friendly waiting room just outside the doctor's office while he and my parents replayed previous conversations, replete with clichés, better safe than sorry … you can never be too careful … It's always better to be sure when it comes to head injuries, especially with children, and so on.

The children's area was obviously intended for kids younger than me. There was a plastic tub of incomplete toys and a stack of toddler books. I picked up one of the books and thumbed through it with little interest. It was a book of old nursery rhymes, *Little Boy Blue, Jack and Jill and Jack Be Nimble*, among others. I had learned to read late, talk late, walk late, and I was still only just learning how to ride a bike. The only thing that I had not been late for was the due date for my birth; I was a preemie.

***

Preemie is the cute term given to babies that are born prematurely. Full-term pregnancy is usually thirty-eight to forty-two weeks. I was born prematurely at under thirty weeks and had suffered with a multitude of physical problems throughout my infancy.

My life immediately after the womb was spent in the neonatal intensive care unit, or NICU, in a transparent plastic incubator designed to keep the preemie warm and limit the chance of infection. I was fed pre-extracted breast milk slowly through a tube in my nose that went directly into my stomach and placed under special lights to help my jaundiced body eliminate the high levels of bilirubin, which had turned my skin yellow.

In the womb, oxygen for the blood is supplied by the mother and not by the lungs, and after birth, the blood vessel that allows the blood to bypass the lungs closes. In preemie babies like me, it often stays open, allowing excess blood to flow into the lungs, which causes breathing difficulty and often heart failure. I suffered with apnea and would periodically stop breathing, because the part of my brain that controlled the drive to breathe was too immature to function correctly.

My parents feared they could lose their baby at any time, and so they did everything they could to ensure my best chance of survival. After leaving the NICU, I was taken to a high-risk newborn clinic where the doctors and nurses would perform numerous tests designed to check the development of the nervous system. I was monitored closely for the first few years of my life, receiving periodic ear and eye examinations and tests that would show the development of basic motor skills. My speech and behavior were also monitored to see if I would need speech therapy or occupational therapy as I grew.

Even after leaving the clinic, I was confined to a single room in our home and kept away from other children, just in case they had something, a disease or an illness that my weakened immune system couldn't cope with.

I had gone from living in a plastic bubble, in the NICU, to living in the invisible, impenetrable bubble that my parents had created for me. The problem with living in a bubble was that I continued to grow, but the bubble stayed the same size, and once all of the oxygen in the bubble was gone, I began to suffocate.

***

Jack be nimble, Jack be quick, but Jack wasn't a preemie. If Jack had been a preemie, then Jack would have been neither nimble, nor quick and would definitely not have been allowed to jump over anything. Instead, Jack would have sat alone in his room, day after day, reading, feeling sorry for himself, and wondering what it would be like to be a normal, healthy child like those he could see through his bedroom window, playing and laughing.

CHAPTER 8

The tooth

I returned to school on Friday, and at the end of first period, I was asked to remain as all the other kids were leaving the classroom.

Miss Harper sat on the edge of her desk and asked, "Is everything alright?"

I shrugged and frowned, waiting for the rest of the question.

"Is everything alright at home?" she asked and studied the expression on my face as I searched for a satisfactory answer.

"If you need to talk to me about anything, you can. You know that, don't you?" she added, peering under my hair to make eye contact.

"Yes, Miss," I said, offering an unsure smile.

"Okay, go on, go play." She breathed a sigh through her nose and gave a disingenuous smile of her own.

I hurried outside, scanned the playground for Joseph, and called to him as I made my way over. "Joseph."

"How's your head?" he asked.

"It still hurts a little, but it's okay."

"I can't believe he did that," Joseph said as he leaned in to view the bandage under my chin.

"Who? What are you talking about?" I asked.

"Scott." Joseph raised his eyebrows, as if waiting for me to recognize the name.

"Who's Scott?" I asked.

"The dick, the kid that pulled your legs from under you, the reason you have a bandage stuck to your chin," Joseph said.

"What?"

"I tried to warn you, but it was too late," Joseph started.

I turned and scoured the yard for Scott and ran toward him. The other kids around him stopped laughing as Scott turned around with my fist inches away from his face. He screwed up his eyes as my fist made contact with his cheek and he fell to the ground. I dropped my knees into his stomach and brought my left fist down on his face.

"Does it hurt?" I yelled and threw my right fist at his no longer smirking mouth.

One of the kids grabbed my arm and pulled me backward. I kicked at Scott as he stood up, blood and snot smeared across his face and tears streaming from his eyes. He lunged at me, pushing me backward and collapsing all three of us in a heap. As we hit the ground, Scott's face smashed into mine, and he recoiled with a howl and with blood dripping from his open mouth.

"What is going on here?" Mr. Copeland snapped.

With a firm grip of Scott's arm in his left hand and the scruff of my shirt in his right, he hoisted us both to our feet.

"Well, answer me?" He looked back and forth from me to Scott, "Right, both of you, come with me."

Mr. Copeland loosened his grip and led us inside, to the school infirmary.

"What do we have here, Mr. Copeland?" the nurse said.

"Two silly boys that decided to fight on the playground; one of them lost a tooth," he said as he folded his arms in front of him.

"I see that," said the nurse, "and what about you?" She turned toward me. "Come here, and let me have a look at you."

She had her glasses balanced almost at the end of her nose and had to tilt her head back to look through them.

"Didn't we send you to the hospital earlier this week?" she asked rhetorically, shaking her head. "Your cheek is bleeding a little"—she pressed two rubber-gloved thumbs against my left cheek—"and what's this?"

"Well, Mr. Copeland, I think we've found the tooth," the nurse said.

Mr. Copeland leaned in, squinting at my cheek. "Looks like you've earned yourself another trip to the hospital for a tetanus shot."

"So, do you want to tell me why you were fighting in the first place?" he asked.

Scott spat, "It was him; he ran up and just hit me for nothing."

"He pulled my legs off of the bench on my first day. That's why I have this bandage on my chin and a lump on the back of my head," I snapped.

"Is that true?" Mr. Copeland asked as he looked down at Scott.

"He pushed me," Scott sobbed.

"Alright, I've heard enough. I'm going to call their parents while you finish getting them cleaned up," he said.

The nurse gave a nod and continued to clean the blood from Scott's face as I sat shuffling in my chair, thinking about how mad my parents were going to be when they got the phone call.

CHAPTER 9

Shadows

When we arrived home from the hospital, my parents made me confess the reasons for instigating the fight. My mother said that two wrongs don't make a right, and my father said that I should have told my teachers instead of wading in with my fists, even if it had been justified.

"Fighting is never justified, John," my mother snapped.

A deep frown formed across my father's face. "He needs to stick up for himself and fight back."

"He wasn't fighting back; he attacked the other boy," she said.

"What about what happened on Monday?" my father said.

The two of them stared at each other and then at me.

My father said, "Go to your room, and don't come out until I say so."

I did as I was told without hesitation or question.

With my elbows on the windowsill and my fingers in my ears, I knelt on my bed, watching the world outside, trying in vain to ignore the alternating high and low octave exchange from another fight, instigated by me.

***

The dissonant duet tapered off in time with the fading daylight, and the orange street lamps blinked on outside, compelling moths to gather, bouncing off the shielded lights in response to instinctive Icarian tendencies.

The scene diffused to an amber haze behind a filter of condensation as my warm breath settled on the cooling glass. I dragged my hand flat against the wet glass, revealing the reflection of two figures standing behind me, silhouetted against squares of amber light on the back wall. My warm breath hung like orange smoke in the cold space around me, trailing my open mouth as I turned toward the figures. Despite nondescript facial features, I perceived their heads as turned toward my bedroom door that hung ajar, letting in a soft beam of light from the hallway.

I returned my attention to the shadows in the corner. They began to move, their heads rotating back slowly to face me. It was the first time I had seen them move. The cold spread from my spine, freezing all motion, save for an involuntary shiver.

There was a brief flicker in my periphery, and I turned my eyes to the door. Multiple silhouettes passed by the crack of light, visible between the door and the doorframe, and at once, my bedroom door swung open. Three of the same creatures from my nightmare burst into my room, screaming and snapping at the air and scrambling toward me on all fours, snorting and each pushing, clawing at the next, trying to be the first to reach its prey.

While two of the creatures rolled into a violent frenzy of snapping jaws and limbs, the third leapt onto my bed with its mouth open, exposing its sharp-pointed silver teeth and dripping black tongue. The creature lurched forward, snapping its jaws at my face, and I flinched, recoiling toward the window with my arms tight to the side of my head.

There was an intense rush of pain. I opened my eyes and snatched my chin up off my arms, folded on the damp windowsill. I whipped my gaze around to the door and breathed a sigh of relief; it was closed and the mud men were gone.

I climbed inside of the covers and stared at the two shadowed figures, still standing in the corner of my room, somehow able to survive beyond my nightmares to share my reality.

CHAPTER 10

Permission

When I arrived at home from school on Friday, my mother was in the kitchen preparing dinner, and my father was sitting on a chair at the kitchen table reading the newspaper. I dropped my bag by the back door.

"How was school?" my mother asked.

"Joseph asked if I could go to his house after school but I didn't think that you'd let me, so I asked him if he wanted to come here tomorrow, is that okay?" I asked, barely stopping to take a breath.

"I don't see why not," my mother said.

"You should have asked first," my father said from behind the newspaper.

"I know, I'm sorry, I will next time," I said.

"What time is he coming?" my mother asked.

"I don't know, but he said he's going to bring his bike and we can go for a bike ride," I said.

My mother frowned and asked, "A bike ride? Where?"

"I don't know, but I was wondering if Dad could take the training wheels off my bike before he comes. I don't want Joseph to think that I'm a baby," I said.

My father folded his newspaper. "If you give me a hand, then maybe we can get it done before dinner."

I smiled and ran to get my bike.

***

My father got me to hold the bike steady while he unbolted the training wheels and reset the loose chain. When it was done, he told me to try it out. My first attempt ended in a wobble and with me falling into the fence between the neighbor's yard and ours.

"Get up and try again; you'll get the hang of it, and don't tell your mother you fell off, she'll only worry," he said and returned into the house.

I continued to practice until my mother called me for dinner. I leaned my bike up against the wall of the house and went inside.

"I don't like the idea of you riding your bike off somewhere that you don't know," my mother said, "What if you get hurt or lost?"

"Joseph knows his way around. I'll be fine, Mom," I replied.

"Maybe you should stay out front of the house," she said.

"But Mom," I started.

"You can't keep him wrapped up in cotton wool forever, Helen," my father added.

My mother dropped the roasting pan down on the table, hard enough to rattle the cutlery, the echo of which resonated in my father's glare as they sat and ate in silence. I wasn't hungry, but ate as much as my shrunken stomach would allow, so as not to antagonize my parents further and run the risk of being relegated to my room for the rest of the weekend.

CHAPTER 11

The lion's den

"Want to build a ramp?" Joseph asked through a wide grin.

I didn't want to refuse and have Joseph know that I was scared. My fear was not of falling, but of the subsequent telltale graze that would cause my mother to worry and possibly revoke my newly acquired independence.

We gathered bricks and scraps of plywood, left over from the recent renovation at the back of the church and arranged them in the empty parking lot.

"Watch this." Joseph peddled fast toward the ramp, stood up on his peddles, and jumped about three feet in the air before landing and skidding to a stop.

"Try it out; it's pretty sturdy," Joseph said.

I walked my bike backward in a circle, lined myself up, raced toward the ramp, stood just as Joseph had done, and launched into the air. I landed hard, pulled my back brake, and skidded to a wobbling halt.

"How was that?" I asked with an uncontrollable grin on my face.

"You went farther than I did. Let's mark it with a stick and try to beat it," Joseph said.

The stick moved away from the ramp, a fraction with almost every turn, as we continued to better each other's previous jump. Soon after the stick stopped moving, the ramp lost its appeal and Joseph suggested we go someplace else.

"Do you want to see the lion's den?"

"What's the lion's den?" I asked.

"It's at the end of the snake trail."

"Snake trail?"

Joseph smirked and raised his eyebrows. "It's awesome, trust me."

"Alright, lead the way," I said.

***

Snake trail was an aptly named dirt path, comprised of a series of alternating S-curves that led down a steep hill, replete with small rocks and fallen branches. Joseph started down the dirt path and shouted back over his shoulder for me to try to keep up. I followed closely behind Joseph and mimicked his movements during the high-speed slalom as he swerved to avoid the various obstacles.

"We're almost there," Joseph yelled.

We slowed to a stop at the bottom of the hill, and Joseph put his bike down. "We have to go through here," he said, gesturing for me to follow him through a small gap in the brush as he crawled in. I dropped my bike and went in after him.

"Where does this go?"

"You'll see. It's just a little farther," he called over the sound of snapping branches and rushing water. We clambered through the makeshift tunnel, and as we emerged from the brush, Joseph exclaimed, "There it is."

The stream flowed quickly through a large tunnel at the base of a monolithic concrete dam. There were thick metal bars running vertically every eight inches at the mouth of the tunnel.

"Wow," I said.

"Told you," Joseph replied with a smirk and climbed up on top of the wall where it met the steep grass bank.

I took hold of his extended hand and followed him up. The wall was about four feet thick and had a guardrail at one edge. Joseph leaned against the railing. "It's the storm sewer; it feeds down into the river. Come check it out."

I peered over the railing and watched with awe as water rushed out of the other end of the tunnel and poured down to the river about twenty feet below.

"I heard that a kid fell into the river, hit those rocks down there, and drowned," Joseph said.

"Is that true?"

"It's just what I heard," he replied with a shrug.

He walked over to the opposite edge and sat down, dangling his legs over the side. I moved slowly to the edge and did the same. We sat and talked about everything and nothing while skimming flat rocks across the surface of the water.

***

The air began to cool, and Joseph checked his watch. "We had better go if you have to be back by six. It's a lot slower getting up the hill than it is coming down."

We climbed back through the brush, picked up our bikes, and started the long walk, pushing our bikes back up the dirt trail.

CHAPTER 12

Made of glass

We arrived back at my house just before six. My mother must have heard the squeak of the front gate because she was waiting at the back door when we wheeled our bikes into the yard.

"How was your bike ride?" my mother asked.

"It was great. We rode around the park for a bit and then—" I started.

"Then we rode down to my house," Joseph interjected.

"Where do you live, Joseph?" my mother asked.

"Just down past the school," he replied.

"Do you want to stay for dinner?" my mother asked.

"No, thank you. My nana is expecting me back," Joseph said.

"Okay, maybe another time then." My mother turned to me. "Dinner will be ready in twenty minutes so put your bike away and go wash up."

"Okay, Mom," I replied.

My mother walked back into the kitchen, and Joseph followed me to the shed at the back of the house.

"I figured you would get into trouble if you told her where we really went," Joseph whispered.

"You're smarter than you look," I replied with a grin.

He smiled. "I told my nana that I would be back around dinnertime, so I should probably get going." We said goodbye, and Joseph grabbed his bike and left.

I washed up and returned to the kitchen as my mother was putting dinner on the table. "So you had fun today?"

"Yeah." I took a seat at the table.

"Joseph seems like a nice boy."

"Yeah, he's my best friend," I said with a smile, "Where's Dad?"

"Your father had to go out for a while."

"Where?" I asked.

"Eat your dinner before it gets cold," my mother snapped and turned away. She breathed a sigh and returned to me with a practiced smile. "There's some apple pie for dessert."

I mirrored her smile with equal conviction and picked through the food on my plate as my mother busied herself with the dishes in the sink. I refused dessert and retired to my room.

***

I watched through my bedroom window as my father pushed open the gate and staggered up the front path. Within minutes, my parents began arguing, loud enough that I could make out almost every word.

"You walk out and then come back drunk? That's great, John," my mother yelled.

"Well, I wasn't going to sit there and listen to you harping on about how fragile our little boy is," my father slurred in response.

"Harping on? I'm worried about our son," she blurted.

"I worry about him too, but he's not made of glass. He's not going to break. Every other kid his age is out having fun. He's not a baby anymore; when are you going to realize that?"

A door slammed shut, followed by the rapid stomping of feet, growing louder on the stairs. My mother's sobbing was momentarily harmonized by the squeak of the front gate.

Children often blame themselves when their parents argue, but in my case, the blame was not misplaced—they were fighting because of me. I lay on my bed for hours, listening for the gate as my mind churned over my parents words.

***

It was almost four A.M., and my father still hadn't returned. I crept down the stairs, into the kitchen, filled my school bag with various cans from the cupboard, and exited quietly through the back door. I wanted to get as far away as possible, or at least where nobody could find me. I got on my bike and rode to the only place that I could think of.

CHAPTER 13

Confessions

The sound of snapping twigs and branches caught my attention over the sound of the river rushing beneath me. Joseph crawled out of the small brush tunnel, stood and brushed the leaves and dirt off his clothes.

"I guessed you'd be here," Joseph said as he climbed up onto the concrete ledge.

"Did you go to my house?"

"Yeah, your mom said she didn't know where you'd gone and asked if I knew where you might be," Joseph replied.

"What did you tell her?"

"I told her I didn't know, but I'd ride around and look for you. I figured you would be here, but if you wanted her to know that, then you would have told her where you were going before you took off," he said.

Joseph grinned as he peered down at the cans of food sitting in my unzipped school bag. "You planning to stay here for a while?"

"I wasn't really thinking. I just grabbed whatever," I replied.

"Do you have a can opener?" he asked.

A smile appeared on my face as I realized how ridiculous the whole thing must have seemed. I shook my head, and we both began to chuckle.

"There's one on my knife. Let's see what you got." Joseph laughed as he rummaged through the bag. "You were going to live on canned tomatoes?"

"It was dark when I left." I shrugged.

"Oh, here we go," he said, retrieving a can of ravioli.

"I did grab matches," I offered as consolation.

"Alright, let's make a fire. I'll grab some sticks and then we'll have us a canned feast." Joseph jumped down to the riverbank and began to gather sticks.

***

While we made a fire, I told him what had happened the previous night. Joseph removed the top from one of the cans and centered it within the flames as I confessed the details of my inexperienced, over-protected childhood.

"So your parents don't let you out at all?" he asked. "You must get really bored."

I shrugged my shoulders and gestured to the bubbling can. "Does that mean it's done?"

"Yeah." Joseph carefully picked up the can using two sticks and placed it down on the concrete. "We should probably let it cool down for a minute." He whittled a stick to a point and handed it to me. "Here's your fork."

I took the stick and stabbed it into the steaming contents of the can while he worked on making another. "It works," I said as I retrieved the speared pasta parcel.

"I wish that my parents would just let me be normal."

"I never knew my parents," Joseph replied, "My mom died in a car crash when I was a baby."

"What about your dad, was he in the car too?"

Joseph squirmed a little. "No, he was at home looking after me, I think. My Nana told me that he was such a mess after finding out about the accident that he asked her to take care of me for a while so that he could get help."

"What kind of help?"

"She said that he checked himself into the hospital," he replied.

"Do you visit him?"

Joseph looked over at me with an uneasy expression and stabbed at the fire with a stick. "My nana used to say that he wasn't well enough for visitors."

"Where is he now?" I asked.

"About a year ago, I heard a bunch of kids talking about the empty house on Fern Road, saying that the guy who used to live there went crazy and hung himself," Joseph said and then paused for a deep breath. "I knew that my parents had lived on Fern Road and when I asked my nana about the abandoned house, she started crying. She told me that she'd lied about my dad because I wasn't old enough to understand."

"You mean that guy was your dad?" I asked.

"Yeah, he never went to the hospital. He killed himself," Joseph replied.

We sat in silence for a minute while we finished off the can.

"What are your grandparents like?"

"They're nice. I've never had any other parents. I don't know, it's just weird that the crazy guy that killed himself was my dad," Joseph replied.

We kicked the fire into the stream and sat for a little while, throwing rocks into the water. "Are you going to go back home?" Joseph asked.

"I don't have much choice. I don't really like canned tomatoes," I replied with a smirk.

CHAPTER 14

Spite

I entered the kitchen, and my mother rushed over, dropped to her knees, and threw her arms around me. "Where have you been? I was going out of my mind."

I made no attempt to reciprocate the embrace. "Sorry."

"Why did you leave without letting me know where you were going?" She held me by the shoulders, her words shaking my skinny arms dangling loose by my side.

"What if something had happened to you? What if you'd been hurt?" she asked. "I'm not mad at you, I just …"

"Mad at me? Why should you, be mad at me?" I snapped. "You and Dad don't want me. You fight over me because you think that I'm weak and pathetic."

"What? Where did you get that from? We are just worried about you." My mother's voice reduced to a plea.

"I heard you screaming at each other last night, just before Dad left," I said.

"The argument between your father and me was not because of you." She gave my shoulders a squeeze, and I turned my eyes away.

"You've been sick ever since you were a baby; you can understand why I worry about you, can't you?" she said.

The mental translation echoed, *You've been sick ever since you were a baby; you can understand why I resent you, can't you?*

With anger welling up and in spite of moral instinct and the stirring feelings of pre-emptive guilt, I snapped, "I'm not made of glass."

My mother let go of my shoulders, sank onto her heels, and began to cry. In my mind, I heard my mother's glass heart shatter inside her shaking chest. I had wanted her to feel as I did, but felt deeply ashamed of my success.

Ignoring the urge to apologize and beg forgiveness, I withdrew into a run, through the house, up the stairs, and into my room. Tears dampened my pillow, and the pillow dampened my cries as I lay face down, wishing that I could rewind time and take it back, but I couldn't, and the damage was done.

***

It was dark outside when the countdown began; the squeak of the front gate, the slam of the front door, and the beginnings of another fight between my parents, like rolling thunder, getting louder and closer. I held my breath and listened intently to the low murmur echoing my father's bark, until it stopped, replaced by the sound of heavy footsteps charging up the stairs.

My door swung open, and my father stormed into the room. "What the hell did you say to your mother?" he yelled.

"I …"

My father's eyes shone reflecting all available light, a glaring expression, the likes of which I had never seen before, and he wore it like a terrifying Halloween disguise.

"Come here," he spat as he grabbed my arm, dragging me from the bed and pulling me like a rag doll into the path of his arcing right hand. The hand impacted the side of my face, turning the room and bouncing me off the wall into a heap on the floor.

He yanked me up by shirt and skin, pointing a thick calloused forefinger an inch away from my nose. "Don't ever speak to your mother like that again, you hear me?"

"Yes, Dad," I gasped between involuntary yipping hysterics and with my hands shaking in front of my face.

"What?" he screamed, slapping my hands down to meet my streaming eyes with his piercing ice-blue stare.

"I s-said y-yes, Dad," I said, my voice cracking and wavering with every yelping syllable.

"I guess you're not made of glass after all, smart-ass," my father sneered and dropped me into a cowering, quivering mess on the floor

CHAPTER 15

Excuses

At the end of the previous week, Joseph and Scott had been made to trade seats in order to keep the peace. From his new desk, Joseph whispered, "Hey, you're not even going to say hi?"

With my elbow on the desk and my head on my hand to hide the deepening, darkening colors still spreading around my left eye, I turned my body to view Joseph through my good eye.

"You alright?" he asked.

I nodded with my hand still in place.

"Move your hand," Joseph whispered.

I hesitated, but relented to appease his curiosity before attracting further attention.

"Ouch, that looks painful," he winced.

My fears were met as his exclaimed response earned a glance from Miss Harper, who was now weaving her way between desks with purpose in her step. I panicked at the thought of having to explain and did the only thing that I could think of, pushing my chair back and bolting out of the classroom.

As I ran down the hallway, I heard the door swing open and the sound of Miss Harper's heels on the hard floor as she attempted to catch up to me. "Hey, where are you going?"

I turned only halfway around and slowed my pace. "I have to use the bathroom, Miss."

"Come here for a second." Her tone softened to that of someone beckoning an injured animal.

"I have to go," I said and ducked around the corner en route to the boys' bathroom, knowing that she would not follow me in there.

I stood in front of the mirror, studying my battered, rawboned reflection. My cheek and all around my left eye was swollen and bruised, and the outside corner of my eye was blood red where it should have been white.

Heavy footsteps grew louder out in the hallway, and I dashed into one of the toilet stalls and closed the door. I was shaking, imagining my father bursting in and dragging me from the stall.

"Are you in here, boy?" Mr. Copeland's voice echoed.

I remained quiet, save for stifled whimpering breaths.

"Miss Harper is worried about you. She sent me up here to check on you," he continued.

"I'm fine, sir," I mumbled, sniffing and wiping tears from my tender face.

"Miss Harper doesn't seem to think so," he said. "She must really like you, to have me come in here to see if you're okay, don't you think?"

"I guess," I said

"Well, are you going to come out here so that I can let her know you're alright?" he asked.

I reluctantly opened the stall door and walked out into the bathroom, knowing that he wasn't going anywhere until I did. Keeping my head turned and Mr. Copeland in my peripheral vision, I peered up at him, but he wasn't looking at me. I traced his eyes and met his reflection in the mirror. My heart sank, and my eyes welled up as I realized that he could see perfectly what I was trying to hide.

"That's a pretty nasty black eye you've got there," he said.

"I fell off of my bike, sir," I replied.

"You're lucky you didn't scrape your arms up too in a fall like that," he said, and I could tell by the look on his face that he didn't believe me. "You seem to get hurt quite a lot."

"I guess I'm just clumsy, sir."

"Miss Harper is your teacher, and she cares about you. You can talk to her any time if you have a problem, or you can come and talk to me if you'd like."

I stood staring at the floor tiles, feeling vulnerable and fighting harder to keep from bursting into tears. "Yes, sir."

Mr. Copeland's clasped hands squirmed together as he seemingly struggled to find the right words to say.

"Can I go now, sir?"

He sighed through his nose. "Alright, go on and get back to class." He pulled his lips back to a straight-line smile and held the door open for me as I walked out.

CHAPTER 16

Human silhouettes

"Where did you go?" Joseph whispered.

"I went to the bathroom. Mr. Copeland came in and asked what happened to my eye. I told him I fell off my bike on the snake trail," I replied under my breath.

"What really happened?" Joseph asked.

"I'll tell you later, but if anyone asks, then that's what happened, okay?" I replied and turned back around to face Miss Harper at the blackboard.

"Okay, class. I want you ..." Her eyes stopped on me and her voice trailed off at you, her mouth hung open as she recomposed her thoughts, "to turn to page thirty-seven and continue with exercises four to eight."

There was no point in hiding behind my hand. Mr. Copeland would relay what he had seen and heard to Miss Harper, and she would inevitably see through my excuse. As the rest of the class busied themselves with their textbooks, the events of the recent days taunted and teased my emotions, and at the first tingle of my tear ducts, I breathed deep, stood, and marched to Miss Harper's desk.

"Excuse me, Miss Harper, I'm not feeling well; can I go home?"

"What's the matter?" she asked.

"I just don't feel well," I said, avoiding eye contact and trying to hold myself together.

"Do you want to go and see the nurse?" she asked.

"No, I just want to go home."

"Is there something that you want to talk about?" she asked.

A lump formed in my throat, and I couldn't hold it in any longer. I ran out of the classroom, through the exit doors, and across the school grounds.

With my heart pounding and eyes streaming, I bolted through the top gate, crossed the road, and clambered over the cemetery wall. I sank down clutching my knees and let it out. The stabbing in my chest and shortness of breath warned of a looming asthma attack, and I tried to calm myself with long deep crackled breaths, held and wheezed out slow, squeezed from sore, aching lungs.

There was a scuffling, panting, and sniffing to my left. I spun toward the sound expecting to see the mud men. As I tried to focus my tear-filled eyes on the thing that was now inches from my face, hot breath pushed against my wetted cheek followed by a wide lapping tongue.

I recoiled, wiping away the tears and saliva to see the snout of an old black-and-white Border collie as it continued to lick at my face. The dog wagged its tail vigorously and barked as my crying evolved to wheezing laughter.

"What's your name?"

The dog cocked its head to one side as if contemplating my question and barked a response.

"Barky?" I chuckled as he tried again to lick the side of my face. "Oh, your name is Licky." I held his head just out of tongue's reach of my face and read his nametag aloud, "Gabriel, what kind of name is Gabriel for a dog?"

Gabriel's ears perked up, and as though by the simple act of uttering his name, we had become friends. I stroked the grey-black fur of his neck as we sat side-by-side, and I let my attention wander to the various angelic statues and stone dominos casting long shadows across the graveyard.

Gabriel lay with his head on my lap, whimpering as he dreamed. When I looked up again, the statues were many but not all were made of stone. Shadowed figures like the ones in my room filled the graveyard, all motionless, but all seemingly facing me. As I studied the featureless faces of the shadows, my fear dissolved, giving way to curiosity. They were different from the creatures in my nightmares; they were human silhouettes, shadow people.

Gabriel twitched awake and scrambled to his feet, sniffing at the air and barking repeatedly as the fur on his back stood up on end.

"Can you see them?" I asked as he continued to bark and growl. "What is it, Gabriel? Is something there?"

"Gabriel's always barking at shadows," said a male voice from the crowd.

I frantically scanned the faces of each of the shadow people until the voice added, "Hello?" The church pastor leaned into view between them. "Are you alright? You look like you've been crying?"

I breathed relief. "I'm fine. What is he barking at?"

"He's old and his eyes are going. He's probably just barking at the wind." He raised his arm and tapped a finger to the side of his head. "I think he may be going a little crazy in his old age."

"Gabriel," he called, "Gabriel."

I glanced around the cemetery, and the shadow people were gone.

"Come on, old fella," the pastor called. Gabriel went and sat at his master's feet. "He's going a little deaf too," he added.

The pastor frowned and asked, "Shouldn't you be in school right now?"

I nodded and stood with a sigh. "Can I come back after school and see Gabriel?"

"I'm sure he'd like that. He likes making new friends," the pastor said, smiling down at Gabriel.

"Guess I should go." I exited the cemetery and trudged back to school.

CHAPTER 17

White noise

I entered the classroom against the flow of squealing traffic bottlenecked at the door as my classmates filtered out for break. I paid little attention as I pushed my way through and made my way to Miss Harper's desk. "I'm sorry I ran out, Miss."

"Where did you run off to? I had people looking for you." Her tone was soft and kind, as was her expression. "I was almost about to call your parents."

I shot a panicked glance and watched her eyes flash at my reaction. She gripped her bottom lip in her teeth and sighed through her nose. "That looks like it really hurts."

I shrugged a response, aimed back at the floor.

"I'm going to ask you something, just between us ok?" She reached forward and took my hand in hers. "Did one of your parents do this?"

"I told Mr. Copeland what happened. I fell off of my bike," I said and searched all around the room for somewhere to hide the truth seeping from my eyes.

"And is that what really happened?" she asked.

Emotions danced erratically in my throat and behind my eyes as conflicting thoughts fought hard for resolution, growing louder to a crescendo of screaming and then nothing. I felt nothing. I was numb.

My mind settled somewhere between vacancy and indifference, and my eyes settled on hers. "Yes, Miss, that's what really happened," I said and took back my hand.

"Okay." She spoke in a whisper and leaned back into her chair.

***

I spent the remainder of break alone in the cloakroom, not thinking or feeling, just sitting, staring at the blank space in front of my eyes and breathing to the rhythm of blood pumping hard through my veins.

When the bell rang, signaling the end of break, I walked back into class and took my seat, and a minute later, my classmates flooded in.

Joseph tapped me on the shoulder before sitting down at his desk. "Where were you?"

"What happened? What's going on?" he asked, "Hey, are you even listening to me?"

"Nothing happened," I replied, my eyes fixed forward.

"Are you alright?" He leaned over his desk and into my periphery.

"I'm fine," I said.

An awkward silence evolved to an electric hum. Stacey raised her hand to get Miss Harper's attention, and they began to converse in a language translated as white noise. I stood and pushed my chair back on the linoleum floor, listening for the screech, but there was no sound. I turned to Joseph, both of us chewing on vowel shapes and spitting only air, before his attention dropped to my feet, and I followed his eyes to the blood. I touched a hand to my face and pulled back a wet, red glove. The blood, streaming from my nose, turned black like tar between my fingers.

Joseph's pen rolled away as he leaned over his desk, his mouth opening and closing with inaudible commentary, while his eyes yelled at mine. The pen fell as though lowered slowly on a spider's thread, and I watched it settle gradually into the black oily liquid, spreading from under Joseph's desk.

A thick black arm stabbed up through the surface and wrapped its talons around Joseph's leg, while another dripping arm with its claw spread appeared from behind him and tore through the shirt and skin of his shoulder. Joseph's expression contorted with agony as the creature anchored its talons into his flesh, pulled itself up out of the mud using the makeshift rungs of its human ladder, and clamped its jaws around his midsection. It ripped away a strip of flesh, and the red poured from the wound, streaming down the chair leg to the black at Joseph's feet as he screamed in silence.

The desk sank down into the mud and was then thrust up into the air as a third creature burst through the surface sending a spray of oil in every direction. Its massive jaws opened, and the muscles on its neck tensed, revealing thick veins that stood proud, like ropes over the surface of its skin. It shook its head violently and drew back as if about to attack. I lunged forward and threw my arms around Joseph, putting myself between him and the creature and pulled him to the mud.

One of the creatures wrapped its talons around Joseph's arm and dragged him up and away from me. As I struggled to maintain my grasp on his other arm, I caught a glimpse of the pen that had fallen and snatched it up with a handful of mud.

The last thing I remember before everything went black was stabbing the pen as hard as I could into the arm of the creature and watching it scream.

II

CHAPTER 18

A butterfly

"Where's Joseph?" I asked.

The balding man opposite me, breathed a disappointed sigh and asked, "Where do you think you are right now?"

We sat at a desk inside a pale peppermint box with frosted windows spanning the top of the back wall and a single metal door with a narrow glass and mesh window.

"In the hospital?"

"And who am I?" he asked.

I read aloud the ID card hanging from one lapel of his tweed coat, "Dr. Liam Thompson?"

"That's right, you're doing very well," he replied.

"Where's Miss H-Harper?"

"Do you feel bad about what you did to your teacher?" he asked.

"Because I l-lied to her about m-my eye?"

Doctor Thompson tucked his pen into his breast pocket and leaned back in his chair. "What do you remember?"

"J-Joseph was screaming … they were attacking h-him. I t-tried to s-save him … is he okay? D-did I s-save …" My spine stiffened in salute of a sudden and incredible pain.

My jaw muscles twitched and contracted, slamming my teeth shut to grind the inside of my cheek and the tip of my tongue caught between.

"Mmmm ... " I yelped through gritted teeth, which served only to amplify the pain.

My right eye flickered open and closed as I attempted to resist the violent contraction of the muscles in my neck, pulling my face hard into my shoulder.

The doctor said, "It will subside in a second or two; just try to stay calm."

It was over as abruptly as it began, and I was left twitching, aching, and scared. The door opened, and a large man, dressed in white, walked in.

"He bit himself again," Doctor Thompson said.

I looked down at the light blue gown, spotted and streaked with a dark red pattern.

"Alright, come on, let's get you cleaned up," the large man said.

"W-what's g-going on ... where's J-Joseph?" I cried the words, spat through red drool.

He took a firm grasp on my arm, and I tried to pull away. I kicked and squirmed as he dragged me from the chair and hoisted me up.

"Where's Joseph?" I screamed, "Where's J-Joseph?"

With one thick arm wrapped around my waist, he carried me out and into the hallway. I continued to scream my question over and over again, until it was no longer a question, just alternating vowels. The meaningless siren-like murmur accompanied the rhythmic squeak of the man's shoes on the off-white linoleum floor, now striped down the center with a sporadic trail of spattered blood. I screamed again, spitting a new red pattern on the floor, a butterfly.

CHAPTER 19

Side effects

"Are you going to behave?"

    I looked up at the large man in white. "Why am I here?"

    "Because you're crazy. Now take your pills," he said in a dismissive fashion.

    "I'm not ..."

    "Take your pills." The impact of his tone demanded obedience.

    I tipped the pills from the first paper cup onto my tongue and washed them down with water from the second.

    "Get up and come on; it's group time."

    I picked myself up off the floor and followed him out.

***

The door opened to a large room, colorless save for blue gowns and the rectangle of colored light emitted from a television in the center. Several children hovered around the buzzing light-box, gathered like moths, while others occupied every inside corner of the outer wall, each appearing as a small blue column against the large white backdrop.

"Have fun." The large man pulled the door shut behind him as he exited the room.

I traced a path around the perimeter of the room, and as my eyes adjusted to the watered down color palette, subtle rings appeared around the eyes of each child, growing red like fresh wounds. I came near a child whose grey skin seemed borrowed from the plastic chair on which his blue gown draped over in the shape of a seated skeleton. His confused expression remained pointed somewhere far behind me until something warned him that I was too close, and he began to scream. I fled to an unoccupied corner and slouched down with my arms tight around my knees.

***

Doctor Thompson entered the room carrying a clipboard, and I immediately ran to intercept him. "Where am I?"

"You're in the hospital," he said, smiling.

"But why am I here?"

He paused for a breath. "What's my name?"

"Doctor Thompson," I replied.

"When was the first time we met?" he asked as though reading from a checklist.

"What? I met you in that room … I bit my tongue, and the man dragged me out."

"Do you know when that was?" he asked.

"Today, or yesterday." My thoughts distorted to static as I tried to recall any time elapsed since the incident in question.

"That was Thursday of last week, but you remember it?" he cocked his head to the side and frowned.

I nodded, followed the lean of his head, and mirrored his frown.

"Do you remember anything before that, or why you're here?" he asked.

"I remember Joseph and Miss Harper ..." I began.

"Yes, go on, what happened to Miss Harper?" His eyebrows rose, prompting me to continue.

"I ... I don't know," I yelled.

"It's okay; calm down." He set two of the plastic chairs facing each other and gestured for me to sit.

"Why won't you just t-tell me what happened?" I said and slumped into the chair.

"Do you know how many times we've had this conversation?" He read the confused expression on my face and continued without waiting for an answer. "At least once a week for over a year."

"But ..." I started.

"We've only just met?" Doctor Thompson sighed. "About a year and a half ago, you attacked one of your classmates, the boy that you keep asking about."

"Joseph? But Joseph is my best friend." I shook my head.

"When your teacher tried to pull him away from you, you attacked her too. Do you remember that?" he asked.

"I ... attacked Miss Harper?" A pain swelled behind my eyes as I tried to process the information.

"You stabbed a pen into her arm," he said.

"No ... I stabbed ..." My thoughts became lost in a fog.

"After it happened, you collapsed, and when you woke in the hospital, you refused to eat or sleep, screaming that monsters were coming to get you. You were clearly in great mental distress. You had to be sedated and fed on a drip for a while."

My heart sank, along with any hope of waking from this nightmare.

"Your parents brought you here to get better," he added. "Do you know how old you are?" he asked.

"Eight," I said.

"You'll be ten soon," he replied. "You've been here with me at this clinic for over a year."

"So I am crazy?" My eyes welled up with tears.

"You're unwell, and we're here to help you get rid of the monsters," he said.

"Is that what the … p-pills do … get rid of the monsters?"

"The pink ones help balance certain brain chemicals, the blue ones help you sleep, and the white ones help manage some of the extrapyramidal side effects," he replied.

"Side effects? You mean the t-ticks … like today in the room?"

"Today?" He squinted and his head reset to its angled position.

"When I b-bit my t-tongue."

"That was last Thursday, but yes, those ticks," he replied.

"Are the t-ticks … b-because I'm sick?"

"Sometimes there's a downside to getting rid of the monsters," he said.

"It hurts," I said.

"What hurts?" he asked with a frown.

"The t-ticks, they … it h-hurts … I d-don't know where, but it hurts … like … I'm b-being attacked from inside and … I c-can't stop it." My eye began to flicker. "Do I still see m-monsters?"

"Not anymore." He smiled, leaned back in the chair and crossed his legs.

"D-does that m-mean I'm … b-better n-now?" As I formed the last word, my jaw seized then clamped shut in spasmodic reply to a painful message surging through my body.

Select muscles cramped and contracted. My eye twitched rapidly, and as my head jutted involuntarily to one side, I screwed up tight what parts of my face I still had control of and curled forward in the chair. I tried frantically to call out, but the sound that I heard was more the howling whine of a wounded dog than of a frightened child begging for help.

***

Within minutes, the sharp stabbing pains and vicious muscle cramps rounded out to a dull, throbbing ache, and the howling transformed to an uncontrollable sobbing.

"It's okay; try to relax," Doctor Thompson said.

"It hurts when I t-try to think about what happened," I managed as I wept through my trembling hands. "Why don't I remember anything after that day at school?"

"The brain is a complex machine. There is no way for us to know exactly what occurred. The only thing we can do is try to help you get back to normal," Doctor Thompson replied.

I cringed inside as my brain reorganized and replayed his words: *You are not normal.*

"You're doing a lot better than you were," he added.

"C-Can I go home soon?"

"Let's give it a few days and see how you are doing?" he replied.

I looked up through tear-filled eyes and asked, "How many times have you told me that?"

CHAPTER 20

Different pills for different monsters

Over the next few weeks, the meetings with Doctor Thompson were a little more varied in topic and subsequently more distinguishable from one to the next. He had said that the marked increase in my short-term memory function was a good sign, but continued to avoid my questions as to when I would be deemed well enough to return home.

"Is that what you meant before, by unresponsive?" I asked, gesturing to a child in the opposite corner, slouched in a plastic chair and wearing a vacant expression.

Doctor Thompson sought out the subject of my question and gave a slow nod. "It's as though you disappear, and when you come back, you don't remember where you've been."

We both stared for a time—Doctor Thompson at the outwardly lifeless child, and me at the small three-dimensional shadow standing just behind him.

"Are there different pills … for different monsters?" I asked.

"Why do you ask, are you having nightmares again?" He turned his attention back to me and studied my face.

"No … I mean, I don't know. I don't remember sleeping." I looked down at my hands. "I just want to know … how the p-pills work."

"The pills help your brain separate what is real from what is imaginary," Doctor Thompson said.

"So I d-don't see anything that's not real anymore?" I asked.

The doctor paused seemingly awaiting eye contact. "I think that is something that *you* would have to tell *me*."

"I guess not," I replied, "It's hard for me to think, is that … b-because of the pills too?"

Doctor Thompson shuffled in his seat. "If you continue to show improvement, then maybe we can lower the dosage."

"Will the t-ticks go away?" I asked.

"I think that they will likely subside or …" He turned toward the escalating commotion that had broken his concentration.

I traced his eyes to the boy in the corner; the shadow was gone and the boy was awake, flailing wildly in his chair. A trail of vomit arced from his mouth, propelled by the upward motion of a violent convulsion as he twisted and shook before slipping to the floor in a twitching heap.

Doctor Thompson called to an orderly and marched over to the child as the room erupted into a hyperbole of unfiltered emotion. While some remained unaware, wading in slow motion through a chemically induced stupor, others screamed, ran, pushed, and kicked over chairs. The room became the stage of a dueling ballet between medicated serenity and interpretive chaos.

The doctor turned the boy onto his side, and the boy turned from red to blue. The orderly hooked a finger into the child's mouth and snatched it back as the boy's teeth snapped shut. More white coats rushed into the room and began ushering the rest of us out as the blue child convulsed in the corner, flapping around like a fish on land. I glanced back as I was led out of the room. The boy lay still and over him stood the doctor, the large man in white, and a child-size silhouetted figure.

CHAPTER 21

A hard pill to swallow

Soon after the boy had choked to death, the facility was made to cease operation, temporarily at the least, pending the result of an investigation, and I was returned to my parents.

Save for the making of my bed, my room had been left the way it had been almost two years earlier. The same half-peeled curl of white paint on the cast iron radiator leaned out toward my pillow like a bookmark between the pages of a bedtime story, beckoning me to continue from where I left off, but all of the characters in my story had changed.

Doctor Thompson had warned my parents that I was likely to appear unresponsive at times, but had not warned me of the same regarding my parents. My father had switched to working nightshifts and between sleeping or working, spent most of his time elsewhere, while an actress bearing vague resemblance to my mother, now played the maternal part with lackluster effort and talent, appearing much older than my mother and scarcely remembering her lines.

Every morning, I was brought a glass of water and two of my three daily pills, the pink one and the white one. I would take the white pill first and swallow it with a sip of water. The pink pill, I would push between my lip and teeth, sip and swallow the water, then wait for her to leave, and spit the pill back into my hand. The blue bedtime pill was spat out and joined the pink pill, wrapped in tissue, waiting to be fed to the toilet and flushed away.

    The insomnia returned soon after the toilet's introduction to the blue pill, but in disregarding the white pill, there seemed no change in the frequency or intensity of the ticks. The demonic creatures, imagined by a younger mind were slain, but the shadow people remained unaffected by the use of medication or abstinence thereof and would keep me company during the long sleepless nights.

CHAPTER 22

Method acting

She took the role of my mother and made it her own. Her best performance since my return was during a scene played out in the kitchen, in which she would witness for the first time one of my more intense seizures.

She stood with a shaking hand cupped to her mouth and tears rolling down each cheek, as I lay clamped to the kitchen table, howling in response to the internal and uncontrollable spasmodic riot attacking every muscle and nerve down the right side of my head, neck, and torso. The expressions of shock, pity and helplessness washed over her face with seamless transition and expertise as she portrayed the devastated mother. With her eyes closed, she held her posture for dramatic effect while the tension throughout my body waned and ownership of motor control was handed back to me.

I scanned the lines and creases across her forehead, and stretching from the corners of her mouth to the corners of her nose, were lines that my mother didn't have. Her skin was rough, dry, and pale, and the hair-dye, used to make her look more like my mother, had grown out, exposing dark roots and a failing actress.

She opened her eyes to me staring at her and wiped away the tears. With a quivering impression of my mother's voice, she asked, "Are you okay?"

I continued to stare, picking holes in her disguise. She forced a smile, walked over to a bottle of pills on the kitchen counter, and popped the cap. There was a high-pitched clink from her wedding ring as she took an upturned glass from the cupboard and filled it from the tap. I expected her to place the water and pill on the table in front of me, but instead, she slapped the pill to her mouth, chased it down with water, rinsed the glass, and returned it to the same exact place in the cupboard. She then pulled on a pair of bright yellow rubber gloves and began scrubbing vigorously at the kitchen counter with a wet cloth.

For the next few hours, she cleaned the same areas repeatedly, only stopping briefly to push back with her forearm the few strands of two-tone hair that kept falling in front of her face.

CHAPTER 23

A second opinion

The older boy offered no insight or wisdom, as we each studied the details of the other's face with synchronized skepticism. I turned away from the mirror and flushed the toilet again to remove the pink spiral drawn on the porcelain by the perphenazine as it had swirled with the water and slipped into the U-bend.

I was met, descending the stairs, by a rising chemical odor that immediately settled as a taste on the back of my tongue. The bleach and citrus fog stung my eyes, and beyond only a few shallow breaths, my chest tightened around a sharp stabbing pain, a searing reminder that I was an asthmatic.

I held a single shallow breath of poison-scented air as I ran through the house and to the medicine cabinet in the kitchen. The maternal stand-in climbed down from the chair on which she had been standing to reach and scrub the upper cabinets. She dropped the chemical-soaked rag into the sink and rushed toward me.

"Don't touch that. I've only just got them clean." She intercepted the door with a bright yellow rubber-gloved hand and pulled it open. "What do you need, dear?"

Her feigned smile and posture read like an audition for the part of prize-girl on a television game show. I ignored her question, snatched one of the blue inhalers from the bottom shelf, shook it to make sure it was full, and left through the back door.

Once outside, I pulled two gasping breaths through my inhaler and down into my tightened chest. The sound of a thousand people crying desperately and faint from inside my throat accompanied the short in-breaths, stolen during the brief pause between each coughing expulsion of inhaled mucus.

The coughing slowed, and I wheezed two more medicated breaths through the inhaler and into my aching lungs. As I peered back through the open doorway, the actress had set to scrubbing the tiled floor on her hands and knees, and in spite of my interruption, she had not let it break her out of character or hinder the completion of the scene.

***

The gap in the park fence was smaller than I remembered, and as I squeezed through, the realization set in that it had been over two years since the last time I had done so, and in that time, I had grown more than a couple inches.

I sat alone on one of the tire swings, thinking about Joseph and the day we built the ramp. The wind whistled past my ears and against my face as I swung, and I closed my eyes. The daydream, projected onto the back of my eyelids turned to black, interrupted by the swelling of distant chants. I opened my eyes and dragged my feet to stop the swing. Three males, maybe just beyond their teens, crossed the church grounds, laughing and pushing one another as they neared the park entrance. My heart and stomach were pulled up on a drawstring, where they bunched together and hung in my throat, beating and churning. I ran to another hole in the mesh and struggled through it, taking with me any opportunity for the intruders to justify rising fears and paranoia. The many mantras of Doctor Rodgers played over in my mind. *It's better to be safe than sorry ...*

you can never be too careful when it comes to children ... and potential head injuries.

As they entered the park, I scurried across the parking lot and around the church, peering back to make sure that they were not following me. I hid behind a memorial statue and watched as one of the group swung the tire over the crossbar, wrapping the shortening chains, as the other two stood blowing clouds of smoke and passing something back and forth.

I scrambled away and out of sight through the cemetery and over the wall. As I slowed at the curb, my mind returned to the biological underlay of the path I had taken. I stepped away from the cold shiver, grazing the length of my spine, and crossed the road.

***

I held a stick against the vertical spindles of the school railings, and each clanged and chimed as the stick bounced from one to the next. I focused on the building beyond the scrolling striped blur, and the chiming slowed in time with my pace as I neared the top gate. Clang, what if this was a recurring nightmare? Clang, what if when I woke, I was back in the hospital? Clang, two years older and ... the stick hit nothing and I stopped at the open gate. What if all of what Doctor Thompson had told me was a lie? What if it wasn't?

My mind was offered the distraction of possible scenarios and conversations played out between Miss Harper and me, as my body sneaked by my senses and made its way through the school entrance closest to Miss Harper's classroom. Before I had given permission, my insubordinate limbs had opened the door to Miss Harper's classroom and carried me in.

The female teacher turned from the blackboard. "Hi, can I help you?" she asked. It was not Miss Harper.

"No ... s-sorry," I replied.

The children were all turned over the backs of their chairs and staring at me. In spite of familiar laughter, I didn't recognize any of the children as I scoured the multitude of smirking faces for Joseph.

"I m-must have the wrong room." I closed the door behind me as I left, and my chest deflated with a sigh. I sat down on the bench across from my old peg, where another boy's coat hung, and cupped my head in my trembling hands.

"Are you alright, boy?"

I wiped my face and stared up at the robust man by my side. "I was looking for M-Miss Harper," I replied.

Mr. Copeland squinted through his glasses and opened his mouth to speak.

"Is it t-true, I attacked her?" I asked.

He frowned, and in a measured tone, he asked, "You don't remember what happened?"

My heart sank upon hearing that same question, and I swallowed the lump in my throat. "I wanted to … t-tell her I'm sorry."

"She transferred to another school." Mr. Copeland put his hand on my shoulder and squatted down next to me. "I still speak to her sometimes. I could tell her that you're sorry if you'd like."

I nodded. "I wasn't well."

"How are you now?" he asked.

I looked him in the eyes and shrugged. "I … feel the same as b-before. Do you know where J-Joseph … is?" I added.

"I'm sorry. I don't know who that is," he replied with a subtle dismissive shake of his head.

"He was m-my … best friend." I stood and dragged my forearm across my face. "I have to go … home."

"Are you going to be alright?" Mr. Copeland asked.

I shrugged again and pushed my way through the exit doors, feeling dejected and alone.

CHAPTER 24

The small print

The days ran into each other, as did the weeks and months, with me sat watching reruns of a drama situated mostly within the kitchen of number thirteen, my house. Derived from sporadic and fragmented conversations, I realized that the lead actress was in fact my mother, and in my absence, she had succumbed to an overwhelming guilt for having given me away. The depression had sapped her will to function and had reduced her to a grieving bedridden surrogate of her former self. Her doctor had prescribed pills to remedy the situation. The pills were a form of amphetamine, an upper, speed. The pills had cured her lack of enthusiasm, but as with all drugs, hidden within the small print, were the side effects.

For every problem, there is a drug claiming to be a cure or control. For me, the cure was perphenazine. For my mother, it was amphetamine, and for my father, although not in pill format, it was whisky.

During television commercials for whichever brand name drug urging viewers to consult their doctor and ask if, insert name, is right for them, my mother would make a cameo appearance, down on her hands and knees in the kitchen, scrubbing furiously at the imaginary stains in the pristine white grout between floor tiles. In small print, the warning read: Temporarily restores normality by removing you from it.

Prolonged use may result in compulsive behavior and a detachment from reality.

Commercials for the fine taste, refined flavor, or beautiful blend of whatever for whichever whisky, starred my father, whose performance was neither refined, nor beautiful. In small print, the warning read: Temporarily alleviates stress; however, prolonged use may result in violent mood swings and the eventual destruction of your family.

My parents maintained their roles in the monotonous routine, re-enacting a series of predetermined scenes that would shape each week into a degraded copy of its predecessor. My father would wean my mother off the speed, then she would call him on his drinking, he would call her a hypocrite, she would cry, he would leave, she would pop a few pills, and within half an hour or so, she would pull on the bright yellow rubber gloves and clean the already cleaned surfaces of the kitchen.

As part of their weekly routine, they would argue about me, or more precisely, about who was to blame. They would blame each other or themselves. If my father had drunk more than his daily quota, then the blame fell back on me, and I would run and hide, waiting for the slam of the front door to signal the end of the hunt.

The duration of my father's periodic desertion escalated from days to weeks, and the longer he was gone, the more intense was the fight upon his return. In my father's absence, I enjoyed the calm and would pass the time reading, writing, or painting; each served as a necessary emotional outlet. My sketchbook and notepad were substitute friends with whom I could share my thoughts and secrets. Just like the shadow people that remained motionless night after night in the corner of my room, these substitute friends would never judge or reject me; they would listen to my pleas and absorb the overflow of emotion.

CHAPTER 25

Maternal sugar pill

The front door slammed shut, the gate squeaked and clattered in response, a car sped away, and I sat in my room like Pavlov's dog, waiting for the familiar pop-clink, commencing countdown to fumigation.

    I drifted down the stairs and through the house, expecting to find my mother with a cleaning rag in her rubber-gloved hands, but instead, her hands were cupped under her face as she wept into them at the kitchen table.

    The air was unscented and breathable, rendering my planned evacuation unnecessary. As my mother sobbed, I watched at first with conditioned indifference. Her emotional breakdowns were common during the weekly cycle, although typically fleeting, transitioning between my father's last words and the metabolizing of her medication. Neither the robotic maid, nor the crying woman, was the same over-protective mother that had nurtured me from birth, but of the two modes, the latter was of closest resemblance. Without medication, she was at least capable of emotion and more likely to notice me as her son and not just a freak interruption of her daily routine. I wanted her to notice me, coax me out of my silence, or comfort me in spite of it. I wanted to tell her that I was sorry for the day my father's words spilled from my mouth and broke her heart.

It took a while for her to notice me sitting opposite her at the kitchen table. When she did, she wiped her eyes, stood, and walked over to the pill bottle on the counter, where she could exchange in equal parts, the ability to care for the ability to cope.

"Mom, don't." The words came out on their own, leaving both of us stunned and staring at one another.

"You don't n-need the pills," I said, but it was obvious to both of us that what I meant was that I needed my mother.

"I'm so sorry," she said softly, as she returned to her chair.

We sat for a while in silence, each trying to think of something sufficient to bridge the gap since the last time we had spoken.

"Are you hungry?" She tested her question with little confidence.

I wasn't, but nodded and attempted a smile. It wasn't about food. It was about routine, hers as a mother and mine as a son.

She responded with a smile I recognized but had not seen in years, before pulling open the sparkling-clean and almost bare fridge. Her smile withered as the few remaining condiments seemed to whisper the truth of how long she had been away.

I had been living off of the non-perishables in the cupboard for over a year, sneaking into the kitchen in the middle of the night, being careful to return everything to its rightful place so as not to upset my mother's new routine.

As my mother's hands searched through the cans in the cupboard, her eyes searched around the room for the missing years.

"Soup okay?" Her smiling mouth was countered by the apologetic plea in her eyes. I acknowledged both her question and her apology with a nod.

I joined her at the stove where she stood, locked in a dream and stirring the pot. She mouthed her part of a silent conversation, frowning at her thoughts and squinting to read an invisible script.

"Mom?"

She snapped awake and turned to face me as I put my arms around her and squeezed tight. She hesitated for a moment, seemingly unsure of how to respond to the now foreign gesture, then cradled my shoulders and head in her arms and began to cry.

"I really did miss you," she sobbed.

"I know ... I missed you t-too, Mom."

The embrace lasted until the pot boiled over. She released me, turned off the stove, and set the pot aside. "You'll have to wait for it to cool a little."

"Do you ... want to see m-my drawings?" I asked.

"Drawings?"

She had picked them up from my bedroom floor and stacked them neatly a thousand times but had never seen a single one.

"I'll go and ... g-get them," I said, pushed back my chair and ran to fetch them from my room.

I spread the drawings out on the floor and sorted them according to subject matter, collating what I thought would be considered appropriate for a normal child and setting aside sketches made from memory of the mud men, of the blue child laying at the feet of his small shadow, and countless others inspired by emotional scars. With the pictures spread out, they read like a storybook, one which made my stomach churn as I questioned how much of the story had been fact or fiction. I gathered the story pages together and placed them face down next to the small stack I had chosen to show to my mother.

When I returned to my mother, she was pressed flush against the kitchen wall, held still by the thick hand of my father, clasped around her neck. He spat and cursed through gritted teeth, inches from her face; she turned her eyes away and found me.

I lunged toward them and was stopped abruptly by a dark blur and a bright flash. The pain from impacting the hard floor tile was quickly suffocated by the immense swelling pain, burning away the side of my face, where the back of his hand had caught me.

    The door slammed shut with a dull thud and a whining echo as I peeled myself up from the cold floor and opened one eye wide to a greasy blur. Something touched my head, and I scrambled back in response. The ringing sound evolved into that of my mother crying uncontrollably, and she made no further attempt to touch me. I crawled around on my hands and knees, picked up all of the loose sketches strewn across the floor, stood, stumbled into the wall, and followed it out of the room. From behind me came the rattle of pills, a pop, clink, and seconds later, the loud crack and tinkle of shattered glass.

CHAPTER 26

Attention deficit and disorder

I moved my hand through the silhouetted figures, and they offered no physical resistance as my hand passed through one, then the other. The dark air that formed the shadow people was cold in comparison to that which filled my room. The chill spread from my hand, and traveled up my arm, and I withdrew with a shudder that scurried over my shoulder and down my spine. I brought the cold hand to my face and held it against my cheek to validate the change in temperature, then repeated the process over and again. The two figures remained inanimate, each as nothing more than a cold dark space in air, in the shape of a man, but the human resemblance seemed to end there. They appeared no more living, nor supernatural, than an image in the clouds, or a man-shaped stain in the carpet.

I returned to my sketchpad on the floor, retrieved my paintbrush loaded with a watered down brown-black acrylic, and traced the pencil outline of the figure with a translucent stroke that wrinkled the page.

I sat staring at a dry, finished painting. My mouth was dry with crusted drool at the corners, my leg buzzed with the tiny stinging pains of pins and needles, and it was now light outside. My body had evidently switched into autopilot mode, seeing as I had no recollection of completing the painting, an increasingly common occurrence since disregarding the blue pill.

It was a pseudo-awake state, whereby, I was allowed to daydream in standby, while my body continued with its current task, a robotic employee not too dissimilar to the robotic maid that spent her days scrubbing at the surfaces of the kitchen in both a physical and mental fog.

Time had begun to blend without logical transition; one minute it was day, the next it was night. One minute, I was massaging the pins and needles from my outstretched leg, the next, I was staring into my father's piercing eyes and gritted, spitting teeth. One minute, the blur of my father's fist was racing toward me, the next, I was peeling my swollen face up off my sketchpad, dividing the scabbed blood between the torn-open wounds about my face and the now red-stained painting of two dark statues.

CHAPTER 27

Paid in blood

Air groaned out of the downed man as he received another kick to the mid-section. Three men stood over him, one shouting, one kicking, and one watching. The security light attached to the church and the street lamps at the road cast long widening shadows from the feet of the three men, resembling the negative of a child's painted representation of the sun's rays. The amber light offered little enhancement to the details of the scene, save for the wet shine of blood, glimmering over the angles of the victim's face.

I remained hidden in the bushes with no delusions of courage compelling me to intervene. I had no wish to accompany the man who was now curled up in a limp, fetal position, no longer groaning or flinching. The tallest of the three standing, pulled the others away from the crumpled, bloodied man on the ground, and led them across the church parking lot and out of sight.

With enough time elapsed to appease my instinct for self-preservation, I slowly approached the bloody heap in the middle of the asphalt. I studied the man, who appeared to be of around the same age as my father. A strange and morbid curiosity similar to that which compels a child to poke at road kill with a stick crept up inside, and I reached a hand down to touch him. His eyes flashed open and his limbs tensed up, shielding his face and body in defense of another blow.

"They're ... g-gone," I said.

The man lowered his arms and scanned the area for any sign of his attackers. "I thought you were one of them," he said, spitting blood as he did so.

I shook my head. "I was ... hiding in the b-bushes ... s-sorry. Why were they ... hitting you?"

He wiped a hand across his face and looked at it. "I don't know. They jumped me from behind, I went down, and they started kicking. Next thing I know, you're standing over me."

"You should get out of here, just in case they come back," he said and stood, clutching at his side.

According to the church clock, my father had left for work. I complied with the beaten man's advice and walked on home.

CHAPTER 28

Pressure release valve

As almost perfectly correlating to my father's work schedule, my days were wasted away leaning over the guardrail at the Lion's den, watching the river below and daydreaming about the boy who had drowned. I imagined the railing giving way under my weight and me falling to the rocks below, suffering the same fate as that boy and thinking that maybe I would be better off.

      I spent my evenings in and around the cemetery, waiting for my father to leave so that I could return home and not have to chance his mood or blood-alcohol level. I had managed to time my ingress and egress well enough to avoid him; save for the odd time that he left his car at the bar and had passed out drunk on the couch. He would wake up sore and late for work, roused by the sound of the back door, opened and closed by someone he could take it all out on. On a one-to-ten scale, the severity of the beating equaled the consecutive days since the last. Nine days without incident meant a nine-out-of-ten melee, allowing me to spend the night unconscious, time that would go toward the next ten-day countdown. I never made it more than nine; maybe I wanted to get caught before the ten days were up, fearing what he would become without the periodic release of pressure.

On the rare occasion my mother was cognizant, she would cry and tell me that my father didn't mean it. He didn't know what he was doing; it was the drink, not my father. She was unable to save me from him and unwilling to try. Instead of defending me, she defended his actions, adding insult to injury, real physical injury. It was as obvious to me as the bruising about my face that she had chosen to sacrifice her only son to appease the insatiable temper of a vicious drunk, while she crawled off and hid inside a bottle of pills, out of his sight and out of her mind.

CHAPTER 29

Smoke and mirrors

I rounded the corner of the church and was met by a thick cloud of smoke that stung my eyes. I waved my hand, pushing the smoke away to reveal three silhouettes standing next to the wall of the church, backlit by the security light. A red glowing ember rose to head height of one of the silhouettes, grew brighter, and disappeared behind a cloud of smoke blown into my face. I began to cough and splutter and tears streamed from my stinging eyes.

"Don't cry, kid, it's just weed," one of them said.

Amid the apprehensive dread, brought on by the assumption that they were the same three who had made a limp bloodied mess of another man only a couple months earlier, I wiped my eyes and quickened my pace.

"Where you going, kid? Come here. I want to talk to you," he said.

I kept my head down and ignored the quiver in my heart and bladder.

"Hey, you little shit, I'm talking to you," he barked, pushing me from behind, and I stumbled forward into a run.

From behind and in a dry tone, another said, "He's just a kid; leave him alone."

A hand tightened around the sleeve of my shirt, and I was pulled back and around. I balled my right hand up into a fist and swung as hard as I could. I felt the snap of something against my knuckles before the momentum of the interrupted chase carried us both to the floor. I scrambled to my knees and saw the blood about his face, but it wasn't his face. I leaned in and drove my fists, one after the other into the bleeding surrogate of my father.

An arm wrapped around my neck, pulling me back as I kicked at nothing but air above the imagined paternal mask. The arm tensed and tightened, emphasizing words, spoken in the same dry tone as before. "Alright, kid, that's enough."

"You broke my fucking nose, you little shit," yelled the man, now cradling his bloodied face.

"I said, 'that's enough.'"

"Fuck you, Panda. He broke my fucking nose."

"Shut the fuck up, Si, you deserved it," came the unenthused response from behind my ear.

Si glared back at the man behind me and then hocked a mouthful of blood at my feet. The arm loosened and I was let go. I backed up a couple steps and turned to face the man referred to as Panda. The blond stubble around his mouth and jaw created a bright haze that served to outline his angled face in the low light.

"How old are you?" Panda asked, looking down at me.

"Almost ... twelve," I replied.

"You got your nose busted by a twelve-year-old kid," Panda said and began to laugh at Si, who was now clambering to his feet, still holding his dripping nose and wiggling it from side to side.

"Yeah, fuck you," Si replied.

"I'm ... almost twelve," I corrected, unintentionally spawning more laughter from Panda and the third man, who was peering around Si's hands to view the damage.

"This is Michael," Panda said and nodded toward the shorter, wiry man, wincing as he stared at Si's broken nose.

Michael ran a hand through dark messy hair, hanging to just below his shoulders, and tucked a few strands behind his ear as he lifted his head in acknowledgement. "Looks like you gave the kid a black eye at least," he said and turned his attention back to Si.

Si's hard stare softened as he looked at my eye. "That wasn't from me."

"Who'd you get the shiner from, kid?" asked Michael.

I felt something bubble inside my chest and stomach as I said the words, "My dad."

Si and Panda glanced over at each other, then the ground.

"Alright, enough of this depressing shit, let's go smoke a joint," Michael said, and they started toward the park gate.

Panda turned back to face me. "You coming?"

CHAPTER 30

Paradise Lost

Simon sat back on the couch, took a long drag from the joint, and closed his eyes. "I idolized my dad when I was a kid. I wanted to be just like him," he said, exhaling a large billowing cloud of smoke into the hazy air about the living room. "When my parents divorced, I had to choose which one I wanted to live with, so I chose my dad."

Simon passed the joint to Panda and picked up the bottle at his feet. "Soon after they split, my dad fell apart. He was drinking and crying all the time. It was weird seeing my dad cry. I didn't know what to do. Not even a year after the divorce, my mom announced that she was engaged to someone else, and my dad lost it. He trashed the house, and when I tried to calm him down, he beat the shit out of me." Simon stopped and took a drink. "That was the first time he'd ever laid a hand on me; beat me unconscious. Pretty soon after that, it was every night."

"Why didn't you l-leave and … go live with your mom?" I asked.

Simon breathed a disingenuous whistling laugh through his almost healed, but crooked nose, and stared at the bottle in his hands. "She started a family with her new husband. They had a new baby on the way, and she never said it, but I could tell that she didn't want me there."

"So you r-ran away?" I asked.

"I stayed," Simon said, shaking his head. He gestured to the bottle in his hand. "I'd steal his whiskey and get so fucked up that I'd remember about as much of the night before as he did. The only giveaway was the fresh black eye or split lip staring back at me in the mirror the next morning."

He stared intently at the fresh cut and bruise on my cheek. "Whenever I see you looking all beat up like that, it takes me right back to when I was a kid, standing there in front of the mirror." He *glugged* from the bottle. "I was fourteen when I ran away. I left for school in the morning and never went back."

"Where did you … go?" I asked.

"Michael's beat-up trailer," Panda interjected with a smirk. "We couldn't afford a house like this back then; we were just kids."

Simon continued, "I went to the same school as Panda. He came in one day with two black eyes and his head down. That's how he got his name. He got caught stealing, and his dad broke his nose. A couple of months after, we both left home and went to stay with Michael, three of us cramped into that piece of shit trailer."

"Did Michael g-go to your school?" I asked.

"Yeah, but he left a few years before us. He only came back to deal weed to the misfits. We were his best customers," Panda said.

I stared at Panda with a question on the tip of my tongue.

"What is it?" Panda asked with a smirk.

"What d-did you steal?" I asked.

Panda shook his head and laughed. "A book."

"A book?"

Panda smiled, "*Paradise Lost* by John Milton. The most expensive book I'll ever own."

CHAPTER 31

Disparate gifts

On the day of my twelfth birthday, Panda had left early in the morning, saying that he had a few errands to run. Running errands usually meant that he was delivering product for Michael, seeing as he owned the only car, a red and rust hatchback, and was the only one with a driver's license.

I took a sip from the bottle of Jack Daniels, handed it back to Simon, and returned both my attention and pencil to the sketchpad on my lap.

"Cheers," Simon said, and *glugged* from the bottle.

"Let me see," Michael said and gestured toward my sketchpad.

I hesitated, then passed it over and watched as he flipped through it, expecting and awaiting his criticism.

"Told you he's pretty fucking talented, didn't I?" Simon said.

"How'd you get this good?" Michael asked.

"Are you … m-making fun of me?"

"No, these are really good. I'm no art critic or anything, but I'd buy these," he replied.

I waited for him to crack a smile, but he didn't.

"We should frame some of these and put them up," Simon said.

I heard the front door open and Panda's voice, "Alright kid, close your eyes."

He entered the room to my confused expression.

"Just do it," he said with a reassuring nod.

I closed my eyes, listened to the rattle and rustle of whatever he was carrying through the living room, and waited there until I was told to open my eyes.

"What's going on?" I asked, staring at a bed sheet draped over a large shape in the corner of the room with Michael and Panda standing next to it, grinning.

"Happy birthday, kid," Panda said and pulled off the sheet, revealing a painting easel and canvas.

"That's … for me?" I asked.

"We got you some paints and brushes too," Michael said.

I sat with my mouth open, but at a loss for words.

Panda asked, "You like it?"

I nodded and swallowed the lump in my throat. "Thank you."

"You should thank Simon; it was his idea," Panda replied.

Simon sat rolling a joint and spoke before I had a chance. "Happy birthday, kid."

He peered up at my grinning face and smiled back. "Don't get all sappy; just go and fetch me a beer."

Up to this point, birthdays had been a non-event. Being an asthmatic, I had been steered away from excitement, the way that most kids are steered away from fire. I returned to the living room where we spent the rest of the day telling stories, laughing, smoking, and drinking.

***

I didn't remember getting home or falling asleep at the kitchen table. My head was pounding and made worse by my father's yelling. My eyes seemed glued shut, and it took a couple minutes and a slap across the face before I was fully awake. My father was shouting about me smelling like booze, and still drunk from the night before, I heard a laugh escape my throat. He slapped me again, hard across the face, and I continued to glare, as he continued to shout and scream. The slaps and strikes no longer hurt the way that they once had, whether owing to physical calluses at the surface of my skin or the emotional calluses beneath, I was as close to numb, as not to care.

"You keep staring at me like that, and I'll knock that smirk off your face, you hear me?" he screamed.

"John, stop, please," my mother whimpered as she entered into my periphery.

Without taking my eyes off him, I said in a flat and even tone, the last words I would ever say to my father, "Fuck you."

A vertical line creased my father's forehead, his nose and lips wrinkled into an animalistic snarl, and his thick arm propelled a white knuckled fist at my face. The blow hammered me backward over one of the dining chairs that broke as we collided against the wall and crashed to the floor. I heard my mother pleading with him to stop as I rubbed at my eyes, trying to steady the room and clamber to my knees. Through the blur, I watched my mother fall back and slide away as I fumbled around, trying to find my feet. My hand found a broken leg of the chair, and I held on to it as I stood. My father centered in the room as it stopped moving and I swung the chair leg with everything I had.

The makeshift bat connected with the side of his head. The hollow sound bounced back from the walls, a second before his body fell limp and his head bounced off the tiled floor with a dull crack. Blood spread away from under him, following the channels of previously pristine white grout. I stared at the red pinstripe grid framing my father's outwardly lifeless body, not knowing what to think or feel. My mother cried hysterically into the phone for an ambulance, as the chair leg clattered to the floor at her feet, and I continued out through the back door without looking back.

***

I ambled along in a surreal blur, letting my feet find their way to Panda's house. I pushed open the unlocked door and stepped inside with the learned stealth of small prey among large predators. Simon sat on the couch with a plastic tube gripped between his lips and a lighter poised under a piece of tin foil, directly under the tube. A single flame licked the underside of the foil, and the powdered contents turned to liquid, bubbled into white smoke, and rolled up into the tube.

"What is that?" I asked.

Simon's eyes flicked open as he whipped around. "What the fuck are you doing here?"

I trembled on the spot, with my chin tucked into my chest, and taking up as little room as possible.

"Sorry, kid, you fucking scared me; you shouldn't sneak up on people like that," he said.

An inaudible apology bubbled over my twitching lower lip as I raised a reluctant glassy gaze to meet his. Simon winced, "Holy shit, what happened to your face?"

"I think ... I killed him." My words fell to the ground wrapped in tears.

"What? Who, your dad?" he asked.

"He wasn't m-moving. There was blood everywhere, and ... I did it."

"Calm down. What happened?" Simon said slowly.

I lowered myself to the couch and let the rest of the story filter out through my hands as I wept.

"Do your parents know about this place, that you come here?" he asked.

I shook my head.

INFINITY

Simon sat back and let a large breath of air out between his lip and teeth. "I'm sure your dad's fine; he's probably just knocked out."

I wiped my sleeve across my eyes and nose.

"Nobody's going to find you here; even if they did, you think we'd let them take you away?" he said and raised his eyebrows.

"What's that?" I asked, nodding toward the tin foil.

"Medicine. It helps make the pain go away," he said, and in response to the look on my face, he added, "That's not for you, kid. Panda would kill me if he caught you chasing the dragon."

"Chasing the d-dragon?"

"Just leave it alone, kid," he replied.

Waves of expression rolled over his face like sped-up video footage of bad weather. "It's heroin. Do you know what that is? It's not like weed, kid, this shit is bad, you understand?"

"Then why ... d-do you do it?" I asked.

Simon shook his head and threw his hands up. "Fuck. You want it? Then go ahead, but if you get fucked up on this shit, then it's your own fault."

I retrieved the book and placed it on my lap. I wanted to get fucked up. I wanted to forget, and to escape from this life, my life, any way I could. Simon continued to shake his head but did not stop me as I loaded the tin foil and brought it up to my face. I exhaled, flicked the lighter and inhaled deeply through the plastic tube, breathing in the first breath of my new life.

III

CHAPTER 32

No one ever catches the dragon

I lay there on the bare mattress, doubled up with my arms clutched around my cramping stomach, sweating and shivering simultaneously. My legs shook spasmodically and itched beneath the skin. Imagined insects crawled through my veins, but I was too weak to scratch them out. Without so much as a point in two days, I was suffering from the beginnings of heroin withdrawal.

***

Number three heroin, is cut with caffeine to help it vaporize more efficiently when heated. Number four heroin, is regarded as the purest form of heroin, also known as China-white. These had become Michael's top-selling products.

Heroin, when heated from underneath, on a piece of tin foil, liquefies into a reddish brown glob, "The dragon," to be chased by a flame underneath the tin foil as the emitted vapor is inhaled through a tube. Another, more common use of the term, "chasing the dragon," refers to the pursuit of replicating the very first high. As tolerance for the drug builds, so does the desire to achieve that elusive high, and so grows the dosage. As

Michael would say, "you can chase it, but no one ever catches the dragon."

After four years of regular daily use, most people would call me an addict, but up until three months before, Michael had referred to me as a chipper, or part-timer. Before the accident, I would typically wake up, medicate, and then sleep or go, "on the nod," for another hour or so, before getting up and painting whatever I had dreamt. Since receiving the easel and my first canvas on my twelfth birthday, I had painted almost every day.

Michael had convinced one of his clients, a gallery owner named Paul, to display some of my more fridge-worthy artwork in exchange for a reduced rate on whatever Paul needed, to cater whatever high-class function was scheduled that week.

Michael had also introduced me to one of his suppliers, a tattooed bear of a man named Craig, always leather clad and adorning the flaming-skull patch, denoting which particular chapter of the biker gang he was part of. Craig would give me an envelope, an address, and a time to deliver. I was told never to open it or ask what was inside, and I never did. I didn't care what was in the envelopes; it was an easy job, and between the money I received being a runner for Craig, and the thirty percent cut from the occasional sale of a painting, I typically had enough money to stay dry, high, and fed until my next payday. But I hadn't sold a painting in just under three months and had not turned up at the clubhouse in over a week. The latter, was the reason that Michael had stopped leaving my medicine and was also the reason that he had not been home in two days. He had introduced me to Craig and had vouched for me, and me letting Craig down was the same as Michael letting Craig down.

Michael had always kept his relationship with the bikers strictly business—cash for drugs and vice versa, straight trade, no favors. Letting me off the hook for neglecting my responsibility as a runner was Craig's favor to Michael, and now one of us would have to repay that favor.

***

Simon kicked at the mattress. "Here, fix yourself up; you've got to go sort this shit out with Craig or Michael's going to be pissed."

I roused to a seated position, legs outstretched, took the preloaded foil, and fondled around for my lighter. Simon pulled a lighter from his pocket, rolled up a bill from his wallet, and handed them to me. As Simon left the room, I heated the foil and inhaled the smoke. Within minutes, I was slouched back down against the wall, somewhere between awake and asleep. In the same way that the pink pill had once worked to remove the monsters from this world, heroin was now my way of temporarily removing the world itself.

CHAPTER 33

Obligation

The room grew darker, and my body became lighter, rising slowly from the mattress. The people standing around me dissolved, and in their place, the shadow people stood, silent and motionless. The room melted, twisted, and stretched into a thin wet membrane, before folding and turning inside out. I watched this new world being born.

A strange vertigo-like sensation swept through me, decaying any lingering allusion of earthly position. I was suspended in darkness and becoming part of it, seeing in all directions simultaneously and no longer able to decipher the confines of my own body. The blackness became calming white light with no shock or transition as if it were the same thing.

With colors like that of light shone through a prism, a bright halo exposed the partial outline of a figure, casting faint rays of shadow in the space around it. I could hear the glowing figure whisper and seemingly from inside of me. As more figures materialized around me, I understood what was being whispered and knew that I was not welcome. I began to drift backward and the scene froze like a photo, stretched back into the distance leaving only tracers, copies of the image overlaid into infinity.

I was back in the expansive darkness and falling toward the unfolding wet skin. Something foreign clasped around me, restraining me as the walls of my room stretched into place. I was held, wrapped, and bound by my own body, becoming heavier, solid.

As I stared at the shadow people now standing all around me, masks materialized, faces belonging, perhaps, to the people they once were, superimposed over the now animated figures. The longhaired man in front of me frowned as he opened his mouth to speak, and I reached out to touch him. With my fingers only inches away, he recoiled to a black shape, set once again with the rest of the shadow people in my room.

Sounds grew louder and brighter, as I struggled to surface from sleep. I took a deep gasping breath and strained to view the blurred figure that now introduced itself as the source of the sound. I waited for my eyes to readjust to the light and for the figure to sharpen into focus.

"Come on, get up, we've got to go." Simon kicked at the mattress again. "Hey?"

"I saw people," I mumbled as I rose up on my elbow and rubbed at my eyes.

"What?" Simon asked, but continued without waiting for elaboration. "You've been on the nod for half an hour. Get the fuck up; we're going to see Craig."

Simon marched out, and I sat up, trying to shake off the fog. My eyes fell on the painting, clamped to the easel in the corner of my room, and a familiar sadness swelled in my throat. Simon called from the other room for me to hurry up.

"Alright, I'm coming," I shouted and struggled to my feet.

My attempts to stand worked against the cramping muscles in my stomach like an old well pump, forcing acid up and into my throat. I staggered into a run with my hand cupped over my mouth, dropped to my knees in front of the toilet bowl, and spewed burning, clear acidic bile through my hand and hair. With my head rested on the cold porcelain bowl, my body ran through the programmed cycle, tensing and heaving but expelling only air and sound.

Simon stopped at the doorway to the bathroom as I rinsed my mouth out at the sink. "You okay?"

Our eyes met in the mirror. "How do I look?"

"You look like shit," Simon replied with a smirk.

"I feel like shit," I said and returned my gaze to the gaunt, glassy-eyed stranger in the mirror. I rubbed at the dark-ringed sockets of my eyes and rinsed the bile from the hair hanging matted to below my jaw. Red blotches from ruptured blood vessels stood out in contrast to the otherwise pale blood-drained tone of my skin, fading in and out behind the adolescent and sporadic dirt-like facial hair.

"Are you ready to go?" Simon asked.

I nodded and turned away from the disheveled, diseased teenager in the mirror.

***

After a long wait in the foyer of the clubhouse, Craig entered from the back room and tossed a small packet of white powder into Simon's lap.

"What's this?" Simon asked.

"China-white," Craig replied.

"I thought you were mad at us?" I asked.

"Why would I be mad? You let me down, and now you're here to make it up, right?" Craig said in a flat, gruff tone.

"Michael wanted me to come and see you. I didn't realize that it was such a big deal; they're just envelopes," I said, not heeding the glare from Simon.

"It's not the envelopes that are important. It's what's in them. Do you know what's in them?" he said, enunciating every syllable.

"No," I replied.

"So how the fuck do you know, how big of a deal it is?" Craig said through gritted teeth.

"I ⋯" I started.

"How can we make it up to you?" Simon interjected.

Craig kept his glare fixed on me for a moment. "There's a job on tonight. Kev needs someone to keep six, do the gig, and we're square."

"What about you and Michael?" Simon asked.

"I do a lot of business with Michael. He and I will be just fine," he replied.

"What about the kid?" Simon asked.

Craig looked me up and down. "We're done; he's out."

***

Simon returned from the kitchen with a couple beers and loaded a piece of foil with the now brownish powder, cut from the small packet of China-white.

"What did he mean by keep six?" I asked.

"Kev has a job to do tonight, and I am going to go with him and watch his back. When this is done, we're out of debt with Craig, and you should stay away from those guys, you hear me?" Simon said.

"Panda's gone, Michael's gone, are you going to leave too?"

"I'll be back later, kid, and Michael will be home in a few days. Drink your beer and do your hoot. There's enough to last you until Michael gets back," he replied.

I picked up the tin foil and a plastic tube from the table, did the hoot, and sipped from the bottle with my eyes closed until it was pried from my hand.

"You go on the nod with a beer and you'll wake up wearing it." He placed the bottle on the table. "It will be right there for you when you wake up."

My eyes closed again and I was gone.

CHAPTER 34

Altered state

Of the men, women, and children standing about the living room, only the man with the long dark hair made an attempt to speak. He was mouthing words through thick facial hair, and for a brief moment, there was sound, "... remember this."

The rest of the people in the room crooked their heads in a contorted and unnatural fashion, flicking their attention from the man as he spoke to me as though awaiting my response.

"Who are you?" I asked.

The man frowned. "I asked the same thing."

I was compelled to reach out and touch him, to see if I could touch him, seeking confirmation or validation that this man, bearing ancestral resemblance, perhaps a long-dead relative of my family, was real and not just a figment of my imagination or psychosis.

The man receded into darkness, and my hand passed through the cold silhouette as the walls and ceiling began to soften and sag around me. The goose-bumped flesh of my arm blistered like a burning photograph, while the room's shell stretched thinner, revealing the dark and seemingly endless void beyond. I was enveloped by it, becoming part of it, without body, shape, or form, and all was replaced with brilliant white light.

The glowing figures materialized before me, haloed by a plethora of colored light and casting faint rays of shadow.

"Who are you?" I asked.

The reply was soft and clear but occurred as a thought and as an echo of my question, "Who?"

"Where are we?" I asked.

The voice echoed, "Where?"

"We are nowhere. We are no *when*. We, like you, are but a thought," the voice said.

"No when? I don't understand," I replied.

"Time is a concept of matter," the voice said softly.

Multiple voices spoke simultaneously, "The present, or now, within the constraints of time, is only a brief sliver of existence. It is merely the reading of events. The past and future should be thought of in the same way, as events, infinite possibilities."

"Events?" I asked.

"Events, without time, existing only as potential. You were an event within our existence. We enjoyed your life. It was an important event." The voices overlaid and coalesced into one. "You were special."

The uneasy feeling, having been referred to in the past tense, was subdued by a warming smile from somewhere within the figure.

"You have to go, little one," the voice trailed off.

"But I …" My voice, along with the light, raced into the distance, leaving only echoes of the image curving to form a tunnel of light. I slipped backward, a mirror staring at its own reflection, as everything separated into nothingness, no sound, no light. Nothing, forever.

Sensation returned as a surge through my shaking body. I opened my eyes to the reddened face of Simon. His voice escalated from a low murmur to a frantic shout as he shook me by the shoulders. "Breathe, Breathe, kid," he screamed.

I lurched forward, coating both the floor and myself with projected bile, drew in a deep gasping breath, and collapsed back onto the couch.

"What the fuck?" Simon shouted.

My heart pounded in my chest as I glanced all about the room.

"You alright?" he asked in a tremulous tone.

I wiped my mouth with my sleeve and peered down at my legs, now glazed with bile.

"Hey, talk to me. Are you alright?"

"What happened?" I slurred.

"You were turning fucking blue," Simon said and breathed a sigh. "Fuck, kid, I was freaking out."

"I saw people," I said.

"How much of this shit did you take?" he asked and snatched up the blackened tinfoil.

"Just what you gave me …"

"Bullshit. That was this afternoon. How much have you done since I left?" he snapped.

"Nothing. I did what you gave me. You were right there," I replied.

Simon stormed off into the kitchen, and I picked up the beer from the coffee table to wash out the taste in my mouth. The beer was warm, flat, and stale, causing me to gag and almost spit it back out.

Simon returned to the living room, stood, and stared at me for a second. "Are you alright?"

"I think so. What's going on? What happened?" I asked, wincing and trying to scrape the taste from my tongue with the back of my teeth.

"Craig must have given us some bad shit; you weren't breathing. I thought you were going to die," he said and exhaled loudly through his nose.

"I think I talked to God," I said.

"That's not funny, kid, I'm fucking serious, you almost died," Simon said sternly.

"I …" I started.

"We're going to go back to the clubhouse to see Craig," he said, cutting me off.

"I thought you wanted me to stay away from those guys?"

"I need to see Craig right now, and I'm not leaving you on your own, so come on," he said.

"Can I change my clothes first?" I asked.

"Hurry up; we're leaving in five minutes," he said, leaving no room for compromise.

CHAPTER 35

Square

I had to break into a run every couple of steps to match Simon's pace as we made our way back to the clubhouse. It was late when we arrived. Craig and a few others stood outside under plumes of cigarette smoke, talking in hushed gruff tones.

Without waiting for Craig to acknowledge us, Simon stormed on up to the group and blurted, "What the fuck did you give me? That shit almost killed the kid. He wasn't fucking breathing."

"Slow down and lower your voice, Si. That was China-white, that shit's pure," Craig said.

"Pure? It almost fucking killed him," Simon replied.

"You use that tone with me again, and I'm going to have you put down; you guys stomp on this shit not me. What I gave you is as pure as it gets." Craig seemed to grow larger as he stared down at Simon. "Maybe you shouldn't give bad drugs to a sixteen-year-old kid."

"He's an addict; what fucking choice do I have?" Simon snapped.

The seemingly child-sized version of Simon was swallowed whole by Craig's shadow, as the looming bear snatched the scruff of Simon's shirt and pulled him close. "This is the last time I'm going to say this. Watch your fucking mouth."

The no longer stomping child was lowered back to the ground, and in a calm, almost fatherly tone, Craig said, "You did well tonight, Si, let's leave it that way, unless you want to owe me another favor to make up for your attitude?"

Simon shook his head and lowered his eyes to the ground.

"You come here shouting like that again, and I'll have you put down like a dog. You understand me?" Craig said and waited for Simon to make eye contact. "We're done, square. Now get the fuck out of here."

Simon turned and held me in tow by my shirt as we hurried away. Once out of sight, he let out a nervous laugh and took a deep breath, which stammered to the rhythm of his pounding pulse.

"Well, that fucking showed him," Simon said through an awkward smirk, and we both laughed. The near-miss nervous laughter, compelled by shock, fear, or perhaps relief, died down as we started up again toward home, and Simon asked with sarcastic intonation, "So what did God say to you?"

"That I was special," I replied.

Simon smirked and shook his head. "No shit."

CHAPTER 36

Angel-bugs

Morphine hydrochloride or morphine base is mixed with acetic anhydride in a stainless steel pot. A dampened towel is stretched over the pot and the lid secured, the towel acting as a gasket or seal. The mixture is heated to around eighty-five degrees Celsius until the morphine has dissolved. The pot is opened and the solution allowed to cool. It is diluted with water, stirred, and left to stand for twenty minutes. Sodium carbonate is dissolved in hot water and added slowly to the mixture until it stops frothing, precipitating solid heroin base, which is filtered through a fine cloth and set aside. Once dry, the granular white powder, a crude water insoluble freebase product, is dissolved in hot alcohol and filtered using activated charcoal. Hydrochloric acid is then added to the solution before it is diluted with ether. The precipitated heroin hydrochloride is then collected and filtered once more. This is number four heroin, China-white, the purest form of heroin collected by filtration, and allegedly what was in the bag given to us by Craig.

 Whether my tolerance had decreased during the two days of reluctant abstinence or it had been dirty heroin, as was Simon's immediate assumption, the powder from Craig had been flushed and replaced with a more costly, "but guaranteed-pure," product from a rival dealer, while I was still sleeping.

I woke up late, and there was a small hoot waiting for me on the coffee table in the living room—enough to stay the sickness but not enough to get high or send me on the nod.

"So what happened yesterday?" I picked up the foil and did the hoot.

"You almost died, that's what happened," Simon replied.

"I meant the gig with Kev," I said, exhaling the smoke.

"Kev went into a house, and I kept watch until he came out," he replied.

"What was in the house?" I asked.

"I don't know; who cares? Fuck it. It's done, it's over, and we're out of debt with Craig," Simon replied.

"Will Michael come back now?"

"He'll be back tomorrow."

"Where is he?" I asked.

"What's with all the questions? He had to go to another supplier because of all this shit with Craig. Right now, he's probably on a bus, on his way back with a shit load of H in a carry-on bag," he replied.

"What if he doesn't come back?"

"He'll be back tomorrow, kid, and then everything will go back to normal," Simon said with an exasperated sigh.

"Panda's never coming back though."

Simon's chest deflated, as did his expression. "I need a drink. You want one?" he asked, and I nodded in response.

He returned with a couple beers, and we sat for a short while, each searching for the right thing to say. Simon stared at the floor, shaking his head.

"What is it?" I asked.

"I've had my nose broken twice in my life; once by you, and once by Panda, because of you," Simon said and smirked.

"Sorry," I said and stared back at the bottle in my hand.

"Don't be. It was my fault. I shouldn't have let you try it," Simon winced, "Fuck, that hurt. It had only just healed."

"That was the only time I'd ever seen him mad," I said.

"He was pissed. You can still see the blood stains in the carpet, all the way to the bathroom," he said, and I followed his gaze to the trail of dark spots leading out of the living room.

"The day he caught you, he said that you were my responsibility, and if you overdosed, it would be my fault," he said, "Yesterday when you turned blue, that whole conversation came flooding back. He was right. If you die on this shit, it'll be my fault."

"Why would it be your fault, I'm ..." I started.

Simon shook his head. "He made me promise I'd get you off this shit. He made a point of reminding me every time he saw me getting your medicine ready."

"You know how hard it is to get off this shit?" he asked rhetorically. "You've only gone a few days. Wait until you've gone a week or two without a fix."

A resurrected sense of shame colored my words as I spoke to the beer in my hands. "He snatched the foil out of my hand and called me a fucking idiot. He said that if he ever caught me doing it again, he would throw me out of the house." I paused and took a drink. "He didn't speak to me after that for about three weeks."

We sat and drank, both silently replaying private memories. "I miss him," I said somberly.

"Me too, kid," Simon replied.

***

More than a couple beers in and we were trading stories back and forth, degraded versions of Panda's infamous trivia.

"Did you know that heroin and Aspirin were made by the same company?" Simon quoted, with caricatured mimicry.

With my eyes closed, fond memories played out. Panda perched forward on the edge of his seat, his elbows on his knees and drawing pictures in the air with his hands as he spoke. He was never short of a relevant tidbit or anecdote, no matter what the subject. I would always stop and smile when I heard those three words, "did you know," and those were the conversations that had replayed on an endless loop in my mind for the last three months. "Did you know that the magi cicada spends seventeen years underground in the dark as one kind of creature," Panda began.

"and then climbs out of the dirt, scratching its way to the surface to become something else," I said, reading Panda's words out loud, as he mouthed them in my mind.

"What?" Simon asked.

"It's known as the seventeen-year locust," I continued with my eyes still closed, unwilling to let go of the daydream.

"Flying-fuck-bugs," Simon said.

I opened my eyes and glanced over at Simon.

"They live underground for seventeen years, crawl out, sprout wings, fly up into a tree, fuck, and die," Simon said and took a drink, "Flying-fuck-bugs."

"Angel-bugs," I replied, "I'll be seventeen next year; maybe in the spring, I'll shed my skin and grow wings. Like an angel."

"An angel?" Simon said, rolling his eyes. "You're just going to sprout wings and turn into a magical junkie fairy?" he said and laughed through his nose.

"The cicadas grow wings after being without them for seventeen years," I argued.

"The cicadas are a freak of nature, a one off," he said, shaking his head and becoming visibly irritated.

"What about butterflies?" I asked with a smirk.

"You know what, kid? Maybe you will grow wings and fly the fuck away, do us all a favor," he snapped and downed the rest of his beer. He placed his empty bottle on the coffee table and read the expression on my face. "Alright, kid, I'm sorry, I didn't mean it."

I shook my head and attempted to laugh, as though his comment hadn't hurt as much as it had. "It's okay."

"You've got to stop with this God and angel shit though, you sound fucking crazy," he said in a defensive manner, "there's no such thing as angels or God."

"I've talked to God," I murmured.

"Yeah, and tomorrow, maybe you'll tell me you rode home on a fucking unicorn. It doesn't mean it's true," he said, sarcastically and with an undertone of spite.

I stood and stormed toward the kitchen, ignoring both the pain in my shin from catching the corner of the coffee table, and the noise from empty bottles as they rattled and rolled off the table, dripping stale beer dregs into the carpet.

"What the fuck, kid? Where are you going?"

"To get another drink," I snapped.

I pulled two beers from the fridge, set them on the counter, and wiped my eyes with the back of my hand. I popped both caps and dropped the bottle opener down on the counter. It clattered to a stop next to a small bag of white powder, and I stared at it, a slave staring at his master's whip. I snatched the bag and slipped it into my back pocket.

I slammed a beer on the coffee table in front of Simon. "Alright, kid, calm down," he said.

"I want to go and visit him," I said.

Simon let out a big sigh. "Kid," he started.

"Today," I said, cutting him off and with no intention of backing down.

"Why don't you sit down, drink your beer, and calm down," Simon replied. I remained standing and continued to glare.

"Alright." Simon raised his eyebrows and the bottle in his hand. "We'll go after these."

I retrieved my sketchpad from the table, ripped a selected page along its perforated edge and folded the page into quarters. We sat in silence until both bottles were placed empty on the coffee table.

"You sure about this, kid?" Simon asked.

I gave a brief nod and followed him out.

CHAPTER 37

Lithobates sylvaticus

It took a while to find the stone, and if Simon hadn't been there, I wouldn't have known what to look for. Steven Andrew Clarke, beloved son and brother, followed by his date of birth and date of death. These were the details engraved on the headstone over Panda's grave.

"I didn't know that his real name was Steven," I said.

"He wouldn't have answered to it anyway; he'd hate that it says Steven on his gravestone," Simon replied.

"Do you think he's in heaven?"

Simon snorted, "You know where he is? He's about six feet under us, in a wooden box."

"I mean," I started.

"I know what you mean. I miss him too, but when you die, you're gone, that's it, there's just nothing."

"What about ghosts?" I asked.

"When you're dead, you're dead. Ghosts aren't real," he said, emphasizing every word.

"I've seen ghosts," I said.

"Yeah, and they put you on anti-psychotics," Simon sneered.

"I could still see them even when I was taking the perphenazine," I said, unsure of whether I was trying to convince myself, or defend my all but diminished pride.

"Can you see them now?" he asked. "This is a cemetery; it must be full of ghosts and angels and goblins."

I shook my head, and a smirk spread over his face.

"I've seen this whole place crowded with them," I snapped.

"What? When? This is the first time we've been here?"

"I used to come here to avoid my dad," I said, as my eyes began to well up.

"So it's when you're stressed or upset, that you see things, right?"

"What are you getting at, Si?"

"I'm saying that maybe stress is what brings it on," Simon replied.

I glowered at him. "Brings what on?"

"Whatever it is, that's wrong with you, maybe stress causes it."

"Whatever is wrong with me? There's nothing wrong with me," I yelled.

"You hallucinate, chasing the dragon. Heroin's not a hallucinogenic drug." Simon shook his head. "Maybe you should go back on the pills before you end up back in the hospital."

"Fuck you, Si, I'm not going back to the hospital, and I'm not taking any more pills. There's nothing wrong with me. I'm fine."

Simon glanced around at the scornful expressions, dotted around the cemetery and all staring back at us. "Whatever, kid, I've got better things to do. See you later." He walked away and into the periphery of disapproving mourners, offering them a direction and purpose for unresolved anger as they each tracked his egress.

The onlookers, one by one, faded back into dutiful grief, paying their respect and placing flowers, and I returned my attention to the headstone before me. "I brought something for you," I said aloud and retrieved the folded sketch from my back pocket.

I knelt and placed the sketch face up, with a rock on top to stop it from blowing away. "Did you know that there's a frog that can freeze itself in the cold. Its heart stops, its breathing stops, and it seems as though it's dead, but it's not, it comes back to life," I said with a quivering lip and tears welling up in my eyes. "I miss you."

With my head in my hands, I wept. The rock darkened in wet streaks and the paper under it wrinkled, as the tears dripped from my chin, blotting and blurring the penciled impression of a wood frog.

CHAPTER 38

Simon says

I awoke to view the ripped curl of cardboard and blackened foil lining, torn and removed from a discarded cigarette packet, while a mess of flattened grass tickled and stabbed at the side of my face. I rolled onto my back and winced at the bright blue sky. Even with my eyes closed, the back of my eyelids glowed bright red, causing me to look away and shield my eyes with a draped forearm. I wiped the grass and dirt from my face and fingered the new crosshatched grooves pressed into my cheek by the tangled makeshift pillow, and I waited for the large bright yellow-green spot in front of my eyes to fade.

The graveyard came slowly into focus as my eyes adjusted, but the scene remained dim, darkened by a forest of human silhouettes. A smile crept over my face as I scanned each of the motionless figures, wondering if Panda's shadow was among them, saving a place for him in the world. As I studied one to the next, I became aware of movement, distant in my peripheral vision. Warped and partially obscured, the shape advanced quickly through the cemetery, closing the gap between us and strobing into focus, brightness and clarity as it passed through each of the dark, man-shaped filters.

Preceded by a series of stomping footsteps over hollow earth, a hand broke through the shadow and snatched a hold of my arm. I was pulled to my feet, passing through cold dark air and into the accusing glare, burning from Simon's reddened face.

"The dope?" he snapped, "Where the fuck is it?"

As if anticipating my inability to process the question, my hand reached back, seemingly of its own will, bypassing the chain of command to retrieve the bag of powder from my pocket.

"Do you want to join Panda, is that it? You've already almost died on this shit." Simon snatched the packet from my outstretched hand. "Well? Answer me, kid."

"Can you see them?" I turned my gaze left and right. "They're all around us."

"See what? Don't start that fucking shit with me again," Simon snapped.

"Ghosts, shadows," I said.

"Are you trying to make me angry?" Simon released my arm with a push, and I stumbled to the ground.

There was a beating, scuffling sound, followed by a guttural growl from behind my shoulder. Simon traced my gaze to the exposed teeth and gums of the snarling animal at my side. "It's okay, it's Gabriel, the pastor's dog," I said.

"You are fucking crazy, kid, or you think I am." Simon stared down at me with a disdainful sneer. "What fucking dog?"

I flicked my attention back and forth, from Gabriel to Simon. "You don't see him?"

"The only thing I see is a piece-of-shit-junkie who should be locked up in the nut house," he spat.

I rushed to my feet and put all of my weight behind a punch, thrown at Simon's face. He leaned away and let the momentum of my swing carry my head into the path of his responding fist. As I brought my hands up in front of my face, he pulled me forward into a knee, driven hard, up into my abdomen. The air in my lungs escaped all at once, and I collapsed to a gasping heap.

"Are you done, kid?" Simon's fists hung, clenched at his sides as I sputtered on the ground. In a blur of teeth and fur, Gabriel lunged forward and bit at Simon's leg as I expelled sharp dregs of air, stretching a hand out in retroactive protest. Simon recoiled, joining the ranks of a newly formed circle of people, watching and talking in a collaborative murmur.

From the crowd, I recognized the man with long dark hair as he stepped forward and said, "It's not real."

"It's not real?" I replied in a stammered whisper.

"You know it's not real," Simon shouted.

The man glanced about him and back down at me with a frown.

"You're not real?" I gasped.

"You can see me?" the man asked, almost in a whisper.

"Who the fuck are you talking to?" Simon asked.

"Yes, I can see you," I replied, ignoring the glare from Simon.

"You need to go back on your pills," Simon said.

"Who are you?" I asked.

"Kid, you're hallucinating, and you're freaking me out," Simon said.

The man raised a hand to his face and hair, mouthed something as his eyes searched the cemetery, and then returned to me as if having found the words to say, "I'm your friend."

"You're my friend?" I asked.

"Of course, I'm your friend, and I'm fucking worried about you," Simon replied.

The man blurred to a dark featureless surrogate, followed by the rest of the crowd, and in the time it took for my eyes to flick to Simon and back, they had gone, leaving only Simon and me, over Panda's grave, in the warmer air of a brighter cemetery.

"Kid?"

"They're gone," I said through a somber sigh.

"Come on, we're going." Simon leaned in to take hold of my arm and I grabbed and fumbled, trying to lift his pant leg.

"Knock it off." He pulled me to my feet and clasped my head firmly in his hands and brought me reluctantly back to his stare. "What the fuck is wrong with you?"

"There's no bite mark," I mumbled.

"There's no what?" Simon asked.

"There's no bite mark where Gabriel bit your leg."

Simon frowned, hesitated and spoke sternly. "So what does that tell you kid? They're not real."

I turned my eyes away as they glazed over.

"Come on," he said and tugged me by the arm, "We're going home. You going to walk on your own, or do I have to drag you all the way?"

I relented into keeping pace, following closely behind him, and although the journey was silent, Simon's words echoed in my mind, all the way home.

... So what does that tell you kid? They're not real.

CHAPTER 39

Repressionist primer

The bruise darkened to the hue of a rotting plum, outlining my yellowed eye socket and spreading away like blotting ink, absorbing into the expanding canvas of my cheek as it continued to swell throughout the evening, while I sat alone in my room, nursing a warm beer and my tattered pride.

A storm of emotion accompanied a cascade of violent flashbacks, memories brought back to life by the visual triggers coloring my face, and all starring my parents, him with that flaring temper and glaring eyes, and her with that vacant, robotic smile.

Long since the last physical trace of abuse, the memory of his hateful glare, and the smiling mask worn over her face, emoting only that she didn't or couldn't care, remained, carved into my mind and lurking behind every other memory of my childhood, emotional scars that would open up, never able to fully heal, periodically weeping and frequently infected.

To treat the wounds, I would medicate with heroin, dulling the world and removing life's sharp edges, before stretching a new cloth bandage over a wooden frame and painting my own exit, an escape into wet pigment, colors mixed from bitter memories and rearranged over each canvas as a colorful cryptic remedy. There were canvases with paint over half an inch thick, paintings over top of other paintings, and buried inside each, were scenes of domestic violence or demonic creatures. Sealed under a red butterfly, was a lifeless blue child, lying at the feet of his small shadow.

The final subject of each painting was unimportant; my catharsis was in the process, hiding memories where no one would ever find them, and where no one would ever think to look. I would add a new layer with every bad dream or memory until Michael would remove it from the easel, with only the last impressionist, or repressionist, distraction visible.

Often I would wake up to the skeleton frame of an empty easel and with red smears over myself and the mattress, Michael having used my limp hand to moniker my work with a thumb print in the bottom right corner, before delivering it to the gallery with a pocket full of powder to sweeten the deal.

My last painting had remained on the easel, rejected in disgust by Michael, defaced and half-destroyed by me. It was a full color, slightly abstracted version of a photograph from a newspaper article, a red and rust hatchback folded around a streetlamp, the exhaust smoke lit by the tail lights and the road glistening with a thousand tiny cubes of glass. The article describing the image had said that the driver swerved to avoid a jaywalking pedestrian, lost control, and collided with a lamp standard. The driver was pronounced dead soon after the ambulance arrived, and Panda never came home.

CHAPTER 40

A box of memories

Shaking off a daydream, inspired by the morbid remnants of the painting on the easel, I swallowed down a recurring lump, wiped my eyes, and marched toward the canvas. Previous attempts to cover over the offending image had only served to accentuate its macabre nature, enhancing the horrific scene with smeared red paint, slashes, and tears.

I turned my eyes away and turned the painting around as though reluctantly handling the rotting corpse of an animal. One of the depicted taillights still stared at me from the tongue of tattered canvas, hanging from the ripped-open gape of its mouth, as I attempted to shove the canvas behind a stack of boxes in the closet. I wrenched the canvas down against the back wall, kicking at the obstructing boxes and levering against them until one and then another tumbled out of the closet against my leg and to the floor, spilling their contents.

With the canvas wedged and jammed as far down as it would go, I knelt down to the heap of books at my feet, all with the same plain burgundy cover, and one was splayed open. I flicked through it; the number fourteen was written in the front and, with nothing more than a passing glance, I recognized his writing, these were Panda's journals.

INFINITY

***

Slouched back on the mattress, my pillow folded in half against the wall and the journal marked as number one open on my lap, I began to read.

> *So far, I've had no luck finding a job, no one wants to hire a fourteen-year-old dropout. Less than a month ago, I was a straight-A student, now here I am, part of a trio of dropout-runaways, all cramped together in a beat-up old trailer and living off scraps. If you ever read this, I hope you'll realize why I couldn't take you with me, I can barely take care of myself.*
>
> *Dad never laid a hand on you, and I hope to God that doesn't change now his punching bag is gone. I can't bear the thought of you ending up on the receiving end of that asshole's temper. I'm going to come back for you. I just need time to get back on my feet. Michael says that I can work for him until I find a job. I don't want you around this stuff; it's no place for a kid your age. When I can offer you a better kind of life, I will come back and get you, I promise. I'm sorry, Nathan. I miss you, kid.*

As I turned the page, something fell to the mattress, a photograph of a boy, a boy that looked like Panda.

CHAPTER 41

Consequences

I awoke to the sound of muffled voices, picked myself up, still fully clothed, and followed the sound, growing louder as I neared the living room. The conversation trailed off as I entered. Michael and Simon sat staring at me and then each other.

"When did you get back?" I asked.

"I got back into town at about eight o'clock this morning," Michael replied in a somber tone. "Where'd you get the shiner?"

As my eyes fell upon Simon's twitching grimace, he stood and stormed out of the room, shaking his head and cursing under his breath.

"He's still mad at me?"

"Mad at you?" Michael asked with a frown.

"About yesterday, he told you what happened, right?"

"It's nothing to do with you. He's got a lot on his mind right now," Michael replied.

"What do you mean?"

"Just leave it alone, kid," Michael said, shushing me with his hand.

"What's going on?" I asked.

Michael's attention flicked over my shoulder as Simon slapped a folded newspaper against my chest. "Read it."

"What is it?" I asked.

"Just fucking read it," Simon snapped.

On the front page was a photograph of an ordinary looking house, in focus behind the yellow blur of stretched police banner tape and in large letters, "Man stabbed to death in own home." Below the image, the article continued, "Police are investigating what they believe to be a targeted attack that occurred Thursday evening and left a man dead with multiple stab wounds. Local authorities have said that the victim was known to them and had been arrested several times for drug-related offenses."

"Police have several eyewitness accounts describing two males that were seen on the property that evening. Sketches will be released to the public later today. If you have any information please contact …"

"That was the house, the gig with Kev." Simon stabbed at the page with a pointed finger, emphasizing his words.

"I thought you said that nothing happened?"

"How the fuck was I supposed to know?" he snapped.

"You could tell the police that you didn't do it, that you just waited outside."

"Are you fucking stupid? I'm an accessory to murder. They'll throw me in jail or worse," Simon yelled.

"Worse?" I asked.

"The only way that I'm going to stay out of jail is by ratting Kev out to the cops," he ranted and began to pace. "Do you know what happens to rats?"

He kicked at the coffee table, a makeshift ashtray and beer bottles clinked and clattered to the carpet, pouring out new stains and a layer of ash. "Fuck," he screamed, scooped up a bottle and hurled it past my face. It exploded on contact with the wall behind me, sending a spray of beer dregs and glass shrapnel in every direction.

"You watch, those witnesses are going to be on the front page, missing or dead within the next few days, then I'm next. I can go to jail for murder or rat Kev out to the cops, either way, I'm fucked." Simon's eyes met mine and narrowed as he stormed toward me. "This is your fault."

I backed into the wall, flinched, and squirmed; he slammed his forearm into my chest, pushed my face flat to the wall and spat through his teeth, "This is your fucking fault."

Michael pulled Simon away and ushered him into the kitchen, while I remained, shaking, but not daring to move. Simon's bark echoed from the doorway over Michael's futile reasoning, and moments later, Simon emerged, still red in the face, arms and fists tensed like hammers at his side as he marched through the living room. He gestured with a jutting snarl as he passed me, causing me to flinch, raising my arms to protect my face as I cowered and slid down the wall.

The slam of the front door reverberated through the house, a tremor passed from the wall and floor through my shaking body, settling at my lip and lower eyelids as they filled with hot, stinging tears.

"I think maybe it'd be better if you weren't here when he gets back. I'll talk to him and calm him down," Michael said.

"He's right. It is my fault," I sobbed.

"Kid," Michael started.

"He went in my place, to make it up to Craig," I said, cutting him off.

"Here, just take this and go for a walk or something, until I get a chance to talk to him," he held out a small bag of powder. I wiped my eyes and took it from him.

I washed my face in the sink, unable to raise my head to meet the coward on the other side of the glass, retrieved the journal from my room, and left the house without another word.

CHAPTER 42

Defaced

The cemetery was empty and striped gold by the early morning sun. Behind the church, remnants of the most recent facelift, several cracked stones, a bag of mortar-mix, and various masonry tools, were laid out over a sheet of plywood. I wrestled to separate a stack of empty plastic pails, turned one over to use as a stool, and placed Panda's journal as a tabletop, over the remaining stack. From the garbage, I found an empty cigarette packet, retrieved the foil lining and held a flame under it, warming the glue and separating the paper layer. I rolled a ripped piece of the packet into a tube and loaded the foil.

Having medicated, I returned to the graveyard and tucked myself inside the shadow of Panda's headstone. The sun lit up the old church building; the upper window shone like a lighthouse beacon, beckoning all lost sheep seeking sanctuary or salvation. Moss and ivy had once climbed each of its walls, but had been removed sporadically to facilitate the renovation work. Bare patches now highlighted the grey veins of new mortar, filled cracks in the naked stone façade, spreading up the wall like their ivy predecessor and popping bright like the photographic negative of skinny winter trees.

Turned on my side and propped up on one elbow, I thumbed through the pages of Panda's journal, resuming my place as a fly on the wall during the one-sided conversation between Panda and his brother. The journals were never meant for me, but nevertheless, I found comfort in his words when he wrote of missing Nathan, of missing me. Beyond death, the journals would serve to keep the memory of him alive in my mind. The cemetery blurred, fading behind new conjured images painted behind my eyes, inspired by Panda's words.

***

Averting my eyes from the unfiltered, mid-afternoon sun, I returned to the headstone with a white pail of soupy grey mortar, mixed using stale rainwater and a trowel that was now somewhere submerged beneath the mud in the bucket, and set it down along with an old soaked rag, hammer, and stone-chisel. Wrapped over the back of the chisel, the stretched cloth rag dampened each strike with the hammer as I chipped away at the stone, carving around the n and d of Andrew.

Wrist deep, my fingers spread under the cold, thickened mud, I searched out and retrieved the trowel, wiped off the handle and my hand with the rag, and began spreading the mortar, pushing it into the previously etched name and smoothing it over with my fingers. Using the corner of the trowel, I removed the excess mortar from the new grooves, smoothed the edges with red-raw and wrinkled fingertips, and sat back to view the headstone that now read, Panda.

"What do you think you are doing?"

I turned to see the pastor scowling down at me.

"Have you no respect for the dead?" The white square of his collar seemed to glow, contrasted against the black cloth and the burn-red skin of his vibrating neck and face.

"It's what he would've wanted," I replied.

"He would have wanted you defacing his gravestone?"

"I'm not defacing it, I'm fixing it," I said and dropped the trowel into the bucket to land with a wet slap.

"Fixing it? What right do you have?" he demanded.

I ignored his question and began gathering up the tools.

"What do you think the family is going to say when they see this?"

"Do you know his family?" I asked, and while he rearranged his words around the cutting edge of his tongue, I added, "his brother, Nathan Clarke?"

"Yes, I know Nathan, and his father." He paused, exhaling a loud sigh through his nose. "What will Mr. Clarke say when he sees what's been done to his son's gravestone?"

"Panda's dad beat him, until he ran away. We were his family right up to when he died. If you don't believe me, read his journal," I said and gestured to the burgundy book at his feet.

"Where did you get that?"

"I have Panda's old room. They were in a box in the closet," I mumbled, not taking my eyes off the ground.

"Do you think he would have wanted you reading his private journals?"

Passing the shameful lump in my throat, the words fell out of me, barely reaching his feet, "I don't know. He's dead and I miss him; it's the only thing I have left of him."

The pastor seemed to recompose himself. Both the tone of his skin and the tone of his voice softened. "Let's just go inside and call your parents, see if we can get this figured out."

He reached down to take my arm, and I pulled away, that single word ringing in my head and triggering a reaction inside me. With my blood brought rapidly to boiling temperature, I rose to my feet among the billowing steam. "My parents? I don't have any parents. Panda was the closest thing to family that I had, and he's dead."

He raised his palms, fingers splayed and facing me. "Alright, look …"

"You touch me and I'm going to start swinging." I balled up my fists.

"Now calm down," the pastor said, growing the distance between us with each careful step backward.

"Are you going to set your dog on me?" I asked, shaking with red-hot adrenaline coursing through me.

"My dog?" The pastor stopped and frowned.

"Gabriel, he won't attack me, he likes me," I blurted.

The pastor stared at me, his expression skewed into something unreadable. "Are you okay?"

My eyes began to sting as hot liquid lined my lower lids. "What do you mean, okay?"

"You seem a little confused."

"Confused? I'm a heroin addict, I'm crazy, I'm alone, and I'm a worthless piece of shit, but I'm not confused," I replied through the now streaming tears, feeling like nothing more than the sum of my words, and somehow dismantled.

"Wait here for a moment," he said, gesturing with his hands for me to stay.

"Are you going to call the cops?" I asked, wiping my face.

"No, I'm not going to call the police. I have something for you," he replied, waiting for me to make eye contact to add a reassuring nod and the same straight-line smile that I had been offered so many times before.

Ignoring the overwhelming instinct to run the minute he was out of sight, I sat and waited. He returned moments later carrying a small book, a pocket-sized bible.

"Read this, I think it may help," he said, holding the book upright to show the gold-leaf title.

"Help what?" I asked.

"Help you find your way out of the darkness and into the light," he replied.

"I don't understand," I said.

"And I will bring the blind by way they knew not, I will lead them in paths they have not known, I will make darkness light before them, and crooked things straight. These things will I do unto them, and not forsake them. Isaiah 42:16," he said, reciting with conviction.

He held out the book, and I took it from him.

"Now, what are we going to do about this?" he asked, glancing down at the headstone.

"About defacing it with a different name?"

The pastor nodded, raising his eyebrows and leaning in to my peripheral vision as I stared at Panda's new headstone.

"Like I said, I already fixed it."

The pastor said nothing as I walked away, and I didn't look back.

CHAPTER 43

Divided

"Did you talk to Si?" I asked.

"Yeah, I talked to him," Michael replied.

"What's he going to do?"

"Sit down for a minute," he said.

"What's going on, where is he?"

"He's gone," he said, tapping his fingers on the arm of the chair.

"What do you mean, gone, gone where?"

"He packed a bag and left. He's gone, and we're going to do the same," he said.

"What? Where did he go?"

"He didn't tell me where he was going. I don't think he knows."

"Is he coming back?" I asked.

"Kid, listen to me, he's gone. If they find him, he's fucked. If they can't find him, they'll come looking for us, so pack your shit, we're leaving," he said, emphasizing each and every word.

"Leaving, to go where?"

"I don't know yet, but we can't stay here."

As I sat, trying to process the information, he snapped, "Kid, go pack, we're leaving."

I went to my room, sorted and stuffed clothes from the floor and closet into an oversized army kit bag, one of Panda's many thrift-store finds. Beyond clothes, I was unsure what I would need, or couldn't do without. I didn't have much, but most of what I owned was given to me by Panda, and leaving it behind would be like leaving him behind. The art reference books on my shelf, each symbolized irreplaceable memories of our time together. Over the four years, he had taken me to almost every gallery within driving range, chasing exhibits of the old masters, indulging his need for knowledge and my love of art. It was his enthusiasm that further fueled my passion to paint, to improve, to impress him, and make him proud of me.

With the olive-drab bag stuffed, I pulled the drawstring, cinching the hole shut and stretching the green fabric tight. The protruding corners of packed books lined one side of the bag like saw teeth, periodically and painfully clipping my ankle as I brushed past it, gathering up priceless memories.

When I returned again to the living room carrying the taped-shut box packed full with Panda's journals, Michael was crouched down beside my bag, pulling at the draw string of the bulging limbless crocodile.

"What the fuck have you got in here, kid?"

"Clothes and my art books," I replied.

"Kid, leave the books; we'll get you some more when we settle," he said and began pulling them out of the bag.

"But Panda got them for me," I replied.

"What's in the box?"

"Journals." I gripped the box tight.

"Kid …"

"I'm not leaving them." I glared at him as he pulled out the last of my reference books and pulled the string tight.

"Fine, you're carrying that shit. Don't cry to me when that shit gets too heavy for you," Michael said, shaking his head.

"I won't." I set the box down next to the bag.

"Your medicine's on the table. Do it before we go; we've got a long bus ride coming," he said.

"Bus ride?"

"Just hurry up," he said.

I knelt down at the coffee table and picked up the foil. "What about the house?" I pulled my lighter from my pocket.

"What about it? The lease is in Panda's name, and he's dead. What are they going to do?"

"I mean all our stuff," I said, ripping a strip from an electronics store flyer and rolling it into a tube.

"We'll replace it."

"And what about Panda's stuff?" I flicked the lighter and pulled the smoke through the tube.

Michael shrugged. "We have to leave it."

I held the smoke for a few seconds then exhaled. "So we're never coming back here?"

"No, we're not." Michael picked up his bag. "Come on kid."

I swung the now sagging olive-drab bag onto my shoulder, picked up the box, and followed him out.

CHAPTER 44

Halfway house

Half an hour into the journey and Michael was slouched in his chair, knees raised, pressed against the seat in front, and snoring through the curtains of greasy hair, hanging and tightly framing his face.

Once on the highway, the bus picked up speed, and the scenery raced by in a blur. The pulse of angular grey shapes slowed to an eventual flat line of green moving in and out behind desolate barns and the rusted skeletal remains of old farming equipment. Centered in an expansive striped field stood a large farmhouse, claiming ownership to the land around it and marking the scenic halfway point in our journey. As if passing through a mirror, a line of symmetry projected from between the farmhouse's double doors, the scrolling background now played in reverse, a plagiarized version of all that had come before it.

The bus arrived at another city center, complete with shopping malls, department stores, parking lots, and finally a bus station, an almost perfect replica of the one we had started from.

I gave Michael a nudge. "I think we're here."

He jolted awake with an abrupt snort, dropped his feet to the floor, and began to stretch, pressing his shoulders against the seat with his back arched and elbows pointed at the roof of the bus. Through a stifled yawn, he groaned, "Home sweet home."

***

I followed behind Michael as we walked around for what felt like hours. Sweat dripped from my forehead down to the large box cradled in my aching arms with its corners biting into the palms of my hands. I was almost about to break my vow of silence, regarding the weight of my irreplaceable luggage, when Michael stopped.

"Oneiroi motel?" I asked, tracing his gaze to the half-lit, half-burned-out sign.

"Looks like a dive, but it'll do until we find something better. Wait here. I'll go get us a room," he said and went inside.

I set the box down and sat leaning against it, palms offered up like a vagrant, begging of the slightest breeze to caress and soothe the blistered skin stretched tight over the swollen lumps of meat, hinged from my wrists.

Looking down the length of the single-story, two-tone-dirt-and-beige stucco building, I found myself almost hypnotized, lost in the repetition. The thin horizontal stripe of glass stretched, tapering into the distance, broken up by blue doors, vertical rungs in the façade, delineating each section as a room and each unit definable by differing levels of dilapidation.

I was snapped out of my daydream by the rattle of keys next to my ear. "We're in number seven."

A dark patch in the paint, in the shape of a seven, centered the upper portion of a sun-faded pale blue door with two small screw holes hinting at where the brass number was once fastened. Michael unlocked the door, and I followed him in, stowing the box against one of the room's dented, scuffed, and smoke-stained yellow-brown walls. Two single beds, each with its own bedside table, alarm clock, and lamp, took up almost the entire space, save for a slim mottled carpet path leading to a chair and small table in the corner with a phone and directory sitting on it, and to a door at the back, hung open to a small off-white bathroom.

"The guy said he'll let us know when there's a room with a kitchen available." Michael set his bag down on the bed and unzipped it.

"Holy shit," I said.

"What? What do you think I've been doing for the last few days, kid?"

"That's a …" I started.

"A shitload of heroin, I know."

He pulled a couple rolls of cash and a handful of point bags from the side pocket. "I'm going to need your help bagging this shit. You've got to be dead-on with the weight though, most junkies are paranoid as fuck, if they think I'm trying to rip them off, they'll go elsewhere."

"I'll do my best," I replied.

"Here you go, chipper." He handed one of the small bags of powder to me, stuffed the rest of the pile into his pockets with the rolls of cash, zipped up the bag, and shoved it under the bed.

"I'm going to go check it out, see if I can get rid of some of this shit."

"What can I do?" I asked.

"I don't know. Write in your journal or something. I'll see you later, kid." The door closed slowly behind him and sealed with a loud click.

CHAPTER 45

Do not disturb

Three of the four unshielded bulbs above the mirror flashed on with a harsh white light, searing through the almost transparent grease-paper skin, worn like a cheap vampire mask over my illuminated skull. I spun to close the bathroom door so as not to disturb Michael, who was still snoring and periodically choking himself half-awake before murmuring a nonsensical lullaby and returning to the rhythmic nasal barrage that had woken me up several times throughout the night.

I stared at the disheveled figure on the other side of the glass, and we acknowledged one another with mutual contempt as we each scrubbed sleep from the corners of dark ringed eyes. The grey-skinned, starved vampire runt opened its mouth, exposing its regular-sized teeth, and we brushed in unison, avoiding further eye contact.

After retrieving the journal from my bedside table, I fumbled around in the low light to find my room key and exited the motel room, careful not to let the door slam behind me. The electrical buzzing sound of the flickering half-lit sign forced me off the motel property in search of a quiet place to sit and read.

***

My concentration was broken by coins as they hit the page, sliding down into the crease between the pages of the journal. I puzzled over it for a second before looking up to see people everywhere, hurriedly walking this way and that on a much busier sidewalk. A man, wearing a business suit, ran with a theatrical bounce, crossing through traffic, one arm up with the palm of his hand flat and facing the cars to stop or thank them as they slowed to let him across. I rubbed at my eyes, stood, and brushed the dirt from my clothes.

On my way back to the motel, a smiling woman stopped to deposit a handful of coins into the upturned hat of a grey-haired, grey-bearded man, sat cross-legged on the ground. Clasped loosely between dirt-ingrained, yellowed fingers and angled to face passers-by, his cardboard sign read, hungry and homeless.

The homeless man acknowledged me with a nod. I tipped the journal, pouring the coins, donated to serve as a temporary bookmark, into the hat and possession of their rightful recipient.

"You're an angel. God bless you," he croaked.

I kept my eyes to the ground and hurried back to the motel, compelled to wash and scrub away the layer of skin deserving of a stranger's pity.

Consulting the plastic tag on my room key, I matched it to the unbleached sigil, centered on the faded blue door and unlocked it. Michael jumped from his chair in the corner of the room as I entered.

"Fuck, I thought you were the cleaner or something; here put this on the door." He held the laminated length of card outstretched in a shaking hand.

I hung the do not disturb sign and put the latch across at Michael's request. "… just in case."

He waited a few minutes to calm his nerves, turned his head to one side, and took a few slow, deep breaths before returning his attention to the table. In front of him was a square plastic tub, lined with a clear plastic bag full of powder. He retrieved the small plastic scoop, and with his other hand pinching open one of the small clear bags, he dug slowly into the powder, tapped the side of the scoop gently with his forefinger until level, then fed the measured dose into the open mouth of the waiting bag.

He turned and breathed deeply over his shoulder before repeating the whole process again. Perched on the edge of the bed, I remained still and quiet, watching and mirroring his breathing so as not to disrupt the delicate process.

After a time, he stood and offered me the chair. "It's time for you to learn the family business, kid."

CHAPTER 46

Alchemy

We soon settled into a routine, and the weeks rolled by, with one day no different from the last. I would bag in the morning while Michael slept; he would wake, wash, we would eat, he would leave with the bagged product, and I would medicate and read until Michael returned, whispering through the inch gap allowed by the brass latch, connecting door and frame, for me to let him in.

Michael's report of nightly success, or my request to replenish diminishing supplies, had become the only topic of conversation between us. Michael insisted that one of us remain in the motel room with the product and cash at all times; by one of us, he meant me.

I worked each day with the curtains drawn, dividing large bags of powder into countless smaller bags. Michael exchanged those small bags for small bills, and those small bills would be rolled together in an elastic band and put with the rest in a bag under the bed.

During this time, my only exposure to a world outside the motel room came in the form of second-hand memories, gleaned from the pages of Panda's journals, an ongoing story that now included a younger version of me, as a member of its cast.

CHAPTER 47

Panda's Journal #9

"... he reminds me of you. He's only a couple years older than you were when I left, although, I figure you'll be turning twenty this year. I can't imagine you as a grown man. In my mind, you remain unchanged from the last time I saw you, the same boy that smiles back at me from the only photograph I have of you.

    I've driven by the house so many times, seems even the better parts of the neighborhood have been reduced to vacant ruins, a ghost town. Our old house has sat empty for at least as long as I've had my driver's license. I wish I knew where you were. I sometimes wonder if we would recognize one another if we passed on the street.

    ... Si's been unpredictable lately, there's something going on with him. His nose is almost healed, but I think it may take a little while longer to mend his pride. He's been collecting unpaid debts for Michael, to cover his share of the rent, he seems to prefer it when they don't pay. Si said that the guy in the church parking lot got what was coming, that he should have paid what he owed. I was there. Si didn't even mention money, just started laying into the guy, and took it way too far.

    'Whoever fights monsters should see to it that in the process he does not become a monster. And if you gaze long enough into an abyss, the abyss will gaze back into you.' — Friedrich Nietzsche.

I don't know how Si would react if I started quoting Nietzsche in front of him. We've come a long way from the days when he would copy my homework. I know what it's like to get beaten every day, to have your confidence stripped and stolen, maybe Si is just trying to steal some of it back.

Between father and son, confidence seems to be a tangible, almost physical commodity with a set value, a finite quantity divided among them. The push-and-pull struggle between alpha male and his successor, is for the acquisition of the other's share. Dissolving of a competitor's confidence dissolves also any legitimate threat to the throne.

It seems to me, that abusive fathers fear the idea of becoming obsolete, the idea that what they are doing is not shaping the next generation to carry their name but training and facilitating a replacement. Maybe it is the instinctive violence that exists in every man, aggression once channeled toward any outside threat to our family, that we now suppress until a threat is found within.

My fear is that if I ever have a family and a child of my own, I will become like him, that the violence lies dormant inside me, waiting for a perceived threat, waiting for me to step into my father's well-worn shoes, to wear away the remaining toe leather, kicking the confidence out of my own child.

... When I look at the kid, I think of you. I hope that you have not had the confidence beaten out of you, the way he has. The bruises about his face are superimposed over the mental image I have of you. I couldn't save you, but I have a chance to help the kid. Even with what little I can offer him, it seems a vast improvement on what he has told me about his way of life.

... Life itself doesn't change, only our knowledge of it, and our ability and willingness to adapt." —Panda.

CHAPTER 48

Resupply

With all of the product bagged up and nothing left to read, I was left alone in the motel room to guard the cash and to begin the mourning process once again over the loss of Panda. His last words, although not intended as his last, were of his hopes of being reunited with Nathan and of his hopes for my future.

His predictions of a better life, his expectations for my career as an artist, gave rise to a sensation not unlike the beginnings of withdrawal, a churning sickness in the pit of my stomach, shame and guilt for having let him down.

***

Michael called through the gap in the door, and I took off the latch. He came inside, closed the door behind him, and began thumbing through a large stack of notes fanning out from his other hand.

After rolling the rest inside a rubber band, he handed the wad of cash to me. "I'm going to give you half of what I owe you now. Don't go throwing it around; people are going to wonder where a kid your age, looking like you do, got that much cash."

"What's this for?"

"It's your cut; it's the same as I gave Si for bagging. Like I said, don't flash it about and get yourself noticed, and I'll give you the rest when I get back."

"Get back? From where?"

"I've got to do a supply run; we're all out," he said.

"I didn't expect …"

"I know, but you've earned it," Michael said. "There'll be no cash or product in the room while I'm gone, so feel free to go out and check out the city."

"Do you mind if I buy some art supplies?" I asked.

"Buy whatever you want, it's your money. Just don't go spending all of it in one place," Michael replied.

"Okay, I won't," I said.

"Fridge is stocked, and I paid for a month on the room. I told the guy at the front that I'm working nights, so there shouldn't be anyone coming by. Stay away from the office. I don't want to give them any reason to start sniffing around the room or asking questions, okay?"

I nodded in compliance.

"Alright, kid, I'll see you in a couple days," Michael said and left with his bag.

CHAPTER 49

Reunion

As I stared at the re-sealed box, my thoughts revolved chaotically around an image of Panda's intended reader. This mental image, evolved and corrected throughout the course of all twenty-three volumes, requested my deepest empathy, fueled by grief over the loss of my friend, our brother.

For Nathan, the grieving process would have begun long before Panda's death, during those years of uncertainty, not knowing if his brother was alive or dead, if they would ever see each other again, or if his brother even cared.

After medicating and on the verge of sleep, scenarios played out behind my eyes, in which I delivered the box of journals to Nathan, and he and I conversed like old friends. As we spoke, Nathan's appearance changed, blending with, until replaced by, his older brother's likeness, and my thoughts morphed into the beginnings of a dream.

***

I awoke with a single thought swimming around through the murky morning fog within my head, my mind seemingly having been made-up by the events of a dream that I could no longer remember beyond the necessity of reuniting Nathan with the memory of his brother.

Michael would be gone for a couple days, allowing enough time for me to make the journey home and back, without having to let him know about it and get mad at me for it. He wouldn't understand why I had to go, and I knew that when he returned, with product for me to bag, I would be trapped indefinitely within the confines of the motel. I medicated, washed up, picked up the box, and exited the room.

***

I had exchanged the rerun of scenery for daydreams and subsequent sleep and was awoken upon arrival at the station by the bus driver. One of the local busses brought me the rest of the way, and I thanked the driver as I stepped down to the pavement next to the padlocked gate of my old school. The bus pulled away, and the loud rumble of its diesel engine gave way to the dissonant drone of organ music, distorted on its way out through large cracks in the stone behind a net of moss and ivy on the non-renovated portions of the church façade.

I set the box down behind the thigh-high wall and meandered, taking the long way around, toward the corner of the cemetery where Panda was buried. At a sideways glance, the deep cracks spreading away from every corner of the upper window frames appeared like crow's feet and laughter lines, urging me to return a smile.

I was expecting to see the headstone restored to its original state, but it was the way it had been the last time I had seen it, save for color. The mortar was cured and faded to the same pale grey as the rest of the headstone, only conspicuous under careful inspection of its rough texture and the imperfect lines that formed the name Panda. Around the cemetery, worn paths of flattened or thinning grass weaved their way to graves and statues. Along the path I had taken, my footprints remained pressed into the otherwise perfectly manicured grass, and I wondered how long that single set of tracks, ending at Panda's grave, would remain.

Having said my final goodbye to Panda, I wiped a sleeve across my face, retrieved the box, and made my way to the church entrance. With the weight of the box supported against my thigh, I pulled open the large wooden door and wedged my foot just inside. The music ended, and the door creaked open as I leaned back against it and struggled through, bumping the doorframe with the corner of the box and rattling the hardware, causing the back row of people to shuffle and turn, squinting into the sunlight flooding in around me. I mouthed sorry and took a seat in the back corner.

The pastor's voice echoed around the packed room. He boomed words like forgiveness, compassion, sin, and light as the seated crowd nodded and acknowledged with a low pitched, collaborative, "Amen."

The pastor said, "We will now say our Lord's Prayer."

The congregation shuffled and stood to a murmuring chorus and the clearing of throats. A couple seconds silence preceded the low, monotone chant as each joined in the collective narration of their sacred mantra, "Our father, who art in heaven, hallowed be thy name, thy kingdom come, thy will be done, on earth as it is in heaven …"

When the prayer finished, belongings were picked up, and the room grew loud with talk and laughter as people filtered through open doors into the sunlight outside. I sat and waited while the remaining few shook hands with the pastor, thanking him for the service, before rejoining the crowd outside.

I approached the pastor as he made his way between the wooden benches, collecting hymnbooks. He looked back to the center aisle where I stood and smiled. "You decided to come to Sunday service."

"I need help with something," I replied.

"Most people do, when they walk into a church." His smile widened.

"I need to find Nathan Clark. I have something for him."

The pastor's smile faded. "I don't feel comfortable giving out the address of a member of this church to a stranger."

"It's important," I said.

"Well, what is it? Maybe I can pass it on when I see them," he replied.

"No, they are for Nathan, not his dad," I stated with an unintentional abruptness that made the pastor stop and set down the stack of hymnbooks.

"What is it that you have for him, exactly?"

I gestured toward the box, sitting on the ground, at the back of the room. "Panda's journals. They're written to Nathan."

The pastor flicked his gaze to the box and back to me.

"It's important. Nathan has to know that Panda didn't just abandon him. He thought about him and wrote to him every day, right up to the day he died."

There was a long and awkward silence, made longer by the pastor's intense examination of my face. "I will have a look through our records to see if I can find the address. Wait here."

I stood waiting and in the back of my mind, wondering if the pastor would instead, call the police, having seized the opportunity to make me pay for "defacing" Panda's headstone, but a few minutes later, he returned holding a square of yellow paper.

"Promise me all you are going to do is drop off the books, nothing else," the pastor said, creasing and crumpling the paper, wrapped tight in his hand.

"I promise. I just want Nathan to know that Panda didn't just forget about him," I replied, almost pleading.

Nodding slowly, he held the paper outstretched, "What if his father answers the door?"

"I guess I'll just wait as long as I have to, until he leaves," I replied and took the paper.

The pastor seemed to have something else on his mind, something else that he wanted to say. I interjected his thoughts with my thanks and turned to walk away.

"God hasn't forgotten about you," he called after me.

I didn't respond to his statement, nor the shiver down my spine, but continued down the aisle, picked up the box, and left.

***

"It's okay, I'll get the next one," I said as the doors opened.

The driver replied, "You sure? Won't be another bus for an hour."

I nodded and thanked him. The doors closed, and the bus pulled away from the curb, like the two that had come and gone before it. The car that I had been watching backed out of the driveway, and I waited for a clear look at the driver, a greying man in his fifties, possibly sixties. I stood, stretched, and made my way to the house, set the box down in front of the doorstep, rang the bell, turned, and ran.

Peering back at the house from behind a parked car across the street, I watched as the door opened and a man, closely resembling the Panda I had first met, glanced up and down the street before kneeling, peeling away the line of tape, and unfolding the cardboard leaves with a frown.

He thumbed through one of the journals, brought a hand to his face and dragged it across his eyes before retrieving another. He raised his head, turning left and right before mouthing words into the air between us, and returning into the house with the box.

Despite sentimental scenarios played over and again in my head, no words were required, other than those on the pages of his brother's journals.

CHAPTER 50

Writer's block

The bright white, pre-stretched, pre-primed canvas stared back at me from my new easel, set up in the kitchen area of the motel room. In an attempt to ignore the mocking effect of a blank canvas to a blank mind, I sat on the corner of my bed, picked and peeled the barcode sticker from each of the various sized brushes, and scratched at the residual glue with my thumbnail.

After unpacking my paint and having rolled each of the removed barcode stickers into thin tacky tubes, I stuffed the garbage back into the craft store bag and reached for the pre-loaded tinfoil square, rolled-up twenty, and lighter.

Panda's advice for overcoming "artist's block" was to paint anything, a stickman, a tree, anything to eliminate the pressure of a blank canvas. "Just paint until you are inspired." He told me that he had read somewhere of a writer who, when she started a new project, would flip to the back of her new note book and write a shopping list, just to take the pressure off of committing the first words to paper.

I picked up three tubes of paint, squeezed out a daub of each onto the bright white square of fabric, and smeared the colors into a black-brown mess with the palm of my hand.

As the medication worked its way through my system, an image worked its way from my mind, through my hand, and onto the canvas. With most of the white space filled, I added yellow ochre, cadmium red, and burnt sienna, reinforcing the form floating somewhere between my eyes and the canvas and connecting the dots between sketch and imagination.

***

Michael unzipped the bag and pulled out a couple neatly folded items of clothing, under which were bricks upon bricks of tightly packed product, negating any inquiry into the success of his trip. He retrieved two of the large bricks, zipped the bag closed, and shoved it under his bed.

He nodded toward the canvas. "You've been busy."

"What do you think?" I asked.

"It's a little morbid, but it's good," he replied.

The painting was of a man, facedown on a desk. Next to his right hand, was a tipped over inkwell with a pool of black ink and quill, and under his left hand, a small pool of red and a razor blade. The pooled liquid on each side blotted into the opposite edges of a single piece of paper, half covered by the man's head and hair. Written at the top of the page, upside down to anyone viewing the painting, were the words "Writer's block," and in the lower right corner was my thumbprint in red.

"I guess you won't be seeing Paul anymore," I said.

"No, but there's probably a gallery out here that will take your stuff, or one of the coffee shops." He set one of the bricks into the plastic tub and cut open the wrapping. "You can check it out tomorrow. I need you to get as much of the bagging done as you can first though. I'm going to catch up on some sleep so I can get back out there tonight before I lose all of my customers."

Within minutes, Michael was sound asleep; the sound was a deep rumbling metronome offering tempo to the repetitive process of dividing and bagging product.

I worked, hypnotized by the cycles of sound and motion, daydreaming of a gallery showing of my artwork. I was centered in a white room and squares of color lined the walls like windows to other worlds. People paced in a circle around me, staring at painted representations of my thoughts, each containing an embedded piece of me. The figures began to drift sideways like hanging sheets, as their attention turned to me. The walls started to glow, becoming warm white light, enveloping the room and everything in it, save for the faint pink echo of smiling faces.

"Kid?"

I turned to see Michael, awake and standing next to me. "Have you been bagging this whole time?"

I turned to view the alarm clock and looked back to the heap of little bags, each appearing identical to the next. "I don't know, I guess so; my mind was somewhere else."

He selected a couple bags from the pile and held them up next to each other, and I awaited his approval, which came in the form of a subtle nod. After filling his pockets, he cupped a hand behind the pile and scooped them off the table into a waiting plastic tub, held just under the edge of the table.

"Alright, kid, I'll be back later. Lock up behind me."

"Okay, I'll see you later," I replied and followed him to the door.

***

With nothing else to occupy my time, I had continued bagging until there were no small bags left. After dosing myself with a generous hoot, I had gone on the nod and had remained asleep until past midnight, when Michael knocked on the door.

"Hey, it's me," he said in a loud whisper through the inch gap in the latched door.

I let him in and said through a stifled yawn, "How did you do?"

"Pretty good at first. I got rid of most of it in the first couple hours." He paused. "There was this guy though; I sold to him last week. He came back tonight with this other guy; it was sketchy, felt like a setup, like they were going to try to jump me or something."

"What happened?" I asked.

"Nothing, I told him that he had me confused with someone else and got out of there."

"Did they follow you?" I asked.

"No, I was checking over my shoulder, all the way back to the motel."

"Who were they?"

"It could be another dealer. I'm probably stepping on someone's toes here, fuck, I don't know, maybe another dealer tipped off the narcs to get rid of me," he said.

"So what are we going to do?"

"I'm just thinking out loud, it's probably nothing. If it were a cop, they'd have to catch me selling to bust me. I'm just going to have to be careful and pick my sales for the next little while," he replied.

I stared at him until the creases across his face relaxed into an insincere smirk. "Don't worry about it. I'm probably just being paranoid, it's part of the job. Just forget about it and get some sleep. I'll see you in the morning."

What felt like hours passed in the darkness, without even the beginnings of a snore. Kept awake by the buzzing sound from the half-lit sign outside, I lay still, staring at the silhouette of Michael's head and trying to guess what thoughts were buzzing around inside.

CHAPTER 51

Shedding skin

Along with my change, I took the slice of pizza handed to me on a paper plate and sat at one of the few tables inside.

The bell rang above the door, and a skeletal figure wearing an old army jacket came in. Patchy red and grey stubble surrounded his dry cracked lips, parted as he lisped his order between two upper canines, housed in an otherwise toothless set of swollen red gums.

He brought the wedge of pepperoni pizza to his mouth, leaving the paper plate and a handful of small change spread out over the counter, and sucked back the slice, snapping his mouth around it, the way a snake devours a field mouse. Flakes of dry skin fell from his neck as he scratched at it with a clawed hand, and I let my food fall with a slap down to the paper plate, cupping a hand to my mouth to keep the rest of it in.

When I looked again, his glassy grey stare was pointed back at me. He sputtered, "What the fuck are you staring at?"

"Nothing, sorry." I dropped my eyes to the table.

"You wanna fucking go, you piece of shit?" the guy spat, and from under my lowered brow, I could see his feet twitching, pacing back and forth.

"Get out of my store crack-head," came a shout from behind the counter.

"Fuck you, you fat piece of shit," was the lisped response.

I glanced up as the hinged part of the counter flew up, and the large hairy man, wrapped in an orange-smeared, white apron, rushed through the opening. "Come here you cocksucker."

The loud jingle announced the departure of each man as he rushed out of the store. The crack-head was turned half around and shouting back at the pizza guy as the chase continued onto the road and into honking traffic. A woman appeared from an alley behind the crack-head, looking like his female twin, her frizzed-out bleach-blonde hair continuing seamlessly into the fake fur of an oversized coat, open to the exposed and sagging skin of her stomach over a short, shiny red skirt. She waved her arms as she swayed, mouthing something, inaudible through the storefront glass and over the sound of multiple blaring car horns.

I returned my attention to the half-eaten pizza, sitting on the paper plate in front of me and noticed a long black hair, braided into the stringy mozzarella cheese, hanging from the crescent shape cutout from my last bite. The bell rang and the pizza guy stormed back through the store muttering, "Goddamned crack-heads." I stared at the large club-like hands curled into fists at his side, hanging from thick forearms, matted with a net of black hair, and returned my hand to my mouth as I ran out of the store.

Far enough away from the smells emanating from Angelo's Pizzeria, my stomach began to settle and I slowed to a walk. On the other side of Main Street, a couple blocks away, was a sign above a storefront window that read, "Shepherd Gallery."

Inside, bathed in soft white light, were landscape and wildlife paintings, each varied in style and medium. One wall housed a series of tall abstract paintings resembling my own efforts to hide each blank canvas before deciding what to paint. I turned around to a white pedestal on which stood the sculpture of a head and torso made from bent strips of rusted metal, like the displayed remains of a long-ago-decommissioned robot. I imagined its working life, deterioration, and eventual salvation from a robot graveyard.

"You like it?" a soft female voice asked from behind me.

I turned to face her. She was a well-groomed woman in her thirties, dressed in a pinstriped grey skirt and jacket. Her sky-blue eyes remained fixed on the sculpture as she spoke. "The artist's name is Karl. He owns the junkyard on the outskirts of town."

"It's beautiful," I said, instantly second-guessing my word choice.

She tilted her head, peering at me through squinted eyes, and a smile spread across her face.

"It is, isn't it? He was an auto mechanic in his day, working on muscle cars and hotrods; now he's a recluse." Her gaze sank to the flakes of rust around the base of the sculpture as she spoke.

"A recluse?"

She nodded. "People call him crazy-old-Karl, but he's no crazier than any of us, just got left behind in the wake of computer technology."

"What happened to him?" I asked.

"He lost most of his business to the bigger garages set up to work on imports. After his wife passed away, he closed his garage, turned his land into a junkyard and locked himself away. You can read that story over and over in every one of his sculptures, tragic but beautiful."

I stared at the sculpture, applying the backstory, and imagining its creator, building the rusted mannequins to keep him company in the absence of his wife, but each one a representation of himself, and his own deterioration.

"It's amazing," I said under my breath.

"Few people know, or care to know, the story; all they see is an ugly rusting statue," she replied with a subtle shake of her head. "I've had it for three years; it's my only permanent piece. I wouldn't let this one go for any price."

She turned to me and smiled. "Sorry, I'm Christine Shepherd," she said and held out her hand.

CHAPTER 52

Snake in the pizzeria

The canvas slipped from under my arm, ringing out like a slack-skinned drum as it made contact with the ground while I fumbled with my room key. I set my bags and the other canvases just inside and checked the third for damage before carrying it in and latching the door behind me.

It was past noon, and Michael was gone. In his place, a couple bricks of powder leaned against his pillow, which I assumed had been left out for me to bag. The bricks blurred in my peripheral vision, behind Christine Shepherd's business card turning between my fingers as I replayed the last part of our conversation. As much for my own desire, as for the last hopes of Panda, I had lied to Christine, selling myself as a prolific artist. In truth, I had only one painting ready to sell.

I removed the painting from the easel, set a blank canvas in its place, and set to work, priming it with thick wet smears of black and green acrylic, and not stopping until all bare-white canvas was gone.

The tin foil rustled loudly in my hands over the sounds of distant traffic and the faint buzz of the motel sign. I sat on my bed, facing the mud-colored canvas and pulled the smoke through the tube, closing my eyes as a familiar warmth washed over me.

INFINITY

When I opened my eyes, images began to appear, dancing in the space before me, thoughts superimposed over the surface of the canvas. Ignoring the shadows to my left, I stood, picked up my brush, and began pushing color across the canvas, tracing the shapes swimming around my hand. As I replayed the details of the day, my hand worked to translate, beginning with the black and white checkered floor of Angelo's Pizzeria, fading into darkness. From that darkness, emerged a snake in mid-shed, its smoky-grey-cataract eyes, framed by hexagonal olive-green scales.

Behind the snake, black cylinders transformed, becoming chess pieces, and caught in the transparent folds of shed skin, were the opposing white pawns. The only white piece standing was the king, positioned inches from the fanged mouth of the snake. I pressed my thumb into a daub of red paint on the body of the white king and stepped back, wiping my hands down the front of my jeans until neither my hands, nor jeans, yielded any more color.

CHAPTER 53

Sorry

The numbers shone a bright red blur in the otherwise pitch-black room. I rubbed the sleep from my eyes. It was past midnight when I had last looked at the clock; it was now ten after eight, and Michael's bed was undisturbed.

"Shit." I scrambled from the bed and ran to the door, the latched door. "He's going to kill me."

I folded back the brass latch and opened the door, hoping that he was outside and at the same time dreading what he would do if he was, but Michael was nowhere in sight. I paced around the room, mentally rehearsing my apology and cursing myself for having slept through his attempts to wake me, his efforts limited by the early hour to a frantic whisper through the inch gap between door and frame.

I snatched one of the large bricks of product from Michael's bed and set it down on the table, thinking that maybe if I could get ahead on the bagging, that it would aid my apology and soften Michael's mood. I returned to his bed, knelt down and reached my arm underneath, feeling for Michael's bag where the supplies were kept, but my fingers found nothing. I dropped, flat to the carpet and lifted the bed skirt; his bag was gone.

I stared at the brick leaning against Michael's pillow, and beside it, where the other brick had been, sat a roll of cash wrapped in an elastic band, half-tucked under the pillow. Underneath, there sat several rolls of cash, each rolled and wrapped the same as the next, all except one. The outer skin of one of the rolls was white, a piece of paper bound with the bills and with a single word written on it.

Sorry.

I slipped the band off the roll, letting all but the note fall into a heap of curled paper leaves on the bed. My stomach churned as I turned the paper over and began to read.

The cash is yours. The dope is yours too. There should be more than enough to keep you going and to sell if you need to, when the cash runs out. I'm sorry, kid, I can't be responsible for you and do what I do for a living; it's not good for you, it's not safe, and you deserve more.

Take care of yourself. I'm sorry. Goodbye, kid.

The note shook in my trembling hands as Michael's words squirmed around inside my intestines, forcing me into a run toward the bathroom with a hand cupped over my mouth. I grasped the rim of the sink, coughing and spitting stomach acid, cursing and crying between desperate breaths.

The pathetic pale-faced child on the other side of the glass made a plea with wet, reddened eyes, and I lashed out hard with my fist, smashing the mirror into a thousand cascading blades.

"Stop crying, you fucking worthless piece of shit," I shouted, looking down past my bloodied hand at the countless versions of the same face, all staring up at me from the red-smeared shards lining the sink. I pulled a long red sliver from the meat between my knuckles and watched the dark bead of blood roll down the length of my index finger and drip to the crying faces below.

CHAPTER 54

Myself and I

The tear-soaked pillow was cold and coarse against the red-raw skin of my cheek. I reached past the alarm clock, digging thumb and forefinger through the picked hole in the plastic and took a pinch of powder.

Propped up on one elbow, I rubbed the powder between my finger and thumb, off and into the waiting silver crease of foil as they stood all around the room, motionless and featureless, but watching me.

With the note rolled and gripped between my dry, cracked lips, I flicked my lighter and watched the powder boil to a smoking glob. The smoke traveled up through the apologetic tube and down into my lungs. I shut my eyes, waiting for the drug to warm me and for the shadows to disappear.

I awoke to something biting at my elbow, digging and grinding against the bone. The sound of crunching, cracking, and snapping glass, accompanied my attempts to shuffle and roll away from the sickly stinging pain. A highlighted shard of broken mirror pointed back at me, inches from my face as I turned my head to see the toilet bowl, smeared with blood and vomit.

My foot slipped and skidded across wet tile and mirror shards as I tried to stand, and I slammed back down to a bed of a thousand blades and needles. Grasping the rim of the sink with a bloodied, sliver-ridden palm, I pulled myself to standing to meet my reflection in the doorway.

Long dark hair framed his expression, mirroring my own, but set with deeper creases and from behind thicker facial hair. I remained still as he pulled back the corners of his mouth into a wince. With the skin stretched tight over his cheek, I could make out a tooth-size scar.

"Sorry," he said, and I traced his gaze to the crumpled, bloodstained curl of paper at my feet.

"Who are you? Are you, me?" I slurred.

His frown deepened as he backed away and into the dark room. I swayed and staggered after him, reaching a hand out for something to hold on to but finding only my easel, which collapsed with me onto the hard corner of my bedside table.

CHAPTER 55

Paint thinner

Putrid air escaped from the unfurled bag, the smell stung my senses, filling my nostrils en route to my rapidly tightening chest. I stood, picking at the green spots from a single slice of bread, the back of my other hand pressed against my mouth and nose in a futile attempt to avoid the invading odor.

My stomach churned as I chewed the remaining bread into a sticky paste, choking it down between hiccupping spasms and trying to ignore the stale taste and smell. An eruption of stomach acid lapped at my insides, burning in my chest and causing me to swallow back the hot froth.

Clutching my chest, I pulled open the fridge and snatched up a carton of milk, hoping to put out the fire in my throat. The sour lumps of congealed milk slid over my tongue as the smell rose up into my nose. I sucked air and sour milk into my windpipe as I gagged, mid-turn, to spew everything in the direction of the small kitchen sink.

I stayed, leaned over the sink dry heaving like a cat with a hairball, letting out air with a groan, as my body tensed and released for what seemed like hours.

When I returned to my bed, my thoughts returned to Michael. I reached into the widened hole in the sagging bag and loaded the blackened foil. The smoke went down hot, and I closed my eyes, waiting for my escape, waiting for the drug to wash over my thoughts like paint thinner, blurring, smearing, and dissolving the layered images in my mind.

CHAPTER 56

Rent

A rhythmic *whomping* sound cut through the high-pitched squeal in my head. My eyes rolled behind heavy, aching lids as I tried again to open them. The *whomping* sound became the knocking of a large-sounding fist at my door, and I struggled to a seated position. "I'm coming; hold on," I yelled.

I pulled open the drawer of the bedside table and dragged the cash, dope, and foil into the waiting trough, and made my way to the door. In a daze, I pictured Michael standing out there, but I knew that it wasn't him.

With the latch folded across, I turned the handle, pulled open the door, and peered out, squinting into the sunlight through the small gap. "Yeah?"

"Open the door," the man said.

"Who is it?"

"It's the guy you owe money to, that's who," said the voice.

"For what?"

"The room you're in," the voice snapped.

"What? Michael paid a month in advance."

"Who's this? Where's Michael?"

"I, we work together," I said.

"Your buddy paid me for one month, exactly one month and two days ago. If you guys plan on staying here, then you'd better pay up."

"How much for the month?" I asked.

The man recited the daily, weekly and monthly rates through the gap in the door as I thumbed the amount from the drawer.

"Why do you have the door latched?" he asked.

"I'm not dressed. I thought Michael told you we're working nights," I replied, and handed the cash through the gap.

"Alright, look, I've had no problem with you guys, but I don't like chasing money down—"

I cut him off. "Yeah, sorry, we've been working so much, I guess we lost track."

"Just don't let it happen again," he said.

"Okay, we won't."

The sound of his heavy footsteps faded, and I leaned against the door, pushing it closed with a click. I returned to the drawer, the open bag had dumped most of its contents. "Shit." I pulled a card from my pocket and scraped the powder back into the bag, dirt, fluff, and all. I loaded my foil with the last of it, tapping the powder from Christine shepherd's business card, the details like ghosts behind a white film. The flame licked the underside of the foil, and the paint thinner smeared my thoughts of her and her gallery.

CHAPTER 57

Evicted

"Get the hell out of here, you Goddamned junkie."

"What, what's your problem?" I slurred, trying to focus on the dark shape in the doorway.

"What's my problem? What's my damn problem? Get the hell out of my motel. I'm calling the police." Rays of sunlight danced in a circle over the silhouette's head and shoulder as he hurried away.

Sunlight poured in through the open doorway, glinting off the broken brass latch and dazzling my unaccustomed eyes. I turned away and dropped my feet to the floor, blinking at the bright rectangle still blazing in front of my eyes and following my gaze.

I scrambled around the room, stuffing the olive-drab bag with everything I owned, dumping the cash and dope in on top of my clothes before zipping it closed. I dragged my canvases, easel, and bag out into the blinding sunlight. My skin burned, on the verge of spontaneous combustion, as I struggled away from the motel as fast as I could move.

I found refuge, tucked with my belongings against a rusted metal door, recessed in the brick wall of a close-by alley and listened over my pounding pulse, to the sound of distant wailing sirens, wondering if they were headed to the motel and if they would come looking for me.

I sat, pulling at the edge of canvas, where it wrapped around the wooden stretcher. With a firm tug, the staples popped, and I followed my hand through the gap between frame and fabric, popping each staple as I worked my way around.

With the canvases rolled together between the handles of my bag, the stretchers worn over my shoulder like a bandolier, and my easel folded under my other arm, I trudged along with a wooden *clatter*, dragging my feet toward the next street over, and away from the Oneiroi motel.

CHAPTER 58

Venom

The street was striped black and gold by the early morning sun, like the abdomen of a wasp, the part that contains the poison and ends with a needle.

I kept my eyes fixed to the cold, dark pavement as I walked, stopping at the bright, hot, gold-washed roads, intersecting my straight-line path to Main Street. In response to an itch at the back of my head, I set down my bag and scratched under the matted hair, but the itch was inside, under my scalp, crawling and burrowing deeper.

A man tripped and stumbled to my right. "Move your fucking bag, you bum." He turned and shoved my chest with both hands.

The pavement seemed to meet me halfway as I fell, catching the parts of me unhindered by my easel and stretchers. The thing, crawling around at the back of my skull, sank its teeth in, holding on as the world flipped over in a blur.

A ringing pain at the back of my head became a high-pitched squeal in my ears, as my eyes rolled back to center on a dreamlike bright-blue sky. I struggled to my feet and followed the waves of people as they ebbed and flowed along the busy sidewalk. The motion made my stomach turn and my vision blur in and out of focus, desperately trying to lock on to a synthetic replica of the world, pulled like a veil, over and in front of my eyes.

My thoughts turned to the bite at the back of my head, a spider-bite, leaking neurotoxic residue into the non-feeling wet mass inside my skull. I reached back and clawed at the wound, trying to dig out the spider, but my nails brought away only blood and hair.

Legs hurried by, dragging me along as they snagged their clothes on my protruding wooden corners, and kicking the over-stuffed bag hanging at my shin. I split away from the pushing, cursing crowd to settle behind a dumpster in the dark half of an alley, where I sat with my eyes closed, waiting for the effects of the spider's venom to subside.

***

When I opened my eyes, the alley was turned around. Light and shadow split the alley down its length, and I was no longer in the shade. My body was soaked with sweat, but the effects of poison and fever were gone.

I traveled the back alleys to Main Street, avoiding the sun and the fast moving crowds, and entered the office of the nearest motel, where a woman sat behind the counter with a phone receiver pressed against her brightly colored face. As she spoke, I stared at the paint on her mouth and nails, vibrant accents against rough textured skin, like a toy fire truck in a sand pit.

She gave a sideways glance, somewhere between a sneer and a frown. "I have to go." She replaced the receiver and looked up at me. "Can I help you?"

"How much is a room for the month?" I set my bag down and pulled a roll of cash from my pocket.

She read aloud the rates, quoting nearly double the price of the Oneiroi. I slipped the elastic band off the roll and thumbed the amount, placing it on the counter between us.

INFINITY

"We need a credit card," she said, glancing down at the cash and back up at me.

"No, I'll pay cash," I replied, returning the sour look and gesturing at the splayed cash.

"We require a credit card, in case of damages to the room," she said, with wincing eyes and a smile as plastic as the color of her lips.

"Damages?"

"It is company policy, sir. We need a credit card and two pieces of picture ID." Without leaving room for me to respond, she said, "Maybe you would be better suited to one of the hostels on the outskirts of town."

I snatched back the cash, stuffed it back into my pocket, picked up my bag, and left the way I came in, letting my easel bang against the doorframe and cursing under my breath.

***

The three men spoke in broken English, interspersed with an occasional word in a foreign language that neither I, nor the uninterested guy behind the counter of the hostel understood. They moved to the wall, huddled around an open backpack and a single pocket phrase book.

The guy behind the counter looked over at me. "Hi, can I help you?"

"I need a room," I said, not wanting to waste my breath on requirements before being informed of company policy.

The guy pointed at the sign denoting the single-room, day price.

"How much for the month?" I asked.

"You pay by the day, buddy," he replied in a manner that suggested he was sick of answering the same questions over and again, probably delivered in broken English, read aloud syllable-by-syllable, from a not-English to English phrasebook.

I placed the cash on the desk, and he exchanged it for a key.

"Check out is at eleven A.M. tomorrow. If you want to stay, then come pay me, or whoever is working the desk, before nine A.M. Shower and bathroom are shared, first come, first served. Have a nice stay," he recited in a flat, automatic tone.

I picked up the key, "Where …"

"Top of the stairs, third on the left," he interjected without looking up.

The third room on the left smelled of bleach with a hint of urine, and the walls were the color of the latter. Black spots peppered the wall and sill, bordering a small barred and frosted window. I leaned my easel, stretchers, and the roll of canvas up in the corner of the room, and dropped my bag down onto the metal-frame bed. The dark green, tucked-in, coarse-hair blanket made me itch at the thought of it against my skin.

I unzipped my bag. "Fuck."

Inside the bag, inside all the creases, seams, pockets and folds of clothing, was a layer of powder. I made sure that the door was locked, returned to the bag, and fished out the square of foil.

Two laminated signs hung on the wall by the door: a map of the second floor, showing fire exits and extinguisher locations, and a sign written in thick black marker.

House rules.

No drugs or alcohol.

No smoking.

The powder liquefied on the foil and I inhaled the smoke.

CHAPTER 59

Derelict Vessel

A ring of scum lined the shower basin as the coffee-colored water filtered slowly through the tangled mess of hair lining the drain. I scrubbed at the shower basin with my soiled shirt, scooped out the wad of hair, and wiped myself dry with a clean shirt before pulling it on damp. I brushed past the line of people, waiting outside the washroom door, as I made my way back to my room with a plastic shopping bag rolled around my dirty, wet clothes.

In four days, I had left the hostel just once to pick up soap, foil, and dry-packaged food goods that would keep without refrigeration. I had been followed around the store by a man, two sizes smaller than the suit draped around him, with a nametag pinned to his lapel that read, Todd, Assistant store manager. The gap in front and behind me in the checkout lineup had been large enough for two shopping carts causing me to check my reflection in the glass of the automatic exit doors before they shushed open, letting me out and letting Todd get back to his assistant-store-manager duties.

Even after scrubbing myself for almost an hour, my skin itched, crawling with invisible or microscopic creatures. Staring down at the green-wire bed sheet, my eyes flicked to every twitching fiber, and back to the red weeping spots in almost every inside crease of exposed skin, my body having served as a nightly venue for blood-feasting bugs.

I moved to the corner of the room, away from the scouring-pad bed-sheet and away from the bugs. Slouched down with my sketchpad across my knees, my thoughts alternated between words and picture as my hand scribbled in eager translation. The picture was of a boat, without crew and missing its oars, adrift in a calm sea; the words read of its chance of reaching land safely and being repurposed, or being forced by the tide into coastline rocks and into painted splinters, unrecognizable and beyond salvage.

CHAPTER 60

Pitch

The roll of painted, unpinned canvas had grown larger, and the rolls of cash had become smaller one by one. Aside from weekly trips to the craft store and supermarket and daily visits to the front desk or bathroom, I had stayed in my room, painting or sleeping, the two modes divided by regulated self-medication.

The money would soon be gone, and I would have to sell the paintings or split and sell the dope. I washed and dressed, calmed my nerves with a pinch of powder, picked up the roll of canvas, and left for Christine's gallery.

***

I unrolled the paintings on the floor at the back of the room as directed by Christine, while she finished up with a client at the front desk. I stood comparing the frayed-edge pieces at my feet to the confidently colored squares around the room. Christine approached with a slender hand outstretched. I wiped a trembling, clammy hand across the back of my jeans before offering it to her.

"Wow, these are wonderful," she said.

My mouth danced nervously around a smile. "Do you think they're good enough to sell?"

"They're a little different from the work that I usually display, but I don't think that you will have trouble selling any of these." She moved slowly down the line of canvas. "Have you priced these yet?"

"Michael usually deals with that," I replied.

"Michael's your agent?"

I turned the question over for a second before responding with a nod.

"Well, if you have him come down here, then we can get these priced and try to find a place for them," she said and continued to move from one painting to the next.

"He's out of town for a while. I don't know when he'll be back," I replied, swallowing back the lump as it formed in my throat.

"Okay, well how about this, you get these re-stretched and bring them all back here in the next couple days and I'll go through my rates with you, and we'll see if we can plan a show, or an auction. We can settle accounts with Michael when he gets back," she said with a smile.

"Okay, that sounds great, thank you," I replied, trying and failing to contain my emotion as an uncontrollable smile spread from my face to hers. I shook her hand to seal the deal and gathered up the paintings.

I thanked her again on my way out, and for the first time, in a long time, the spider in the back of my head was quiet and still.

CHAPTER 61

Exposition

Over the two weeks leading up to the show, I had produced another four paintings and restocked my supply of canvas and paint, using all but the last of my cash. I had cut my medication down to the bearable minimum, enough to appease my addiction and to stay the sickness. The image of the oar-less boat, depicted on one of the four finished paintings, crept into my mind, and I pictured myself drifting in the same cold, dark water, not drowning, not swimming, but treading water, waiting to be saved.

I leaned the stack of paintings against the aluminum doorframe and tapped gently on the glass. Christine looked up, smiled, and came to unlock the door.

"I brought a few more, thought we could add them to the show," I said as I brought the paintings inside.

"That's great; the more, the merrier," she replied. "Wow, these are amazing. Tell me about this one."

"It's the Caduceus, two snakes entwined around a staff, or in this case, a syringe," I replied.

"What is the significance of the syringe?" she asked.

"Panda told me that the staff with a single snake wrapped around it is the Rod of Aesculapius, the symbol for the Greek god of healing. He said that if there are two snakes, then it is the Caduceus, the symbol of Hermes, the god and patron of travelers and thieves, trade and trickery," I regurgitated the words with my eyes closed, as Panda mouthed them in my mind.

"This Panda sounds like a very smart man," she replied.

I opened my eyes to her warm smile. "He was."

Her eyes lingered on mine for a second before returning to the painting, her gaze moving down as she mouthed the words written on the syringe; commerce, trickery, negotiation, medicine, poison.

"They have the Caduceus on the side of most ambulances and outside hospitals, but it has nothing to do with medicine — someone used it by mistake decades ago, then everyone else did."

"Perhaps another one of Hermes's tricks?" Christine replied, flashing her eyes wide with feigned suspense before relaxing to a giggle, stripping years from her face and putting a smile on mine.

"Do you think there will be a lot of people here?" As I looked around, the room seemed much larger with most of the artwork removed from the bright white walls.

"Quite a few of my buyers have confirmed, plus walk-in traffic, and we should have a full house." She glanced down at my tapping foot. "Are you nervous?"

I nodded. "I don't do well in large crowds."

"We have over an hour until the show. There's a nice little Irish pub, a couple blocks down; why don't you go have a drink and calm your nerves while I finish getting things ready."

"I don't want to leave everything for you to do," I replied.

"It's okay, you've already done your share of the work." She smiled and gestured to the large stacks of paintings. "And don't rush to get back on time, it's fashionable to be late."

She handed a small stack of flyers to me on my way out and locked the door behind me.

***

INFINITY

"Do you mind if I put a few of these around?" I held the flyers out, facing the stout bartender.

"Don't think you'll get much business from this lot, but go ahead, be my guest." He glanced about the room and back at me. "You staying for a drink?"

I gave a nod and picked one of the today's-specials, O'something's Irish lagers, from the chalkboard behind him. He poured and set the drink down in front of me. I paid and dropped my change into the tip jar, gaining a nod from the large man.

After distributing the flyers about the tables, I returned to my stool at the bar and watched as most were discarded without a second glance. A young woman eyed the black text written across the middle of the large red thumbprint that filled most of the page, then ripped off a corner, and slid it to the young man with a pen poised in hand, leaning against her table.

"Not the artsy type, this bunch."

I turned back around to face the large man behind the bar.

"These guys are just getting a head start, before the clubs open," he said, "It's Friday night. You want another?"

I finished what was left in my glass and handed it back with a nod.

***

Crouched behind a dumpster in the alley behind the pub, I unfolded the pre-loaded foil and fished for my lighter. I kept my eyes fixed on the mouth of the alley as I inhaled the smoke, which seemed to grab the back of my neck, squeezing a shiver through the base of my already buzzing head.

The gallery was filled with well-dressed people, each gingerly sipping red wine and moving slowly around the room. The pointed features of the woman in front of me skewed to a yearning, wrinkled pout as she seemingly tried to extract each painting's theme by means of smell.

Around the room, among the subtle murmur, I heard, "The varying depth of ... the emotional expression of ... the metaphoric representation of ... the artist's struggle ..."

With a room full of people talking with confidence about what I was trying to capture or convey, I caught myself laughing, wondering what Simon and Michael would make of these people, and vice versa. I made an effort to compose myself, after garnering a few disapproving looks from those immediately around me, then joined the flow of people circling the room, hoping that I would eventually find Christine somewhere in the crowd.

As more people filed in, I wondered how many of them had come for the complimentary wine. I moved to stand among the more casually dressed walk-ins hovering in the center of the room, feeling a touch self-conscious in my paint-smeared, thrift-store attire.

From where I stood, I couldn't see a single painting, or the white spaces between. The gallery was packed with people, some were now staring back at me and seemingly closing in around me. As I backed away, something touched my shoulder. I whirled around to an arc of deep red, the pop and tinkling sounds of an exploding wine glass at my feet, followed by the wet slap of trailing red liquid.

"Jesus Christ, watch where you're going," someone barked as another man reached out to grab my arm. I recoiled, was pushed from behind into the reaching man, passing through him to land flat on the hardwood floor, sprinkled with broken glass, wine, and now blood.

As I turned over, an old woman loomed over me, her face like wrinkled wax and her lips pulled into a grimace over toothless gums. I raised my hand up to hide my face, to hide her face, but it didn't stop her. Led by the wrinkled sneer of her mouth and nose, then her dead, grey marble eyes, she moved through my hand, swooping down to within inches of my face.

INFINITY

"Leave me alone," I yelled, scrambling to my feet, pushing my way through the crowd, and flailing violently toward the exit. I stumbled through men and women who gave no physical resistance, while others backed away, staring at me, each with the turned-down expression of someone handling rancid meat. I pulled open the door and ran. I ran all the way back to the hostel without looking back.

CHAPTER 62

Splinters

Slouched on the infested, scratchy green blanket, the foil and lighter held loose in my hand, and the last of my cash rolled into a tube, hanging and stuck to my lower lip, I let the smoke leak out of me slowly, careful not to move and scare the bugs from their last supper, their final fix of my flesh and blood.

I stared blankly at the scattered sticks and splinters that had been my easel; the boat from my painting floated in the distance, somewhere on the horizon of thought as sleep washed over me.

My head throbbed as I pried my eyes open to the blur of red weeping welts. My sight sharpened to the small curls of glass, woven into the skin of my forearm, draped over my pillow, in front of my face. I sat up and picked at the complimentary glass splinters, each new hole sealing shut with a bead of blood.

I dumped some of the dope into the crease of a red-smeared page, torn from my sketchpad, then folded it in on itself, sealing the powder inside. I stuffed my clothes and packaged food into the olive-drab bag, on top of the folded unpainted canvas, closed up the remaining dope-bag with masking tape, and shoved it into a sock before stowing it with the rest of my things.

INFINITY

I kept my eyes to the floor of the hallway, past the bare and slippered feet of the people in the washroom lineup, down the stairs, and out into the bright morning sun. I turned down the first alley and tucked myself into the shadow of a dumpster, following the directions of a voice in the back of my head.

The voice was cruel and unusual; it was the voice of the spider, spitting profanity, taunting me as I curled around my bag and broke down into tears.

CHAPTER 63

Nocturnal

The spider's web spread like a veil in my mind, spun to intercept my thoughts, wrapping them up comatose, poisoned by its neurotoxin and replaced with ideas of its own. It told me when to eat, when to sleep, when to medicate, and what to dream.

Like the spider, I became active at night, layered with every item of clothing I owned and walking to stay warm. I hid from the sun in recessed doorways, in shaded alleyways, warned away from people and heavily sedated by heroin vapor.

I fed from the packaged goods in my bag and from a water faucet in a back alley, until the food was gone and the wheel to turn on the tap had been removed. My last note was broken down into smaller bills and change, until all paper money was gone, spent on a jar of peanut butter, cans of tuna, a thick three-quarter-length thrift-store coat, hooded sweater, and wool gloves.

One afternoon within my first week on the street, I had woken up still high, groggy, and wet. The handles of my bag still twisted around my arm and the bag pulled tight against me were soaked, along with the clothes I was wearing. The clouds were wrung dry by nightfall, all the while the wet conspired with the cold night air, offering itself as a conduit to the skin of my shivering body. I begged the girl working night shift at a twenty-four hour coffee shop to let me stay and warm up. I was told apologetically that I had to buy something or move on, company policy. I found a dry spot under a bridge, made a fire under a small square of loaded tinfoil for warmth, and waited for the sun to rise.

Over time, I migrated closer to the bus depot for use of the public bathroom, sometimes just for shelter from the rain or to warm myself with hot air from the hand dryer. With the peanut butter jar scraped empty, I was left with only the cans of tuna, and no can opener. After repeatedly hammering the can against the corner of a dumpster for what seemed like hours, a triangular hole appeared in the puckered lid, leaking liquid and the strong, welcome smell of fish. With the can up on edge, I stamped on it, over and again until it bulged and opened up, spilling some of the meat through razor sharp teeth. Ignoring the blood, seeping from sliced fingers and mixing with the water in the can, I scooped all of it into my mouth and drank it down with the pink dregs of water. I sat tonguing the metallic taste from the back of my teeth as my stomach turned over the decision to accept or reject my offering. With my hunger appeased, the spider led my hand back to the square of blackened foil to satisfy its own growing hunger.

CHAPTER 64

Sale

From the mouth of the alley, I heard a female voice ask, "You selling?"

I tore squares from the clear bag, roughed out a point into each, and tied knots in the twisted tails of cellophane. With my bag pushed as far as I could reach into the shadow under a dumpster, I made my way to the street, searching for the girl who was looking to buy.

I turned at the street and made my way to the busy corner, scanning every sketchy, tweaking candidate but careful not to hold eye contact. A female staggered to the crosswalk and stepped into the road, grasping at the air out in front of her. She swayed and lowered herself to a crouched position, bent over and sifting through invisible sand around her ankles. As she rocked on the balls of her bare feet, her shirt rode up, revealing the bumps of her spine trying to break through the stretched surface of her otherwise sagging skin.

Somewhere behind me, I heard the question again. "Hey, are you selling?" I turned and saw a girl, maybe in her twenties, elbows tucked in tight and her hands out, folded together around paper money.

I waited for her to make eye contact, led her gaze to the small bag of powder, held pinched by its tail in my cupped hand, and gestured for her to follow me back into the alley.

INFINITY

"Down?"

"I just need a point." She stood, fidgeting with the money in her hands and switching her weight from one foot to the other. Our hands met and we exchanged bill for bag.

"This better not be shit," she slurred, tipping the bag over a square of foil.

"It's China-white," I replied.

"You got more?"

I nodded and watched the smoke roll up through the clear plastic tube gripped between her dry, cracked lips. When she opened her eyes again, they seemed a paler shade of blue, glazed and glued somewhere behind me, as I stepped away.

I glanced back to the shape of a girl slumped against the wall, and retrieved my bag from its hiding place under the dumpster. I loaded my own foil, wrapped up the dope, and stuffed it back into the sock before leaning back on my bag and closing my eyes with a lungful of hot smoke.

***

I was woken by the spider, biting at the back of my head. I peeled myself from the brick wall and staggered to my feet. The girl I had sold to was approaching from the end of the alley with a man following just behind her. She stopped around twenty feet from me, and he came the rest of the way alone. "You selling?"

I gave a nod. "How much do you want?"

"How much you got?" he asked, leaving no space between his words.

"Three points right now, but I can come back later with more," I replied.

"I'll take all three." He rummaged a hand in his pocket and brought it out to meet mine.

"Thanks," he said, and started back toward the girl.

"Hey wait, where's the money?" I called out, looking down at an expired bus ticket in my hand.

"I gave it to you," he replied, grinning through a few yellow teeth.

"No, you didn't."

"You calling me a liar?" he snapped.

"No, I'm saying—"

"You're saying what? You saying I'm a thief?"

"Look, just give me the bags back." I took a step toward him, and there was a white flash.

The second hit rang out, amplified by the dumpster as my head bounced back to meet his fist again, this time the sound accompanied a screeching pain behind my eye. I dropped to my knees and took a hard kick to the face, slamming my jaw shut with a wet clack and sending me sprawling in a daze.

"Thanks for the drugs, bitch." His voice was dull behind the ringing in my head.

I rubbed at my eyes, flinching at the surge of pain all through the side of my face. A smear of dull green settled in my view, and I snatched at it, scrambling to my feet. The walls of the alley swayed to catch me as I ran on rubber legs. I turned the corner and continued on, as fast as I could go, until my legs gave out and my stomach emptied its acidic contents.

Slumped against the wall, rubbing at my aching jaw and spitting blood and bile, my fingers grazed the folded bill in my coat pocket. I caught a breath and let it out slow. The money would keep me fed for a few days, although my diet for the foreseeable future would be comprised of soup and liquids, waiting for the pain and swelling around my mouth and jaw to fade.

CHAPTER 65

Absolution tax

The days, living on the money from the sale of a single point, were spent arguing with the spider about how we would survive. My thoughts of retrieving the paintings from Christine and trying to sell them at a coffee shop were met with disdain. The spider whispered of my cowardice: *grow a spine, get yourself a knife, and go get our money from that grinning, yellow-toothed fuck.*

Stripped down to the cleanest layer, I stuffed the rest of my clothes into my bag, draped my heavy coat between the handles, and started toward Main Street, ignoring the spider's relentless taunts.

A homeless old man with an upturned hat out in front of him, blessed each and every passer-by as he or she fished through a handful of change, trying to calculate the cost of absolution, a daily toll or tax that promised of a guilt-free conscience.

As another deposit was made to pay down a debt to karma, the old man looked up with a puzzled expression. "God bless you."

It was the same hat that had received the change, poured out from between the pages of Panda's journal, but as I looked into the old man's eyes, I recognized another's face, from the later self-portraits of Leonardo da Vinci. Panda's voice interjected the spider's rant; *art is never finished, only abandoned.*

I offered what I could of a smile and continued on to the coffee shop at the corner. After waiting in line, I counted my change and ordered a coffee, in compliance with the "paying customers only" sign attached to the bathroom key, and inquired about the wall-space for art on consignment.

The man replied to the bruised side of my face. "We'll have to see the piece to make sure it's suitable."

The spider teased, *looks like you're stuck between a rock and a hard place, or damp concrete and a cold steel dumpster. Your friend, Christine, is going to laugh in your beat-up face, and what if she lets you take the paintings? What if you bring them all down here and this guy says no?*

"Okay, thanks." I picked up my coffee and left the store.

I dropped my bag at a table just outside and sat down, watching people donate change to the upturned hat of da Vinci. I slapped at the back of my head to jar the spider into silence and unzipped my bag, careful not to let anyone see inside.

With my sketchpad in hand, I approached the old man and asked if I could sit and draw.

"It's a free country." His reply was gruff, but spoken through a smile.

Leaning against the post of a no-parking sign, I sketched page after page, as taxpayers fed the karma meter and were thanked in turn with a blessing.

***

After a while, the old man's tired smile came back to me. "Can I take a look?"

I turned the pages back to the first sketch and handed it over.

His eyes rolled slowly over each page. "You're really good."

INFINITY

"That means a lot, coming from a man that looks like Leonardo da Vinci," I replied with a smile.

"Leonardo da Vinci, is that right?" He let out a breathy chuckle and gave back my sketchpad.

"Thanks for letting me sit with you." I got to my feet and dropped the last of my change into his hat.

The old man's croaking tone cut through the spider's profane disapproval. "You're an angel."

***

I closed the lid of the dumpster on the folded edge of canvas and smeared the hanging sheet with brown, black, and white paint. With my sketchpad open in one hand, I set to work pushing shadows and painting in highlights, smiling in spite of the spider's insults, as the figure began to take shape. I painted until the natural light was gone, layered on my clothes, medicated, and huddled around my bag in a brick doorway, waiting for the spider to sleep so that I could dream.

CHAPTER 66

Sold

Behind the supermarket were stacks of discarded wooden pallets. I pulled one from the pile, leaned it against the wall, and kicked the slats loose. I stapled the seams, front and back, where the slats met to form a rough rectangular frame and wrapped the canvas around it. An inch or so of rough, splintered wood extended beyond the frayed top edge of canvas; on it, I wrote, "Art is never finished …" and across the bottom wood margin, "… only abandoned."

***

As I waited in line, I eyed the artwork on the coffeehouse walls, taking note of the price tag on each, and trying to gauge what mine was worth.

"Hi, what can I get for you?"

I read the nametag pinned to his dark green smock. "Hi, Stephen, I spoke to you yesterday about selling my artwork."

He peered down at the canvas. "Okay, hold on. Sarah, can you cover the till for a few minutes?"

INFINITY

I followed him to the end of the counter and leaned the piece against the wall. We stood for a while, him staring at the painting and me staring at his unreadable expression.

He turned to me, and with a nod of his head, said, "Yeah, we can put this up for you."

I let out the breath I hadn't realized I was holding. "Thank you."

"We take twenty percent on the smaller pieces and fifteen percent on the larger pieces, even if it doesn't sell. We display for two weeks at a time; if you want to display for another two weeks when the time is up, then you have to pay again, fifteen percent of the painting's original price," he said.

"Okay."

"If at the end of two weeks, the painting hasn't sold, and if you fail to pay the fifteen percent, then we keep the painting and sell it for what we're owed." He spoke as though reading aloud from the specialty coffee menu.

I nodded and waited for him to continue.

"So, how much do you want to sell it for?"

"Four hundred?" I watched his face, trying to glean approval.

He wrote the price on a sticker, ripped what looked like a raffle ticket in two and stuck one half to the canvas, like a makeshift paper medal. "Bring this back in two weeks," he said, handing the other half of the ticket to me.

***

The water from the bus depot's bathroom faucet, sloshed around inside my otherwise empty stomach. I had gone past the coffee shop every morning for the last three days, hoping that my painting would be gone so I could eat.

I stood staring through the glass, rubbing at my pounding head and trying to ignore the sickly, churning, sucking ache in my gut. From out front of a store, a few doors down, came a familiar voice, one that made me smile. "God bless you."

I walked over to where the old man sat with his upturned hat and said, "Hi."

"Hey, it's the artist," he rasped, grinning through the long, stray grey hairs grown over his upper lip.

"You remember me," I replied.

"It's all I do, is watch people coming and going."

"Can I show you something?" I asked.

"What is it?"

"A painting," I replied.

"One of your paintings?"

I nodded. "It's just at the coffee shop on the corner," I said and held out my hand. He regarded my hand through the white wires of his furrowed brow, hesitantly folding his hat around the change inside, before taking my outstretched hand and letting me help him up.

He followed me to the corner and followed my gaze through the glass to the painting on the back wall.

"Is that me?"

"I painted it from the sketches I made," I replied.

"Well would you look at that, I'm famous," he followed the glass to the door, and I followed him inside.

"Yeah, yeah, paying customers only," he grumbled and unfolded his hat on the counter. "I'll get a couple of those muffins and two small coffees."

He made a quieting gesture with his hand as I opened my mouth to speak and passed one of the cups to me. I stared at the painting, while the old man filled the remaining space in his cup with copious amounts of sugar and cream. There was now an orange sticker, in place of the paper medal, that read, SOLD.

"Hey, excuse me?" I called, fumbling a hand inside my pocket. "My painting, it sold." I retrieved my half of the ticket and passed it over the counter.

INFINITY

The guy looked over the ticket, opened the till, and pulled an envelope from under the tray with the matching stub stuck to it. "There you go."

I ripped open the envelope and stared at the stack of bills inside its mouth. "Thank you."

The old man sat smiling at the painting while I counted the cash under the table, not caring to calculate the percentage or check if it was right. I took out a hundred and seventy and placed it in the old man's hat. "That's half of what it sold for."

He frowned down into the hat, shaking his head. "You're giving it to me?" he asked.

I nodded and touched his coffee cup with mine. "God bless you."

"God bless you." He sat back in his chair and laughed himself into a chesty cough.

I took a bite from the muffin, and my stomach seemed to scramble up into my chest, reaching for the food even before I had swallowed. "So how did you end up like this?" I asked, and broke off another piece.

"Like what, homeless, or old?" he asked.

"Homeless."

"The usual way. I had nowhere to live," he said with a grin.

"I mean, how did you end up on the street?"

His expression sagged, and in a somber tone, he said, "I got old."

He looked down at my bag, my clothes, and at the dirt on my hands, and offered a thin smile. "I grew up in a small town out east; worked my whole life in the mill. Everyone who lived there worked the mill, until one day it closed down. One by one, the stores closed and people moved away. I sold my house behind the curve, ended up getting less than what the land alone was worth. Thought I'd try my luck in the city, but when I got here, no one would hire me, I was already too old. I begged people to hire me for half of what they'd pay someone else, but no one would. When the money ran out, I went from begging for work to begging for food."

"How long has it been?" I asked.

"I don't know anymore, longer than it's been since my last hair cut or shave," he said, losing his fingers in amongst the thick wiry tangle of grey-white hair.

"How do you survive?" My voice cracked, and I wiped the wet from my eyes before the old man returned his gaze, but not before the voice in the back of my head scorned, *How will I survive? Selfish little boy, only cares about himself.*

"Kindness of strangers, and there's a soup kitchen run by members of Saint Christopher's church. You can get a hot meal there once a week," he replied.

I stirred my coffee with a wooden stir-stick, while self-pity turned to self-loathing in the spider's silk.

"You should come by the church on Saturday. It's not just for the homeless; most people that come are just average, everyday people that need a little help," he said.

"What day is today?" I asked.

He looked at me for a long while. "Today is Tuesday, the first day of the rest of your life."

***

It was raining hard when I left the thrift store. I wrapped the plastic bag tightly around my nearly new church attire, shoved the bag in with the rest of my things, and slung the kit bag up onto my shoulder. My walk had evolved to a run by the time I reached the supermarket, and I took my time while inside, hoping that the clouds would exhaust their reserves, allowing me to get back to the bridge before the sky opened up again.

Shoppers held their breath as they passed me under the storefront awning, blinking at the overpowering scent of splashed-on aftershave from a now-open bottle, still sitting on a shelf in the bath and body aisle. The rain was driving in at an angle, pelting and wrinkling the daily newspapers on a display rack next to the seasonal sale items. The date in the corner of

INFINITY

the ink-blotted page told me that my seventeenth birthday had long since come and gone. I blinked away the stinging tears, forming and trapping the chemical scent as it drifted upward, and walked out into the rain.

CHAPTER 67

Threshold

The medicine dosage increased with my efforts to stay warm and pass the time, trapped day and night by heavy rain, in the concrete recess under the highway overpass.

Traffic rumbled overhead, and the vibration traveled through me as vehicles sped over the wet track, trailed by high-pitched shushing sounds, rising over the furious tapping of cascading liquid bullets. Beyond sound, the place that had become my home was desolate. The only people I had seen during the rains were comprised of shadow, statues risen up from the dead brown tangle of foliage, covering the train tracks between the concrete pillars.

The spider said that they were suicides, some hit by the train before the track was abandoned, and the rest were jumpers. I pictured them standing, arms out, eyes closed, waiting for the impact of a frantically whistling train, or falling, over and again, from the deck of the overpass. When I closed my eyes to the falling figures, my mind replayed Joseph's story, told so long ago over the railing of Lion's Den, about the boy who fell to the rocks below. I recognized the boy on the rocks; it was the blue child from the clinic, flapping like a dying fish as he choked.

I positioned a can of tuna over the sharp edge of stone wedged into a crack in the concrete and hammered it down with the fist-sized rock in my hand, turning the can between every clack. Liquid from the can poured into the crack, filling my nostrils with a sweet promise and churning my stomach in frenzied anticipation. When the can was picked clean, the spider said that it was time to medicate. I breathed the smoke into my lungs, let it out, and lit the foil again.

With our appetites met, the spider said that it was time to sleep. I lay down over my bag and closed my eyes. Behind my eyelids, I traveled back through memories to the living room of our old house, sitting across from Panda as he told the story of the Magi cicada, flying up from the dirt at the end of their seventeen-year life cycle.

CHAPTER 68

Poison

As if for the very first time, my eyes opened and I snapped them shut again, screwed up tight against the bright humming lights. The squealing in my head slowed to a rhythmic beep, cutting through my daze and over the dull, rounded, intermittent vowel sounds coming from somewhere far away to my left.

I let my eyelids flutter open to a squint, and the rectangle of white light flickered back in response. There was a paper-like rustle as I turned onto my side. The dark shape next to me sharpened into view as I blinked at the light around it. It was a man, in uniform, a police uniform. His mouth moved in time to the sound, but the sound was locked away in a box somewhere in my head, all except the rhythmic beep of hospital equipment.

My vision blurred to primary colors, painted on the back of my eyelids behind static white noise, and fast moving yellow stars. When I pried my eyes open again, I caught sight of the clear tubing hanging from an IV bag next to the man in uniform. Behind him stood two shadows, figurines made of glass filled with poisonous black smoke like the fumes from burning plastic.

"What is your name?" the man asked. "What were you taking tonight?"

My attempted response was no more than a monosyllabic slur.

"Do you know where you are?" he asked, slipping out of view behind flickering light.

***

The officer was gone, replaced by a large, hard-faced woman in blue scrubs. Her eyes found mine, and she straightened up. "So you're finally back, among the land of the living."

I tried to speak, cleared my throat, and tried again. "What happened?"

"You tried to kill yourself on the highway, all whacked out on whatever, wandering in and out of traffic," she said, punctuating every other word with a chastising sneer or shake of her head. "You collapsed in the middle of the road, and you were pronounced dead in the ambulance on the way here."

"Dead?"

"The paramedics saved your life, and then you tried to thank them with your fists," she sneered.

"I don't remember—"

"No, of course you don't," she interjected and turned back to the beeping machines at my side.

Her words felt cruel and unfair. I had no recollection of anything she described. As I opened my mouth, my mother's face appeared in my mind, and I remembered her excuses: he didn't know what he was doing, he didn't mean it, it wasn't his fault, it was the drink, and it won't happen again.

"Now that you're awake, the police are going to want to talk to you again." She grinned a middle-finger synonym, and I swallowed my response.

She continued with her duties without speaking another word. The second hand on the wall clock clicked slowly forward between the sharp beep of the machines as I waited, for what seemed like hours, for her to leave.

As the door swung shut, I swung my legs off the bed, pulling the IV stand over, which fell with a metallic clatter, popping the tube from my arm. I ripped off the tape, taking with it a strip of hair and slid out the needle tip hanging from my vein like the stinger of a dead bee.

In one of the base cabinets were two blue, thin plastic bags stuffed full of my clothes. Ignoring the pungent smell of urine from the open bag, I pulled out my jeans and sweater, dressed, and peered through the glass.

I moved through the hall quickly, following the signs to the elevators. The red light blinked five, four, three, and the doors opened with a ding. I slipped inside, hit M, and tapped at the close doors button. The elevator stopped at the second floor, and the doors dinged open to a redheaded woman holding the handles of a wheelchair. Sitting in the chair and pulling his own IV stand was an old man, a grim skeleton wrapped in sagging grey skin; he looked up at me with glassy yellowed eyes and shook his mouth around a smile as they entered the metal box.

Unable to feign a smile, I turned away and fixed my gaze on the buttons. A slender bone-white, freckled hand entered my view, hovered over the controls, and then pressed the button marked G. A shiver climbed my spine as I stared at the lit M, which I realized had not stood for Main.

Outside, an ambulance sat idling in front of the emergency entrance. With my head down, I moved past the paramedics, hoping that they were not the ones who had brought me in, hoping that none would recognize me as the ungrateful kid whose unworthy life they had saved. I stopped at the curb and turned back; none gave a second glance. My attention moved to the Caduceus decal on the side of the ambulance, and the words flashed in my mind, "Commerce, trickery, negotiation, medicine, poison."

CHAPTER 69

Hunger

My stomach was twisted in knots, seemingly chewing on itself, perhaps pumped empty at the hospital or simply by the time elapsed between meals. The whole way back, I tried desperately to remember what had happened to my belongings, while the spider ranted. *You lost the fucking dope ... Right now, there's probably a cop leaned over your bag with rubber-gloved hands, digging through our dope ...our medicine ... how could you be so fucking stupid ...*

    As I scrambled up the steep bank under the concrete deck of the overpass, the dark scab crusted to the sleeve of my sweater pulled away from my skin, reopening the small hole left by the needle. I let go of the bags and rubbed at the itching wound, cursing as one of the blue bags tumbled down the hill, leaving a trail of tattered, piss-soaked clothes. I sank down and wept, staring at the remnants of my life, spread out in a line to the black echoes of suicide, standing motionless between the train tracks below.

    I gathered up my clothes as I trudged back up the hill, relieved that the spider had withdrawn his attack. Tired from hunger and suffering the beginnings of withdrawal, the spider slept. I pushed the bags onto the leveled-out concrete and crawled in after. Sitting in the dark corner between the concrete pad and the highway deck was my olive-green bag. The tears continued to stream down my face as a laugh exploded from my chest. I clawed at the zip and ignoring the spider's demands, pulled a can from the bag and set to work, bashing it open over the wedged stone.

Fighting the urge to throw everything back up, I clawed the dripping pink flakes of tuna into my mouth, not stopping until the can was bare and my stomach was untied, murmuring gratitude. The spider murmured of its own hunger, begged for medication, and screamed for me to listen. I layered on my clothes and curled up over my bag. *Take your medicine, you worthless piece of shit ... you won't survive the cold without it ... you shouldn't be so quick to abandon the only friend that hasn't abandoned you.*

CHAPTER 70

Usurper

With each new day of abstinence, the spider's war against me grew more violent. What began as whispered threats escalated to psychological and biological warfare, poisoning of brain chemicals, and sabotage of nerve centers and temperature regulators. The spider claimed responsibility for every itch, twinge, and pain, labeling each as a warning of further, more sinister attacks in the absence of compliance. *I have found your pain receptors ... can you feel the tickle at the back of your neck? ... this may sting a little ... maybe if I burrow deeper ... I'm eating my way to your eyes ... you can make the pain go away ... you know what you need to do ...*

The spider convinced my stomach to reject food, turned my conscience against me, and replaced my dreams with propaganda, twisted revisions of every bad memory.

The nights are getting colder, looks like it might snow soon ... you'll freeze to death ... if I don't starve you out first ... I can make you pick up the foil, make you dance like an epileptic marionette ... take your fucking medicine ...

My whole body conspired against me, and my will was overthrown by democratic vote, enforced by the realization of slow and painful starvation. With the spider's demands met, it let me sleep while it savored the spoils, and its servants set to work, repairing collateral damage.

CHAPTER 71

Salivation

The ground was wet with slush, and a veil of white highlighted the train tracks. The smoke that billowed out from my lungs hung in the frigid air, moving slowly and drifting past the delicate falling crystals. For days, the powder thickened on the tracks, while the spider's powder thinned to less than an inch at the bottom of the bag. It would soon be gone, breaking the conditions of our symbiosis, and dissolving our fragile truce.

With my bag tucked safely in the concrete recess, hidden by dead foliage, dragged and laid over top like a hunter's makeshift blind, I crossed the tracks and trudged through the slush.

Sandwich boards outside eateries boasted Saturday breakfast specials, while the savory smells emanating from each, were delivered to my nostrils as I passed by. I stopped a couple to ask for directions, but was cut off after, "Excuse me ..." by an outstretched handful of change. I thanked them as they hurried away, and continued toward Main Street.

I asked several people for directions; one man shook his head and waved a hand, shooing me like an insect while the most others ignored me and carried on past.

"Excuse me," I began. A young woman dug a hand into the pocket of her thick red coat, and I rushed to finish my question, "... do you know the way to Saint Christopher's church?"

Her eyes met mine, and she offered a thin smile. "Sorry, I thought ..." She stopped and pulled her gloved hand, empty from her pocket. "It's a couple blocks down on the next street over," she said, pointing the way. I thanked her and followed her directions.

***

I followed the small procession in through the open double doors at the back of Saint Christopher's church, through the smell of cooked food steaming out from the large hall. Rows of people sat, laughing, talking, sipping, or spooning from steaming styrofoam cups and bowls, over the lined-up tables pushed together end-to-end.

A man resembling a cartoon giant or Russian wrestler, with long black and grey hair and a matching bushy beard, ladled stew into the waiting styrofoam bowls as the line shuffled forward. I mimicked the actions of those in front, pulling one of each container from the upturned stacks and setting them on my tray.

A large hand reached over my tray, filling the bowl with stew from a ladle. "That'll be three-fifty."

I shot a glance up at him, "But I thought ..."

The wrestler was grinning. "I'm just pulling your chain."

"Fred, you're awful," came a shaky female voice.

In the line behind me was a middle-aged woman in a wheelchair, her seemingly tiny eyes peering up at me from behind large, thick-rimmed glasses. "Don't you worry about him. He thinks he's funny," she said. Her voice was soft but strained. She winked one of her tiny eyes and smiled. "His cooking's better than his jokes."

The wrestler put a hand to his mouth and with pantomime exaggeration, whispered, "I saved these just for you." He placed a couple chocolate chip cookies on her tray before filling her bowl.

With my tray filled with the offered food and my cup filled from the tall, stainless steel coffee pot, I scanned the room for a place to sit. I sat alone in the corner, slurping the best vegetable stew I had ever tasted and watching the door, waiting for da Vinci.

"Hey, Arthur, how's life treating you?" the wrestler's voice boomed.

"I can't complain, Fred. How are you and the wife?" was the barely audible, croaked response.

They finished their pleasantries, and the old man, dressed in a brown tweed suit, slid his tray along and thanked the wrestler with a "God bless you."

He turned with tray in hand, his grey-white beard covering the collar of his clean white shirt. As he glanced around the room, I waved, smiling an uncontrollable smile, which he returned and made his way to me.

"It's the artist," he said as he lowered himself into the chair opposite from mine.

"I like your suit."

He leaned across the table and said in a grumbled whisper, "These are my church clothes. I paid less than twenty for the suit at the thrift store; don't tell anyone."

I smiled and looked down at my own clothes. From the reactions of the people I had approached for directions, my church attire had not fooled anyone.

He followed my gaze and added, "It's not a requirement. I'm just old fashioned."

"How's the food?" he asked.

"It's the best I've had in a long time, and if it's good enough for Leonardo da Vinci, then who am I to complain?" I replied with a grin.

"Do you know what everyone else calls me?"

"No. What?"

"Hobo Santa Claus," he replied with a chuckle.

I laughed and quickly caught myself. "Sorry."

INFINITY

"What are you sorry for? I think it's pretty funny," he said.

"Do you know anyone here?" I asked, looking around the room.

He turned sideways in his chair and nodded toward the wrestler. "That's Fred, used to be a truck mechanic before his wife got sick and ended up in a wheelchair. Now she's on disability, and Fred stays home to take care of her," he said.

"That's his wife?" I said, gesturing to the woman in the wheelchair, holding a chocolate chip cookie.

"No, that's Carol. She's got some kind of degenerative bone disease. She's been in that wheelchair for a long time. She used to get up out of it whenever she could, but I don't see her do that anymore." He shook his head slowly.

"So what will happen to her?" I asked. "I mean, can they fix it?"

"Oh, no, I don't think so. She's been like that for years and only getting worse," he replied.

"That's sad."

"It is what it is," he replied.

"How can she smile and laugh, knowing that she's going to wither away and die?" I cringed inside at how cruel my words sounded coming out.

"Just trying to enjoy what life she has left I guess." He shrugged.

"What about him?" I nodded toward an olive-skinned man, crossing the room, with slick black hair and a thick moustache.

"That's Tony. Forty-some-odd years old and still lives at home with his old Portuguese mother. He's got a couple brothers and sisters, but they've got their own families. He got left the task of looking after their mother because he's an alcoholic and can't keep a job."

"Do you know everyone here?" I asked.

"All the regulars," he replied, "but there's always new people coming through, down on their luck."

"If you know so many people, then why are you still ..."

He put a finger to his lips shushing me.

"What, they don't know?"

"This is the only place where people treat me like a real person. I'm no more a charity case than anyone else that comes in here," he said.

"You said they call you Hobo Santa Claus."

"That's the name I catch under people's breath on the street. Here, they call me Arthur," he said.

"It's nice to meet you, Arthur."

CHAPTER 72

Praise

During the week, the spider was kept high and sedated, burrowed in its nest among my deepest secrets. I routinely sacrificed my hopes of getting clean to feed and appease the spider, and in exchange, the spider would numb my sensitivity to the cold and allow dreamless sleep to pass the time between meals.

***

My clothes were still layered on under my thick coat, and I had hoped that the cold would help mask the myriad telltale homeless odors, as I shuffled along in the soup-kitchen line-up.

    I scanned the room from under my wool hat and hood, looking for Arthur, as I made my way to an empty table in the corner. Sat with my gloved hands wrapped around the steaming bowl as I sipped, my fingers tingled through cycles of pain and relief, until the trembling slowed enough that I could use a spoon. Hunched over the bowl, the steam soothed the stinging skin over my cheekbones, rising to settle between my hat and brow and forming a line of sweat.

My guts untwisted to accommodate the food that was now working its way around and warming my blood from inside. I laid my head down over my folded arms, wanting to rest in the warmth for as long as I could.

The room came to life, punching through the silence, and at first, I was unsure if, or for how long, I had slept. I pulled off my gloves, circled the sockets of my aching eyes with my knuckles, and stopped to stifle a yawn with the back of my hand.

"You okay?"

I shifted and sat up. Arthur sat across the table from me, dressed in his church attire and wearing a thin, sympathetic smile.

I nodded. "How long was I out?"

"Not long, half-hour or so," he said, in a low crackle.

I stretched in my seat and turned my face to my sleeve as I yawned again. Arthur waited for me to return eye contact. "It's the cold; it wears you down, gets into your blood, and makes you tired. You've got to squirrel away enough money to get yourself a warm bed in the winter, or one day, you won't wake up."

I paused, turning his words over in my mind, slowly shaking my head. "It's all gone. I have enough food to last, maybe another week, then …" I stared down at the empty styrofoam containers and shrugged.

His expression sagged, "I—"

"I brought my sketchpad, like you asked," I interjected, untucked the pad from under my sweater, and set it down on the table, my eyes fixed on it, instead of him.

He moved his hand flat over the sketchpad. The cuff of his white shirt appeared to glow against the dirt-ingrained skin, creased at the hinge of his wrist. "Do you mind if I show off your art to some of the regulars?" he asked.

I wiped my face and offered what I could of a smile.

After a couple minutes, Arthur waved me over and introduced me to the group as his friend, the artist, while flipping my sketchpad open to various pencil drawings, skipping the ones that showed him with his upturned hat. We were invited to sit, and I took my place next to Arthur, as my sketchpad worked its way around the table and back to me.

My embarrassment was abated by collective praise, transferred to those now functioning as models for my scribbling hand. I remained quiet, smiling politely from behind my sketchpad, communicating by means of graphite lines, finger-softened forms, and highlights picked out with the attached eraser. As grey images appeared from blank white pages, I seemed to disappear, somewhere beyond peripheral, ethereal, invisible.

I snapped awake to a hand on my shoulder and turned to see Arthur smiling back at me. "Can I see?"

I flicked back through a dozen pages that seemed foreign to memory and handed the pad to Arthur. As he viewed the sketches, my attention wandered to the dark motionless sentinels, now standing around the room. I closed my eyes, hoping that the shadows would be gone when I opened them again.

"You have an amazing gift there."

I turned to Arthur. "Gift?"

"These are incredible. I wish I had your talent," he said, and passed the sketchbook to the waiting hands of a smiling woman across the table.

***

I drew portraits by request and some at the request of others, a caricature of Fred wearing a wrestling leotard and posed like a growling bear, raised up on hind legs. I tore out the day's sketches, and they circulated the room, each finding its way to the subject matter. A loud belly laugh boomed from the far end of the room, joined by giggling and howling of the few people now standing around Fred, as he mimicked the pose from the caricature, complete with a growl.

Arthur cackled and put a hand on my arm. "Look how happy they are; you did that. Like I said, you have a gift."

I looked around the room at the smiling faces, and my own smile dissolved as my eyes fell on Carol, sitting in her wheelchair, glasses raised and rubbing tears from her tiny eyes. On the table in front of her was a torn out page; a sick feeling crept up in me at the thought of what could have been drawn on it. I made my way to her table as the spider whispered fragments of a week-old conversation: *how can she smile and laugh ... knowing that she's going to wither away and die.*

"I'm sorry, I didn't mean to ..."

She looked up through tear-filled eyes and said, "You made me look so beautiful."

I felt the hot sting of tears as they formed in my own eyes, and a smile spread uncontrollably over my face. A large hand wrapped over my shoulder, and the drawing of Fred slid across the table.

"Take a look at the one he did of me," Fred said, with a deep chuckle.

Carol turned the page and began a shaky, infectious giggling laugh that spurred Fred into a roaring bass harmony.

***

By the time I left the church, my cheeks and jaw hurt from smiling. I was reminded of earlier daydreams—the art show in Christine's gallery, which had turned out so very different. Thoughts of Christine sobered my mood and seemed to tug at the strings of the spider's web.

Wait until they find out, you're nothing but a junkie ... a fraud ... a worthless vagrant ... you're not an artist, you're a piece-of-shit heroin addict who lives under a bridge like a troll ... you're an unclean hobo, just like me.

I pulled a fold of pre-loaded foil from my pocket, lit and inhaled the hobo spider's sedative, so that I could go over what

INFINITY

I would say to Christine on Monday. My mind was made up; Christine's words would be no more hurtful than those I had heard a thousand times over from the spider. She could call me names and tell me to leave, but I would be leaving with my paintings.

CHAPTER 73

Shepherd

Reduced to my cleanest layer of clothing and still damp from my soda-bottle shower, I crouched in the alley behind Christine Shepherd's gallery. I bargained with the spider, leading him away from the half-devoured entrails of my self-confidence and to the sedative wrapped in foil. A breeze wrapped around the dumpster, licking my ear and crawling over my wet scalp, sending shivers down my neck and under my clothes. My breathing was reduced to a dither, and my thoughts froze around Arthur's words, "… the cold … gets into your blood … makes you tired … one day, you won't wake up."

The air inside the gallery was warm, causing the skin of my face to throb, and my eyes to dry out. Christine looked up from behind the counter and stopped at a stare.

"Hi," I said, looking all around for the courage to face her.

"Hi," she replied.

I swallowed and spoke to the corner of her desk. "I'm sorry for what happened at the show. I just came to pick up my paintings."

I heard the air stop and start in her throat, caught on the beginnings of a word and released as a sigh. She stood and came around the counter. "Are you okay?"

Entranced by her clean perfume smell, I was devolved to the eight-year-old boy, standing at Miss Harper's desk, apologizing for running away. Something inside me broke, and I burst into tears.

"I'm sorry," I sobbed.

"It's okay," she said softly and put a hand on my arm. "Do you want to talk about it?"

"I wouldn't know where to start," I replied, wiping at my face and trying to regain my composure.

She returned to her desk, opened a drawer, and began thumbing through folders. "Do you want to talk over drinks?"

"I have no money," I replied, and turned away.

"Thats alright, the drinks are on me."

"What about the gallery?" I asked, looking around at the new art lining each wall.

"It was a slow morning; nobody buys art on Mondays," she replied dismissively.

My eyes stopped on a portrait hung on the back wall.

"Do you like it? It's my new permanent piece," she said.

The portrait was of an old man, and written on a splintered wood margin at the top, Art is never finished ... and at the bottom ... only abandoned. "You bought it?"

When I looked back at her, she was smiling. "It's a beautiful piece. I wouldn't sell it for any price."

***

Christine placed the folder on the table and picked up her wine. "Do you want to go first?"

"I don't know where to start," I replied, staring at the bottled beer in my hands.

"Start at the beginning and go from there. I don't have anywhere better to be, do you?" She lowered her head to peer under my brow and gave a reassuring smile.

"You're just going to leave the gallery closed for the rest of the day?" I asked.

"My clients are usually busy on Mondays, dealing with whatever it is that makes them enough money to allow the luxury of buying art," she replied, rolling her eyes. "You know it's funny …"

I looked up at her, waiting for her to continue.

"… most of the people that buy art from my gallery are people that will never fully appreciate it. The people that do appreciate art can't afford it," she said.

I replied with Panda's words, "Art produced by the common man is produced for the common man."

"Exactly my point," she said, and took a sip from her glass.

I drank from the bottle. The first mouthful washed over my tongue, and I closed my eyes to further savor the taste. I let out a sigh, and before I could open my eyes, the words poured out of me. "I'm homeless, broke, and addicted to heroin."

I stared at the bottle, not wanting her to see the tears filling my eyes, and not wanting to see the inevitable horror filling hers.

"All of my friends are dead or gone. I feel so alone, and I don't think I can take it anymore." The tears began to stream down my face, and I gambled a glance at hers.

Her expression was not one of disgust, but pity. She asked in a gentle tone of voice, "How did you become homeless?"

I told her about Michael and the reasons we had to leave town. I told her about the motel and the note that he had left. I told her everything from as far back as I could remember; getting hit by the car, the nightmares, the shadows, the incident with Joseph and Miss Harper, the child care facility, my father's drinking, my mother's pills, the beatings, and the excuses.

She listened as I told her about Panda, Michael and Simon, how we had met, how I had run away from home, and how they had taken me in. I told her everything, and it no longer mattered what she thought of me, because there was nothing left of me to matter.

"I stay high so it all goes away, and I don't have to think about any of it. I have nothing left, I've tried to get clean, and I can't do it, and even if I could, what then? My life is meaningless, I have nothing." I wiped at my face.

I looked up at Christine. She was staring into her empty glass.

"Even coming here today to get my paintings is pointless; the only piece I sold, you bought. If I can sell one, or all of them, it doesn't matter, the money will run out, and I will be back on the street in a month or two, in a foot of snow and with no dope to keep me warm. I wish they'd have left me on the highway to die."

Christine wiped at her eyes, swallowed, and spoke softly. "I want to show you something, but first, I need to apologize."

"For what?" I asked.

"I can't give any of your paintings back to you ..." Her voice cracked, my stomach sank, and she cleared her throat, quickly adding, "They're gone; they all sold."

I stared at her blankly, trying and failing to process what she had said.

"More than half of them sold at the show, and the rest sold over the next few days," she continued.

My head whirred, filled with a mixture of volatile emotion. I felt dizzy and wanted to laugh, cry, and throw up, all at the same time. "I don't get it. Why would anyone buy my paintings after I, after what happened?"

"When I heard people talking about what had happened, I didn't know they were talking about you," she replied. "After you left, there was little more than a mumble, and everyone went back to admiring your artwork."

She placed a hand on the folder. "Do you want to know what they sold for?"

I continued to stare as she opened the folder and began to read from the invoices, one by one.

"Writer's block sold for one thousand, two hundred and fifty. The boat sold for nine hundred. Caduceus sold for one thousand and fifty. The snake on the chessboard sold for eight hundred and fifty ..."

She placed each of the invoices down in front of me after she read them out. "After the gallery's fee, you made just under eight thousand."

"I don't believe it," I murmured.

"It's all there, in black and white." She smiled. "So what are you going to do now?"

"Probably wake up under a bridge and realize that all of today was just a cruel dream," I replied.

"You're not dreaming," she said, and her smile widened. "You should be proud of what you've accomplished after everything you've been through."

"I ... I don't know what to say." I stared into her eyes. "Thank you."

"I'll have to go to the bank in the morning and withdraw as much of it as I can. I'm guessing that you have no use for a check." She collected the papers and placed them back into the folder. "I can give you what I have in my purse, but it's not much."

Part of me wanted to refuse, but my hand closed around the folded cash, and Christine closed her hand around mine.

"You're not alone, and your life is not meaningless; you just need a little help," she said and gave my hand a squeeze.

"Why would you help me? You don't really know me," I replied.

"I've read parts of your story in each one of your paintings. Your art is both tragic and beautiful." Her eyes begged for me to accept her smile. "You'll be okay."

INFINITY

IV

CHAPTER 74

Support

The first year of recovery had been hell, and had it not been for Christine's support, I would have surely failed. At the recovery house, they referred to addiction as a disease, and I was naive in hoping that there was a cure. I was given drugs to help manage the physical symptoms of withdrawal, but offered nothing to kill the ravenous cravings or to silence the ravings of a desperate strung-out spider, who had sent an army of his kind to crawl beneath every inch of my skin in search of a way out.

For residents of the recovery house, abstinence was sustained through inaccessibility. We were kept away from using circles, dealers, old lives, and old habits, tucked away from the world for a minimum three-week period of acute stabilization and detox. For those like me, who had signed themselves in as inpatients, most would regret, refute, and fight violently to reverse that decision by the end of the first week.

The spider screamed of starvation, cursing the smiling staff who were hoarding and eating all of our food, cursing me for pouring the dope out in the snow and for giving them signed permission to torture and imprison us both. The spider counted down the days to our release, and with only a day to go, I signed the permission form for an additional three weeks, hoping that during this time, the spider would wither away and die.

As I neared the transition from inpatient to outpatient, Christine busied herself, preparing for my release. She had found and secured a second-floor studio in the industrial part of town. It was a brick building stretching the entire block with various businesses along the ground floor and cheap living space above. These were to be the perks and incentives to getting and staying clean, a place to live, her spoken promise of a stable career as an artist, and her unspoken promise that she would be there to help me every step of the way.

The first step was the easiest, admitting that I was an addict, that I had no power over my addiction, and that my life had become unmanageable. I returned to the recovery house once a week to speak with the resident counselor about aftercare and relapse prevention and attended an evening support group for recovering addicts twice a week. The remainder of my time was spent painting, working my way through checklists, and completing recovery assignments. Homework included simple tasks like taking a walk, making lists of what helped me relax or made me angry, and more difficult tasks like staying positive and avoiding self-deprecation.

Each week, new members took their place in the support group's unofficial hierarchy. The tiers were ranked by class of drug, frequency of use, method of delivery, and chance of rehabilitation. As a daily heroin smoker, I was positioned below my heroin-injecting peers, as part of the ongoing tournament to be the most hopeless, the most fucked up. The weekly prize for those elevated and crowned at the top of the hierarchy was relapse, and perhaps vindication of personal responsibility, convinced that for someone who had it so much worse than the rest, failure had been inevitable.

Over the course of a year, there were countless additions to the group, a revolution of new faces, each sneering and dismissive of the lower tier's struggle with addiction. The same escalating tolerance for poison that had grown my daily dosage of heroin served as an immunity to the berating from my peers, for I was only a smoker and should be able to quit with ease. It was made clear that anger and denial were natural symptoms of the detox process, and all that made it through the first couple of weeks would focus less on the others in the group and more on themselves. One by one, another sad and unique twist on the same basic story would be added to the support group library.

In addition to the recovery counselor, and in response to Christine's passive, yet persuasive advice, I sought out a psychiatrist to help me work through unresolved issues. Our weekly appointments evolved from timid, fragmented accounts, each a diluted parody of memory, to full disclosure, an unabridged, uncensored version replete with tears and a full cast of personal demons.

The psychiatrist had asked that I keep two separate journals, one to record my day-to-day actions and emotional responses to be used as reference when we met each week, and another starting from my earliest memory, detailing the events that I thought had shaped me into who I had become. He said that in writing of my experiences, I would have the chance to reflect and perhaps resolve some of the issues of my past, to properly mourn and grieve for those estranged to me through death or circumstance. In our ongoing sessions, he used terms such as, abandonment issues, parental surrogates and substitutes, responsibility, and transference. He said that heroin had perhaps functioned both as an escape, and as self-administered punishment for all the things that I had blamed myself for throughout my life.

Meditation was encouraged as a way to relax, an escape from physicality, and a way to unlock repressed memories and emotions. I would close my eyes and fill my mind with color, starting with red, transitioning through orange, yellow, green, blue, and violet, to white as he called each one out. At this point, he would ask me to focus on my breathing and guided me through documented events from my past, while I provided commentary on the vivid scenes played in high definition behind my eyes. The journal chronicling my past served as our itinerary and my filter. Anything written in my journal was open for discussion, and anything left out was mine to divulge at my discretion.

Over the years, I felt less inclined to hide or omit details, realizing that the past was something that I could neither change nor hide from. The psychiatrist said that escaping the past was impossible, that my only choice was to accept everything that had happened, forgive myself, and move on.

CHAPTER 75

Memorial

I lived alone in the studio kept company by the relentless myriad mechanical noises: large diesel trucks, back-up beepers, mechanics' air-tools whizzing and clanging, trains screeching on the tracks, signaling with loud whistles at every crossing and over the ringing bells. Every sound echoed through the industrial landscape, bouncing off brick buildings, warehouses, factories, spring makers, chemical plants, and every kind of material supplier. To me, the noise was soothing, loud enough to drown out the whispers of a dying spider and to serve as a reminder that life continued beyond the four walls of my studio during the long days between support group and therapy.

Each Saturday, I would leave the studio early and pick up groceries on my way to Saint Christopher's church. Fred had agreed not to mention where the extra food came from but as a show of gratitude would sneak items onto my tray as I shuffled along the line, which I would then place on Carol's tray and whisper that Fred had saved them especially for her.

For two years, I had tried to persuade Arthur to come stay with me at the studio, but no amount of pleading or begging could convince him. He said that he begged for small change every day, but was too old for big change, that during the winter cooped up in a small room at the hostel felt more like being in a prison than a home. I listened to him cough,

INFINITY

watched the skin draped over his fragile frame become translucent, showing blue-green strings beneath and a purple-grey where it stretched over bone.

I brought bags of non-perishable food and begged for him to take money. At first, he would refuse, but as his health diminished, so did my ability to conceal how much it broke my heart every time he did so. Each week, I told him of my progress in recovery and brought photographs of new artwork, handing them across the soup kitchen table, waiting intently, desperate to see the shine in his stare, the burlap smile behind a thinning mesh of white wire, to hear him say that he was proud of me.

The last time I saw Arthur was also the last time I saw Carol. For the two months of Carol's absence, I searched the hostels, alleys, doorways, and bridges for Arthur. At her funeral, I mourned for them both. Placed on a table at her wake, surrounded by countless flowers, was my pencil sketch of Carol, framed, and behind glass. Reflected in the glass, the crying members of Saint Christopher's church placed flowers and said their goodbyes.

I had called Christine that evening and asked her to come over. When she arrived, she said that from my tone of voice, she thought that I had relapsed or was about to. Over wine, I told her about Carol and Arthur and broke down into tears in her arms. In Christine's gallery, the next day, and with her permission, I moved an empty sculpture pedestal to the wall below the painting of Arthur and placed on it an upturned hat and a sign that read, hungry and homeless. The following Friday, and every Friday after, all money left in the hat was delivered into the waiting hands of the homeless along Main Street.

CHAPTER 76

Gateway/Relationships

Christine stood in the kitchen corner of the studio, pulling each of the upper cabinets open one by one. "I just want to make sure that you're eating and staying healthy. I worry about you."

The psychiatrist's description of Christine's role in my life, "... parental surrogate or substitute," worked its way from the back of my mind to the smile spreading across my face.

"I love you too, Christine."

She closed the cabinets, picked up her coffee cup, and returned a smile. "You've been here for three years, and it looks like you just moved in."

I followed her eyes around the room from my easel, unfinished paintings, canvas and art supplies in one corner, to my unmade bed in another. My mattress sat, without box or frame, directly on the hardwood floor with the olive-drab bag next to it, unzipped and with every item of clothing I owned folded or stuffed inside.

My furniture, an old armchair and couch that she had given to me when I moved in, half-circled a stack of wooden pallets, topped with a piece of glass and repurposed as a coffee table, in the middle of the room.

"It's minimalist," I said through a smirk.

"Such a prolific artist, with bare brick walls," she teased, sipped from her cup, and took a seat on the couch.

INFINITY

"If I put all of my paintings up on the walls, you'd have nothing to sell, and I'd have nothing in the bank. I get what I need from the process of painting. It's no longer magic when you know how the trick's done."

"I've watched you paint; it's still magic to me, and I'm pretty sure that setting aside a few pieces for yourself wouldn't break the bank." She raised an eyebrow and offered a sly smile.

I had obtained government ID, opened a bank account with Christine's help, and had put roughly two-thirds of all the money I made into a savings account. Beyond food, cigarettes, art supplies, therapy and rent, I had few additional expenses. After getting my driver's license, my largest purchase was an old retired work van that I bought for a thousand and change. It was white, had rust at every edge, and a crack in the windshield spanning the full width, but aside from minor aesthetic flaws, it ran well and was large enough to transport my paintings. Thanks to Christine, I had become a real person, a fact that I had pointed out many times, and was the reason for her short-lived nickname, "Blue Fairy."

We talked over a pot of coffee, catching up on the events of the week, before saying our goodbyes and returning to our daily routines. I returned to my chair, picked up the journal, and began my daily entry. My whole life up to this point had fit into three journals; everything that I had wanted to forget, written down, a permanent record to be reviewed and relived in weekly installments.

Other than my relationship with Christine, all romantic relationships had been deliberately omitted from the journals. The recovery counselor had warned against romantic entanglement during recovery, and one of my short, failed relationships had delivered the lesson explaining why.

Her name was Mary-Jane, which coincidentally is another name for marijuana, often referred to as a gateway drug. When we met, she had been in recovery, off and on, for two years. In group, she told the story of how she stole from her family to feed her habit, pawning anything of value, including her great grandmother's engagement ring, a family heirloom.

She had broken down and confessed to her parents when they questioned her about it. They had gone with her to the pawnshop to retrieve the ring, the price of which jumped higher with every mention of words like, "precious ... heirloom ... sentimental ... priceless." They signed her into rehabilitation at sixteen years old, scared that if she didn't get off the drugs, she would not only sell everything that they owned, but would resort to selling the only thing left that she owned: herself.

We flirted awkwardly for weeks, talking about her poetry and my art. She brought a poem for me to read, and shuffled nervously from one foot to the other while I inhaled sentence after sentence more vibrant and colorful than any canvas I had ever painted. In my studio, she watched as I painted. It felt strange to have company while I worked, foreign but not unpleasant, and over the course of just a few months, our awkward friendship developed into an intimate relationship that we both agreed to keep secret from the recovery counselor and the support group.

About three months into the relationship, we had our first and last fight. I had just finished a painting. After rinsing my brush, I wiped my hands and took a cigarette from my pack, having picked up the habit as a way to curb some of the residual cravings, and turned from my easel to see her on the couch with my journal splayed open between her hands. Without thinking, I snatched the book from her, yelling about her going through my personal things. She burst into tears, and although I wanted to take it back and tell her that I was sorry, I told her to leave. In group that week, she cried again and told of her relapse. After the fight, she had gone straight back to her old dealer and stayed up all night getting high. Soon after, she checked herself back into rehab, and I never saw her again.

Pairing with a fellow addict doubled the chance of failure. A relationship with anyone outside of recovery meant having to explain that I was a recovering heroin addict or having to lie and hope that they would never find out, both of us growing to love the lie, but one of us eventually hating the liar.

CHAPTER 77

Saviour

The industrial landscape had transformed over the past week from brick, dirt, metal and rust, to sloping mounds of white. I kept to the salted wet path between heaped snow, gathered and piled by machines and the line of brown slush kicked up and pushed aside by the endless convoy of delivery trucks. The alternating deep hollow scooping sound and high-pitched back-up beeper echoed over the loud exhaust of a skid-steer working to clear roads farther down.

Daily walks had been a tedious part of my recovery assignments, but were now one of the more enjoyable parts of my routine. During the summer months, I would leave the studio just before the sun went down to watch as the disparate components of an ugly but functional landscape were washed with a beautiful and unifying haze of amber; brick and rusted metal transformed into gold, a task that had eluded even the most adept alchemist of another era. In the winter, the sun would set during one or more of my weekly appointments, so I would take my walk in the morning, the cold air needling my lungs en route to a coffee shop on the outskirts of town.

I plugged my ears to the loud beep, beep, beep, scrape of the skid-steer as I hurried past on the opposite side of the road. Alongside the chain-link fence, the path disappeared under heaped snow. I returned my hands to the warm pockets of my coat, the same thrift store coat that had once kept me warm during cold nights under a bridge, the same coat that had cost more to have cleaned than it had cost to purchase. The snow crunched down forming deep wells around my boots with each step, soaking my jeans far enough up each leg to make contact with sock and skin above my boots.

Through the fence, a graffitied train car sat half-buried in sloping snow. Portions of a rounded white canopy broke and fell from its roof in clumps, while water dripped steadily from the delicate icicles formed underneath the one non-buried corner. I stared for a moment, hypnotized by the falling droplets sparkling in the early morning light against the shadow under the train car. As I watched, the shadow seemed to move. There was a dark shape, barely visible beyond the dripping water. My thoughts returned to the bridge, tucking my bag into the dark concrete recess, and curling around it to sleep.

I continued to the train yard entrance and ducked under the length of chain, ignoring the no trespassing sign hanging from it. The shape under the train car was not a bag, but an animal, a dog lying on its side. The mass of matted fur shuddered to inflate and deflate as wisps of warm breath leaked from its snout, dispersing into the frigid air.

As the wet soaked through my jeans to one knee, I switched to the other and leaned under the train car for a better look. The dog's breathing seemed to slow, and I reached in to touch it. I saw a flash of pale blue eyes and exposed teeth as the dog twisted, snapped at my hand, and scuffled deeper into the shadows. I withdrew, slumped back on the snow, and peered down at my left hand, now peppered with white dimples and dripping red holes. I shook my throbbing hand and pressed it into the snow, hoping to soothe the bite, but instead, the cold only emphasized the dull ache and amplified the sharp pain.

By the time I reached the studio, my hand was covered with blood and swollen like a semi-inflated surgical glove. I washed the wound at the kitchen sink, wincing more at the sight of flapping skin around the deeper holes than at the constant stinging pain. I wrapped my hand with cloth, ripped from an old T-shirt, and secured it with masking tape.

I followed the trail of red lined pits in the snow, all the way back to a pink footprint at the corner of the train car. I spoke softly into the shadow. "I'm sorry I scared you. I brought you some food." I folded back the lid and tapped the open can of tuna on the wet ground at the entrance of his makeshift cave. "Come on, I won't hurt you." The dog made no sound. I tried to slide the can farther in, and it clattered, rolled, and disappeared into the darkness. I waited but there was still no sound or movement from the animal. I wondered if the dog was still there, if it had seized the opportunity to run while I was gone, or if it was dead.

Icicles snapped over my shoulder, dripping cold water down the back of my neck as I crawled under the train car, flinching each time I pressed my left hand down on the wet gravel. I felt my way in the darkness and jumped at the abrupt scraping sound of the tuna can as I swept it away with my hand. I tucked my head between my arms and braced myself for another attack. Fear shuddered through me with the realization that on my hands and knees, any and all defense would prove futile. The can spun faster to a hum as it settled in the darkness, and then nothing. I shuffled forward, and my fingers found the mass of wet matted fur.

The dog was still breathing but made no attempt to move. I could feel its ribs through the wet fur as it shivered. "I'm not going to hurt you," I whispered as I rolled onto my back and pulled the limp animal up onto my chest. I let out a sigh and pushed the image of the deadly teeth, in reality just inches from my face, out of my mind. Pushing with my legs, I shuffled from elbow to shoulder, shimmying to the opening and hoping to get there before the pale blue eyes flashed open again. Once out on the snow, I rolled onto my side, pulled my arm from under the dog, and stood. My fluttering heart slowed as I breathed deep and sighed large billowing clouds into the cold air. In the bright morning light, the animal looked more like a wolf than a dog. It lay shivering, its mouth and nose twitching, and its eyes open a slit but rolled away, showing only pink and white. As I lifted the dog into my arms, the dank smell of its fur breeched my senses. It was the same smell that my coat had before it was cleaned, the smell of an abandoned creature without a home.

CHAPTER 78

Companion

When I returned from therapy, there was no sign of the dog. The food and water bowls that I had put out for it and the makeshift bed, comprised of towels, clothes, and the coat I had wrapped the animal up in, were empty.

I set down the rest of the groceries, tore open the bag of dog food and refilled both bowls, one with the dry food, and the other with water from the tap. As I tried the bathroom door, there was a guttural growl from the other side, doubled to sound more menacing as the sound reverberated off the tiled surfaces inside. With one hand clenched around the door handle, I slid the bowls in through the narrow opening and then pulled the door shut.

Sat with my back against the wall outside of the bathroom, I spoke in a low, calm register. "You don't have to be scared. I'm not going to hurt you."

The dog growled in response.

"You can't stay in there forever. I'll need to get in there at some point. As soon as you're feeling better, you can leave if you want to, or you can stay here with me, and I'll take care of you. I bought a bag of dog food, and I'm not going to eat it."

I heard the click of its nails on the tile, the lapping of water, and the loud echoing crunch as it devoured the dry food.

I waited half an hour into the following silence before gently pushing open the door and retrieving the empty bowls.

For the rest of the evening, I busied myself at my easel, periodically checking over my shoulder to see if the dog had left the bathroom, and trying to distract myself from the worst-case scenarios playing on an endless loop in the back of my mind.

I wiped the excess red paint from my thumb, and turned to see the bathroom door open and the bathroom no longer occupied. Centered in the curl of coat and towels in the kitchen corner of the studio was a mound of grey fur, and I found myself smiling. Fear was pushed to one side of my mind, making room for hope, hope of an end to encompassing solitude.

In spite of having had little sleep, I woke up early to the overpowering smell of urine and the sound of my reluctant companion sniffing at the gap under the door leading to the stairs and the way out. I relented to an uncontrollable yawn, which sent the dog scuffling back, scrambling for grip on the hardwood floor, and after gaining purchase, it ran back to the kitchen. I pulled open the doors at the top and bottom of the stairs and returned to the studio, rubbing sleep from the corners of my aching eyes.

"Go on. If you want to go, I'm not going to stop you," I said, nodding toward the door and backing away to the window wall.

With its eyes fixed on me, it crept along the opposite wall to around the halfway point, and then bolted for the door. A series of diminishing thuds and clicks accompanied the dog on its way out, and I watched through the window as it crossed the road and disappeared around the corner. I pulled a towel from the makeshift bed to mop up the urine, now soaking into the wood, but left the rest of the towels, clothes, and my now fur-lined coat in place, hoping that the dog would come back when it grew tired or hungry, or lonely.

CHAPTER 79

Duality

I unpacked the baking soda, added the white vinegar to the bowl of warm water, and set to scrubbing the urine stain from the studio floor, as per Fred's instruction. While setting up the tables at the soup kitchen earlier that day, I had spoken with Fred about the dog. From my description, he said it was most likely a Husky, and without a collar, probably a stray. Along with the stain remover recipe, he made a list of items for me to pick up, in case the dog returned.

    I put away the cleaning supplies, treats, bones, flea treatments, and everything else that had been on Fred's list, washed up, and retired to the couch. After making my daily journal entry, I stretched out, closed my eyes, and counted back through colors until calm and relaxed. From nothingness evolved images, formed of gold pinstriped light. As I tried to focus, the scene raced away, repelled by scrutiny, seemingly viewable only in the periphery of focus. From the reset darkness, gold sparks danced in the distance, from a blurred impression, to incredible definition. The scene that unfolded around me was the studio interior, as though created from a luminous gas and solidified to recreate the room in perfect microscopic detail. I could see in all directions simultaneously, a golden panorama with me in its center, lying down on the couch, eyes closed. The room stretched vertically, its contents, including the recreated version of me, dissolved to black, and from the emptiness, vague figures began to glow. The darkness evolved to bright white light behind the glowing figures, the two sources of light separated and definable by slowly spinning shadows, cast like the negative of a lens flare.

"Hello, little one."

I was overwhelmed by a warming sensation; it felt like home.

"You *are* home," they said.

Before I asked the question, lingering in the surreal approximation of my mind, the collective voice spoke its answer.

"Yes, and you are in our imagination; we are part of you, and you, a part of us, as we are all part of everything that exists with and without time." They spoke in a coalesced male and female whisper, neither predominant over its counterpart. "Time is a concept of matter and is what separates us. To escape physicality, is to dissolve time, bringing us closer."

"Dissolve time?" I asked.

"As we speak, you exist beyond time and matter. The event of your life is yet to begin, and has already been and gone."

"I don't understand," I said.

"Duality. You exist within and without time. A fragment of the whole that contains the whole."

The figures receded into the bright light, while their voice echoed in my head. "Like books upon a shelf, the beginning and end are already written. To read is to introduce time. Page by page the events unfold, but when the book is closed, the story exists complete, and without time."

I awoke with a gasp, my eyes struggling to adjust to the room, lit only by the street lamps outside. My limbs felt peculiar and heavy as I rolled onto my side, draping my arm to the floor to retrieve my journal. I wrote frantically with the page turned to face the windows, trying to recapture all that I had seen and heard, racing to record the experience before waking reality could erase it from memory, the way wakefulness indiscriminately washes away even the most beautiful of dreams.

CHAPTER 80

Control

During my session with the psychiatrist, we began as usual with the week's events, read aloud from my journal. We talked for a while about the dog, and about if the dog somehow represented my former self, and if saving the dog reflected my own need to be saved. As the psychiatrist seemingly talked in circles, my mind juggled the words, *save the dog—dog save me—God save me*. I apologized when I realized that he had stopped talking and was waiting for a response to something I missed. We moved on to the full-page entry, chronicling my experience during meditation
"What do you think it means?" he asked.
"I don't know. I was hoping that *you* could tell *me*," I said, trying unsuccessfully to read the inverted scrawl on the top leaf of his notepad.
"Meditation is self-reflection on a subconscious level. Perhaps, thinking of your past as a book that is already written, is your way of coming to terms with, and accepting the fact that, the past is something that you cannot change." He glanced up from his notes. "Not the response you were looking for? In my opinion, dreams are subjective. If you believe that dreams of falling represent failure, then your subconscious could manifest the same symbolism to address unresolved issues. The real question is, what does it mean *to you?*"

"I wanted it to be more than just a dream, or manifestation of unresolved issues," I said, resisting the urge to make quotation marks in the air with my fingers as I did so.

"What do you mean by more than a dream?" he asked.

I hesitated, knowing that I had passed the point of no return. "Do you believe in God?"

The psychiatrist sat back in his chair and smiled. "If I told you that I was an atheist, would it change *your* mind as to the existence of God?"

"I don't know if there's a god. I want there to be a god," I replied.

"Why do you *want* there to be a god?" He leaned his head like a dog hearing its name.

"Because there has to be more than this; either there's life after death …"

"Or what?" he pressed.

"Or I'm crazy, and have been my whole life," I said reluctantly, through a heavy sigh.

"Do you think that you're crazy?" he asked.

"Years ago, *they* told me I was special. I just want to be normal," I replied.

"What is normal?" he said, and for the first time in four years, I heard him laugh.

"Do you think I'm crazy?" I asked.

"No." He took a breath as the smile relaxed from his face. "I think you have a vivid imagination, the mind of an artist. You've had a difficult life, and perhaps this is your mind's way of trying to make sense of it all."

We sat in silence as he searched my face for a response. "Isn't that what everyone is really searching for when they go in search of God?"

I nodded, disappointed that the experience had been so easily trivialized, but relieved that his reaction had not included the up-sale of sanity through anti-psychotic drugs.

He put his pen to the paper and asked, "How did it make you feel when *they* said that you were special?"

INFINITY

"Like I had a purpose, that I would do something meaningful or worthwhile with my life," I replied.

"Do you feel like your life so far, *has* been meaningful or worthwhile?" he asked.

"I feel like my life has only just started."

"How have you been sleeping?" he asked.

"Last night, I dreamed that I was thrown into a river as a baby and swept away by the current ..."

"Go on." He began writing.

"For most of the dream, I was a child, thrashing around in the water, crying for help, choking and half-drowning, pulling away clumps of the river bank as it rushed past. At the end of the dream, I was a man again; the river had dumped me into a calm sea, but there was no sign of land in any direction, and I didn't know which way to swim."

"You've had almost no control of your life until now." He lowered his pad and pen and took a thoughtful breath in. "You're no longer controlled by circumstance, or addiction, and perhaps you're feeling a little apprehensive about being in control of your future. Your need for there to be a god and a higher purpose is perhaps your way of, once again, relinquishing control of your destiny to an outside force."

"So what do I do? Just ignore it all, the light-beings, the shadow-people? Just ignore it and pretend to be normal?"

"No, I don't think that trying to repress anything will be good for you in the long term. Meditation is self-reflection. These light-beings and shadow-people are part of your subconscious mind; light versus dark is a common psychological theme. This is your way of working through questions that maybe you don't even realize you're asking," he said.

"The shadows seem no more good or evil than the glowing figures; they're just ... there, watching, waiting. They were still there with the anti-psychotics, the heroin, and even now, clean and sober, I see them in every dark corner. I don't even write about them in my journal anymore; they're just part of the landscape."

The psychiatrist followed my gaze to the clock and checked the time on his watch. "Saved by the bell. I'll see you next week?"

Our sessions had always ended with *see you next week* phrased as a question, as though he was expecting, or waiting for, me to declare my own sanity and relieve him of service.

I nodded. "Same time, same place, same unresolved issues."

CHAPTER 81

Coercion

From the street outside the studio, there came a loud bark, followed by a scratching at the door. Stood up on my toes, face pressed against the window, I peered down to the amber-lit street below, but could not see the dog. The dog barked again, and I rushed to find and fill the food and water bowls, before heading downstairs. There was a scramble of nails on pavement from the other side of the front door, as I unlocked it and pulled it open. I retrieved the bowls from the stairs, placed them just outside the door, and took a seat on the second stair.

After waiting a few minutes, and with no sign of the dog, I called to the street, "Alright, scaredy-cat, I'll leave it here if you change your mind." I closed the door and went back to peering out of the second floor window.

From under a parked truck across the street, the dog emerged, crawling from the shadows and out into the amber light. The repurposed stainless steel, single-serve salad bowls clanged against the brick as the dog drank and ate its fill, just out of view. I continued to watch the road, waiting for another glimpse of my new and elusive friend. The dog stepped into view, wagging its tail as it sauntered across the road. It stopped, glanced back toward my door, and then crawled into the shadow beneath the chassis of the truck.

I retrieved the empty bowl and poured out the dregs of water from the other onto the pavement. "You're welcome," I called, before returning up the stairs and to the window, to watch the dog scurry from its hiding place and take off at a trot around the corner, the same way it had done a week before.

Over the following week, the dog came back every night, ate the food I put out for him, and hid within sight of the door, watching as I retrieved the empty bowls and ignoring my attempts to lure him from under the truck.

During this time, I had given him a name, a homage to another grey-haired hobo and my departed friend.

***

"See you tomorrow, Arthur," I called out to the shadows, retrieved the bowls, and closed the door behind me.

I finished rinsing out the bowls and placed them next to the sink. Over the sound of the running tap, I heard a noise from outside. I turned off the tap, and the sound came again, Arthur's bark from the street below my window. I snatched a bag of snacks from the cupboard, pulled on a sweater, and made my way downstairs.

"I know you're there, come on." The breath exhaled between my words, drifting slowly in the amber light. "Arthur, come on."

I sat on the curb, a few feet from the door, and rattled the bag of treats before tossing one toward the truck, which landed just behind the front wheel.

"I've got a whole bag of these, if you want them."

Arthur's snout emerged from the shadows, turned on its side, gingerly edging out to gain purchase of the bone-shaped snack in its teeth, before retreating once again into the darkness.

It took around twenty minutes and almost half the bag of treats to lure him to my side of the road. I tossed one of the

INFINITY

treats just inside the studio entrance. "You can go in if you want to. Go on, it's okay, I'm not going to hurt you."

As I stood, Arthur scurried back, circling at a safe distance back toward the truck. I left both doors open and a trail of snacks on the stairs, leading into the studio and to a small pile, placed in the dog's makeshift bed.

I heard the slow timid clicks on the stairs and watched out of the corner of my eye, while sitting in my chair pretending to write in my journal. Arthur's snout peaked around the doorframe, sniffing rhythmically, exhaling small clouds into the cold air that now filled the studio. He crept along the snack trail, his eyes transfixed on me as he gathered them silently between his teeth. When all of the treats were collected, he crept back, brushing against the wall, and once beyond the halfway point, he bolted for the door.

I grabbed my hat, added another sweater to the multiple layers of clothing, leaving my donated coat as part of the dog's bedding, and followed him out. With my hands in my pockets, I trudged along the same route that I had walked that morning, and at least once a day since my recovery began, but this time, my wet footsteps were echoed by the clicking of Arthur's nails on the pavement behind me.

CHAPTER 82

To catch and kill a mocking spider

Halfway across the suspended steel mesh walkway, spanning the width of the train tracks, I stopped, leaned over the railing, and peered back to the base of the steel stairs where Arthur remained, chewing on a bone that I had given to him the day before. During the summer months, the mesh walkway had become my viewpoint to watch the sunset. During the winter, it was a place away from people, all edges softened to subtle glistening curves of ice and snow. The soft white landscape seemed to swallow, or absorb the mechanical montage of sound, allowing a rare quiet for me to hear and organize my thoughts, or temporarily discard them. All things unclean, both mental and physical, were packed and preserved in ice, sealed under several feet of clean white snow, out of sight and out of mind until the spring thaw. I had come to this place every day since around my eighteenth birthday. This was the place that I released the spider.

The week of my eighteenth birthday had been a low point. Skewed sentimentality over the anniversary of hitting bottom brought self-doubt, strong cravings, and even romanticized pseudo memories of using. In support group, I was advised by the recovery counselor to surround myself with friends and family, people who had been a positive influence in my life, people who loved me. That night, I wept alone in the studio, trying to think of someone to turn to. On my long list, there were two names, Arthur and Christine. Since Arthur had no phone, no home, and a day-to-day life infinitely more difficult than my own, the names on my short list were pared down to just one, Christine.

With a half-smoked cigarette in one hand and the phone held in the other, I sat willing myself to call her. The spider seized the opportunity to plead his case, a desperate pitch, and a last-ditch effort to make me see reason, or make me doubt the reasons that kept me clean.

She's not your friend. She only pretends to care, so that you will keep painting for her, and she can get her cut.

I took a drag from the cigarette. "It's because of her that I'm not living under a fucking bridge anymore."

It's because of her that you stopped taking your medicine.

"It's not medicine; it's poison."

So you replaced our medicine with cigarettes that are going to kill us?

"Hopefully they will kill you before they kill me." I stubbed out the cigarette and made my way to the kitchen.

You can't kill me.

"Fuck you." I tapped out another cigarette from the pack on the counter, brought it to my mouth, and drew in the lighter's flame.

What? You're going to try to smoke me out? The spider's laugh filled my mind. I closed my eyes and pictured the smoke rolling around my head, creeping like a heavy fog over the surface of my brain, toward the burrowed hole, the spider's home.

You are trying to kill an imaginary spider; you are crazy.

I opened my eyes, tapped the ash into the sink, and froze. A hobo spider, about two inches across, was trying to climb out of the stainless steel sink. I snatched a glass from the counter, and ignoring the shiver climbing my spine, slammed the glass, upturned over the spider. "Got you."

The spider crawled in a full circle, stopped to face me, and placed its foremost legs up on the glass. "There's no way out."

I retrieved a roll of green masking tape from my art supplies and the top flier from the pile of junk mail on my coffee table before returning to the sink. I slid the two-for-one-pizza flier carefully under the glass, folded the edges up over the glass, and ran a couple lines of tape around it to secure it in place. I lifted the glass to eye height, turned it right side up, and the spider fell to, and filled, the bottom of the glass. It turned and stared back at me, its two front legs raised once again and pressed against the side of the glass.

I took the glass and left the studio, periodically checking to make sure that the spider was still in the glass, periodically cringing at the thought of it escaping and running up my hand, into the sleeve of my sweater and scrambling to find its way back inside via my ear, mouth, or nose. After walking for around half an hour, I came across metal steps leading up to a walkway over the train tracks. I made my way up and halfway across and held the glass outstretched. Without ceremony, I let go of the glass and listened to it shatter a second later on the tracks below.

CHAPTER 83

Equilibrium

I had grown used to the monotony of my weekly routine, appreciative of it, of the reliability and security.

Sunday was my day off from scheduled appointments, my day to do whatever I pleased. I would go for long walks with Arthur following close behind. We made a detour at the end of our usual daily route, through a seldom-occupied trail that led to the river and away from the noise of the city. I would sit on the riverbank, while Arthur explored. When he grew tired, he would return, sit, and pretend to listen to me talk, his head cocked to one side as I relayed my thoughts out loud and over the sound of rushing water.

Beyond my daily walk and journal update, Monday was spent painting, Tuesday was a repeat of the day before plus an evening support group meeting, Wednesday the same again plus recovery counselor one-on-one. Thursday, I delivered finished artwork to the gallery and would sometimes wait for Christine at the bar on the corner, where we would sit on the patio and catch up over mostly virgin drinks. Friday morning was spent at the laundromat, and then delivering the week's collected change from the upturned hat at the gallery to the hands of the homeless, en route to the psychiatrist. Saturday morning, I did the grocery shopping for the soup kitchen, and on my way back from the soup kitchen, I picked up groceries for Arthur and myself for the week.

Arthur sat waiting, edging forward with every pleading whimper, while I searched through the bags of groceries to find the rawhide chew, which over the past couple months had become an essential part of our weekly routine. We settled on the couch, Arthur biting down on the rawhide, and me biting down on the end of my pen, trying to think of something worthy to write in my journal, something worthy of psychiatry.

I closed my eyes and counted back through colors. Beyond violet, the open mouth of teeth grinding against rawhide, dulled and faded into the distance along with the faint mechanical chimes from outside. From white noise, gold sparks gathered to form a kaleidoscopic tunnel of light, collecting colors, like iron filings to a slowly turning magnet. As I was drawn in to the epicenter of spinning light, I began to stretch and dissolve, becoming part of the seemingly infinite light. Outside of the tunnel were figures, shadow people racing by as the light grew brighter, then brighter still, until there was nothing but pure white light. My usual senses were gone. Light and warmth were described only by emotion. The light simultaneously expressed emptiness, nothingness, wholeness, and oneness. It felt like I was home, like I belonged. It felt the way that love feels when dreamed or imagined. This calm love seemed to pulse through the light, through me, and then it was gone, replaced by a single thought. The thought was of wanting to be more than the whole. A hole burned open to a black swirling void, and the pulsing light dispersed in every direction, expanding, thinning, and whispering regret.

The pulse became weak, spreading farther, and was slowly enveloped by feelings of fear and betrayal, while the diminishing light approached solidity, manifestation, and resignation.

I awoke with a gasping breath. The first of my senses to return was met with the rough, wet drag of Arthur's tongue as it striped my face. My eyes struggled to focus on Arthur's nose

INFINITY

just inches from my own as he continued to lap, whimper, and paw at my chest. He tucked his head beneath my chin, and I wrapped my arms around the mass of shaking fur. "What is it boy?" I spoke softly. "It's okay, I'm alright."

For the rest of the night, Arthur remained by my side. When I lay down to sleep, Arthur curled up next to me, whimpering and pawing at my chest each time I began to drift into sleep.

CHAPTER 84

Cured

I spent each day's assigned journal time with the task of trying to write of the dreamlike scene during meditation and found that words simply could not describe what had been almost a purely emotional experience. Not even memory or imagination could replicate the experience, with any degree of accuracy, as I attempted to replay it repeatedly in my mind.

During Friday's session with the psychiatrist, I read aloud the failed impression of my experience and waited for his reaction, hoping for insight, or some explanation of its meaning.

"You speak of this pulsing light being enveloped by fear and betrayal. Do you think, that perhaps, this is in reference to your childhood?" he asked, "That maybe, the diminishing light, approaching solidity and resignation is you?"

"What do you mean?"

"The feelings of fear and betrayal may relate to your own feelings about being forced to give up on the idea of a loving family environment, and perhaps, the diminishing light is the way you see yourself, that only now, are you beginning to take control of your own life. The solidity and resignation could be in reference to the regaining of control and your acceptance of the past." He looked up from his notepad.

"I guess that makes sense," I replied.

INFINITY

"What do you think it meant?" he asked, reading my expression carefully.

"It felt more like ... like it was about more than me, something important."

"Some kind of epiphany?" He placed his notebook down at his feet. "Are you talking about God?"

"I don't know, maybe," I replied.

"I think I know what you need," he said.

My mind raced through words like, anti-psychotics, chemical stabilizers, institution, delusion, schizophrenia, mania ...

"Transpersonal psychology, it's a field of psychology that centers on spiritual subject matter."

"I thought you were an atheist?" I asked.

"I've been referred to as an atheist, an existentialist, and a great many other things over the years, and being any of which would render me unequipped to deal with spiritual matters," he added a sideways smile, "it's not my field. All I can do is help you to understand what these experiences mean to you."

I sat, relieved, waiting for him to continue.

"It appears to me, that you are looking for spiritual guidance, not therapy," he said.

"Did you just talk yourself out of a job?" I asked with a smirk.

The psychiatrist let out a small laugh. "You've been coming to see me for how long, four years? Do you still feel like you are getting something out of our weekly sessions?"

"I don't know. I guess it's just become part of my routine," I replied.

"Look, it's your choice, if you want to continue therapy, but I don't see you getting any more than you would out of talking to your friend Christine."

"Does that mean I'm cured?" I asked with a grin.

"It would be unprofessional for me to use those terms, but it is my personal belief, that you have gotten everything that you will likely get from our weekly therapy sessions," he replied and returned the grin.

"So I guess I *won't* see you next week."

"Let's give it two weeks, and if you feel like you need to come back and see me, then we'll set up an appointment." He stood and extended a hand.

I got up and shook his hand. "Do I get a certificate or anything?"

"I'm afraid not."

"Well, I guess this is goodbye then," I said.

"Goodbye."

CHAPTER 85

Duality of light

"It looks like the pause button symbol from a remote," I said, staring at the first painting in four years to be donated to the wall of the studio, less because I liked it, than because I didn't think anyone else would.

Christine sat next to me on the couch, squinted her eyes, and leaned her head one way then the other. "I like it; it's simple and ambiguous."

"I don't know what it is."

"You *should*, you painted it." She turned with a smile.

"It came to me during meditation; it's titled duality," I said.

"Duality?"

I struggled to recall the dreamlike scene in my mind. "There were multiple parallel vertical lines shining on a dark background. Then the lines merged, becoming just two clear lines as though refocused through a lens, and this voice whispered over and again about the duality of light."

We both stared at the painting, as though looking for the hidden image in a magic eye picture. The concentration and silence were broken by Christine's startled gasp, as a flash of grey fur leapt between us, and Arthur set to greeting Christine with a zealous, lapping tongue.

"Hi, Arthur," she said, ruffling the fur at his neck and shoulders, while I sat with my coffee cup elevated to avoid his excited tail, rhythmically wagging against my face.

As I stood, Arthur jumped from the couch and ran to the door.

"You want out?" I asked.

He sat with his head cocked to one side, shuffling on his front paws, and let out a single bark.

"I'll be back in a second. I'm just going to let him out."

When I returned to the studio, Christine was refilling her cup from the pot. "How are you doing without therapy?"

"I'm doing okay. I can always go back if I need to." I joined her in the kitchen and dumped the rest of the coffee into my cup.

"Do you think that you *will* go back?"

"I don't think I'll need to. I'm cured. Besides, I've got you."

Christine smiled. "What about your journal? Are you going to keep writing?"

"I haven't really thought about it. I haven't *stopped* writing."

"You could turn them into a book. You've had an interesting life." She took her cup and returned to the couch.

"I don't know if I would want people reading about my life; it was hard enough talking to the psychiatrist," I replied.

There was a loud bark from outside. "I should let him in."

"Actually, I'd better get going. It's getting late." She put her arms around me and gave a squeeze. "Take care of yourself."

She followed me down the stairs, and Arthur met us at the door as we said our goodbyes. Arthur and I retired to the couch, him with his rawhide chew, and me with my journal, open to the next blank page.

CHAPTER 86

Refraction

On a whim, I had asked the clerk in the bookstore where I could find anything on the duality of light, and he had pointed me to the physics and quantum physics section. After browsing through thick volumes of Newtonian physics, Einstein's relativity, and books containing the quantum physics theories of Schrödinger, Heisenberg, de Broglie, and Bohm, I found myself missing Panda. He was the one person I could turn to with any question and expect an answer, specifically catered for my intellectual capacity. I decided on three books, selected using the least scientific method of closing my eyes and pulling each from the shelf at random, paid for them, and left.

At the riverbank, Arthur bit at the water's edge, trying and failing to catch fish, understanding as much about the refraction of light, making the fish appear nearer the surface, as I did of quantum mechanics as I re-read page after page, hoping that at least some of it would sink in.

I placed the book down, rubbed at my eyes, and rustled the bag of dog treats. Arthur came running, and sat down at my side. "Do you know what a quark is?" He ignored my question and took the treat. "What the hell is Planck's constant? Do people actually understand this stuff?" Arthur leaned his head and barked.

253

"If the light beings are God, and God made me, then they should know that I'm not smart enough to understand it, right?" Arthur barked again and pawed at the bag of dog treats. "Alright, here you go." I poured the last few out and handed them over.

I found myself thinking of Panda, his obscure analogies, his *did-you-know* facts about everything and anything, and I couldn't help but smile. I thought how my life now somewhat resembled the life he had wanted for me, and that if he was among the peripheral landscape of shadows, that perhaps he would be smiling back.

CHAPTER 87

Double slit

I mixed each color on my palette with titanium white, adding the subdued color to the lens-flare-like detail in the center of the canvas, before blending the tapering rays into the white background with a dry fan-bristle brush. The piece contained a simple figure, the same figure that can be found on almost every male bathroom sign. The figure was white, on a white background, defined only by subdued prismatic color, shining from behind the figure and by flaring shadows cast by the figure in the space around it.

    I penciled the title "Light Being" along the bottom edge and finished the piece with a subdued red thumbprint in the corner.

    I stood back, stared for a moment, and then turned to Arthur. "What do you think, Arthur?"

    Other than the slightest wag of the tip of his tail at the mention of his name, Arthur remained still in his bed and breathed a nasal sigh.

    After rinsing my brushes and scraping my palette clean, I retired to the couch, took a book from the stack at my feet, and opened it to the last of the feathered yellow sticky notes, fanning out from between its pages. I struggled through each new theory, flicking back to earlier explanations of basic principles and referencing the attached yellow note, written by, and for, the layman. I understood very little of what I read and found nothing to validate my emersion into a subject, seemingly so far beyond my intelligence. During each night's meditation, I had tried to contact the light beings, and the harder I tried to concentrate, the harder it became. All I saw were degraded re-enactments, created by my own imagination and desperation, adding to my escalating doubt of them having ever been anything else.

I closed the book, looking down at its fore-edge, at the myriad yellow tongues taunting me from the first eighty pages of the book, of which there were hundreds more to go. I blew out a breath, bent back the slab of paper, and let the pages flick from right thumb to front cover, fanning cool air and the new-book smell of paper, ink, and glue. The figure drawings played like a non-linear, nonsensical flick book, black squares, graphs, line drawings, and then a picture I recognized. I flicked back through the pages to find the image that had jumped out at me, possibly misconstrued, translated inaccurately or skewed to fit my subconscious agenda.

When I found the page, the hair on my arms stood up from the sudden goose-bumped flesh. Under the heading, Double slit experiment, were multiple diagrams resembling the pause symbol Duality painting on my wall; one diagram of a plate with two, seemingly illuminated, rectangular slits, another diagram showing parallel vertical lines of light. The description under the first group of images read, *One of the most important experiments within the field of quantum physics. The double slit experiment shows the wave, particle duality of an electron*. I looked back and forth from the page to the *Duality* painting on my wall.

Whether this proved that the light beings were more than a product of my imagination, my subconscious mind, more than a symptom of unresolved issues or self-reflection, became the nucleus of every other thought, as my mind raced with questions and possibilities. If more than seemingly impossible coincidence, then perhaps I had been given a way, or the language with which to decipher their cryptic messages, or at least, a place to begin.

INFINITY

CHAPTER 88

Wave-particle duality

What at first had seemed like the discovery of the Holy Grail, now seemed like nothing more than rumor of its whereabouts. If there had been a quantum mechanics manual made for children, things would have been easier; instead, I struggled through page after page of text created by minds infinitely greater than my own.

From almost every other page, the yellow leaves offered childish explanations of *The photoelectric effect, Planck's constant, Balmer's constant*, and *Rydberg's constant*. My own constant was the reoccurrence of a quantum physics headache, way beyond that of the quantum scale. Flicking through my journal, which now served also as a companion notebook for home-school quantum physics 101, I paused at the page that seemingly told me to do so. The journal fell open without resistance, it too having memorized the page, and I read over my notes on the double-slit-experiment.

Electrons fired through a plate with two cutout slits created a series of vertical lines, a striped pattern, or wave interference pattern, meaning that the electron behaved/behaves like a wave, not a particle.

Further experiments, performed firing only a single electron at a time, revealed that the same interference pattern emerged over time, meaning that somehow, the single electron interferes with itself after it passes the plate.

During attempts to measure or detect the electron at the double slit plate, to see how a single electron could create a wave interference pattern, a different pattern emerged. The electron, when detected at the plate, behaved like a particle, and went through one slit or the other, which over time, the accumulated data shows as two vertical lines on the back wall.

The simple act of observing the electron as it passed through the double slit plate, determined the behavior of the electron as a particle, and no longer a wave. Observation of the electron collapsed the wave into a particle. This is wave-particle duality.

On the following pages were crude, and possibly incorrect, explanations of super-position and probability phenomena, and near the back of the journal were notes of every exchange with the light beings, or at least what fragments of conversation I could remember, or find in earlier journals.

We are nowhere ... no when ... We, like you, are but a thought.

Time is a concept of matter. The present ... is only a brief sliver of existence ... merely the reading of events. The past and future should be thought of in the same way, as events, infinite possibilities ... Events, without time, existing only as potential. You were an event within our existence. We enjoyed your life. It was an important event ... You were special ...

... little one ... you are in our imagination; we are part of you, and you, a part of us, as we are all part of everything that exists with and without time.

Time ... is what separates us. To escape physicality is to dissolve time, bringing us closer ... As we speak, you exist beyond time and matter. The event of your life is yet to begin, and has already been and gone ...

... Duality ... You exist within and without time. A fragment of the whole that contains the whole ...

Like books upon a shelf, the beginning and end are already written. To read is to introduce time. Page by page, the

INFINITY

events unfold, but when the book is closed, the story exists complete and without time.

... the duality of light ...

Interspersed within the last few pages, were my notes, grasping attempts to glean meaning, or make connections.

A fragment of the whole that contains the whole; little one.

Perhaps meditation is the act, or process of transcending matter and time, becoming non-material, non-linear, unobserved, without time, without matter, changing from particle to wave, dissolving time, and becoming one with God.

At the very end of the journal, I copied a quote from Albert Einstein, "Energy cannot be created or destroyed; it can only be changed from one form to another."

CHAPTER 89

Diamond

I didn't hear the knock at the door, but Arthur woke with a start and scrambled for the door. He lay sniffing and barking at the gap under the door as I made my way to him. "You're going to have to move, buddy. I can't open the door with your snout in the way," I said.

Arthur passed me on the stairs and sat scratching and whining at the front door, while I tried to unlock it. "Calm down, Arthur."

I opened the front door a crack, trying to hold Arthur back with my knee and free hand. Through the gap in the door, Christine said, "Hi, it's just me." Arthur snaked around my legs and out to Christine. "Hi, Arthur," she said, stooped in the doorway, trying simultaneously to pet him, steady herself, and keep his tongue away from her face.

"I wasn't expecting you," I said as we made our way into the studio.

"I haven't seen you in a couple of weeks. I was getting worried."

Arthur followed Christine to the couch, climbed up, and curled up next to her.

"I didn't realize it had been that long," I said trying to recall the last time I had seen her.

"Are you alright?"

INFINITY

"Yeah, I'm fine, guess I lost track of time. My routine's been off since graduating sanity school," I replied and pulled a cigarette from my pack.

"Looks like you've been busy," she said, her eyes flicking over the stack of books at my feet. "Quantum physics?"

I squirmed a little inside at the thought of trying to explain my sudden fascination, which seemed somehow more embarrassing at that moment than if it had been a stack of pornography at my feet. "I needed something to pass the time without therapy," I replied and lit my cigarette.

She frowned around a squint and a smile, knowing that there was something I wasn't telling, but not wanting to push. "Not exactly a light read."

I breathed a laugh through my nose and changed the subject. "How're you doing?"

"My sister called," she said in a flat tone, deepening the frown and losing the playful smirk.

"The sister that never calls?"

She nodded. "She called to tell me that my dad is sick."

"Is it serious?"

"Cancer," Christine replied without inflection, staring blankly at, or out, the window. "She said he's okay, that they caught it early."

"Are you going to go out there and see him?"

She rubbed at the side of her face, then let her hand rest in front of her mouth and nose. "Does it make me a bad person, that even when my dad is sick, I still don't want to go back there?"

"A bad person? No, you are the nicest person I know," I replied quickly.

Her eyes closed, pushing the collected tears up over the lids and down her cheeks. I moved to the arm of the couch, sat, and put my arm around her. "I wouldn't be here, if it hadn't been for you."

She leaned into my chest and sobbed, "I'm sorry, I didn't come here to dump all this on you."

"It's okay, I get it. Whenever you go out there, they make you feel like shit," I said.

"He's my dad though. I should go and see him," she said, and wiped her face.

"Who's going to run the gallery while you're out there?"

"I haven't gotten that far yet."

"I can watch it for you, if you show me what to do," I said.

"What about Arthur?"

Arthur took the mention of his name as his cue to lick the tears from Christine's face. She ruffled his fur and held his head, leaned against her.

"I'm sure he'd be willing, but I don't know if he'll be able to work the cash register," I said.

She looked up at me with reddened glassy eyes and offered a thin smile. "I'll probably just close up shop while I'm out there, but thanks for the offer."

We sat for a minute, both of us lost in the imagined near future, perhaps both of us contemplating worst-case scenarios.

"I have coffee on; do you want one?" I asked, offering each of us a break from our thoughts.

She nodded. "Thanks."

I poured the coffee, stirred in the cream, and called back over my shoulder, "How was your sister, while you were talking to her?"

"How'd you mean?"

"Was she civil at least?" I asked.

"Rachel has two modes, disapproving big sister, and devil's advocate for any opinion that contradicts mine. She never misses an opportunity to tell me what I'm doing wrong with my life, ever since I left for university, which, according to her, was a waste of time and money."

I placed the cups down on the coffee table and sat back in my chair.

"Sorry, I'm ranting. She's always had a knack for getting under my skin," she said, shaking her head.

INFINITY

"She's just jealous because you've done something with your life."

She offered a thin smile, seemingly unconvinced and sipped from her cup. "If I hadn't left for university, I'd be serving breakfast, drinks, or gas. I don't think it's wrong to want something better for yourself. There was nothing there for me. I had to leave, but they don't seem to get it. Growing up in a small town is suffocating; it grinds you down, especially for a girl that wants to be something other than a waitress. I didn't want to end up bitter like the rest of my family. Just thinking about going back there is stressful."

She sat rubbing at her head, while I sat thinking of the right thing to say. "Panda said to me once that 'great art and great people are like diamonds.'"

"How so?"

"'They're formed and produced by immense stress and pressure, and when broken free, they're incredibly strong and coveted for their incredible beauty,'" I recited his words, smiling as Panda mouthed along in my mind.

Christine returned the smile. "That's beautiful; you should put that in your book."

"What book?"

"Your memoir," she teased, gesturing to the journals on the floor.

"Who'd want to read a book about *my* life?"

"I would," she said, looking me in the eyes and causing me to look away.

"Thank you," I said.

"No, thank you."

"For what?" I asked.

"For being a good friend," she replied, "You're a diamond."

Arthur breathed a deep sigh through his nose. "You too, Arthur," she said ruffling his fur.

"It's almost time for our W-A-L-K; do you want to come with us?" I reached behind for the sweater, draped over the back of my chair, pulled it and my shoes on, and stood.

263

"Sure, I could use a walk to clear my head," Christine replied.

Arthur jumped down and ran to the door, having heard the magic word, and we followed him out.

CHAPTER 90

Erosion

Over the next six months, the gallery was closed sporadically for at least half of that time, in mostly one, or two week intervals. Each time, Christine had offered an apologetic prologue before telling me the date of her departure and date of her return. It saddened me to watch her leave, and more so to watch as her father's ever diminishing health status took its toll on her.

When she spoke of her dad, I listened; when she cried, I held her. There was nothing that I, nor anyone else, could say that would change the fact that her dad was dying; no spiritual philosophy heralding death as a part of life would pacify the pain, when death had become more than philosophy and the basis of her daily life.

With each commute, new lines and creases were carved into her face, her eyes remained red-ringed and glazed over, and she no longer tried to cover the wear with makeup. The skin at the inside corner of her eyes became red downward channels, worn smooth by periodic streaming tears, like a riverbed carved out, and eroded over time by the exponential increase of an unrelenting current.

During conversations about her moving back home, the *before he dies* part was never said aloud, but had become the subliminal passing phrase, or precursor, to all topics related to her father. At first, she was reluctant to the idea of going back home, scared that doing so would be like admitting that he was not going to pull through, but over time, it became clear that her admittance was extraneous to the fact that her father was going to die.

She regressed and reminisced about her childhood, the acreage that her family had owned for generations, the rancher style house that she grew up in, and the large red oak out front, whose roots had stretched under the house, lifting parts of the foundation and causing the floorboards to creak when trying to sneak out after dark. As children, Christine and Rachel had carved their names deep into the bark of the red oak, and soon after, the bleeding sap from the wound had attracted a type of beetle, and with it, an infection from neighboring trees on the outer edge of the property. The red oak gave way to wilt over the course of a single summer, died, and collapsed under the weight of heavy snow the following winter.

I made every attempt not to treat Christine like the daughter of a man dying of cancer, skirting around the *before he dies* and *after he dies* that were never said but implied and always lurking in the subtext of every conversation. The cancer worked its way through her father and set up billboard posters in the minds of friends and family, appearing at the first sign of a smile and marketing happiness in whatever brief form as selfish and shameful. They caught the cancer early, giving her father a fighting chance. He reacted well to treatment at first, winning the first few rounds, but the cancer came back stronger each time, seemingly less afraid and knowing that the key to victory was endurance, a war of attrition against the Shepherd family, the gradual spread of infection until wilt, death, and collapse.

CHAPTER 91

After life

During daily interaction with Christine, one of the two previously subliminal phrases, *after he dies*, had become the subject and main focus of all conversation.

Christine sat on the couch across from me, absently thumbing through one of my journals, the one repurposed for quantum physics 101. I cringed inside as she flicked through the last few pages, hoping that she would continue past the chronicled light being exchanges and my scattered attempts to derive meaning from them.

"Energy cannot be created or destroyed; it can only be changed from one form to another," she read aloud from the back of my journal, and after a pause, she asked, "Where do you think we go when we die?"

"I don't know," I said, looking anywhere but at her.

"Please," she added, and waited for me to meet her tear-filled eyes.

"Just like the Einstein quote, I think we change from one form to another, a different form of energy, back to the consciousness or God."

"You believe in God?" she asked.

"I believe in something, a collective energy outside of time and matter, where we go before choosing our next life."

"You think that we choose our life?"

I nodded slowly, trying to recall the answer to a question that I had asked myself over and again. "If we do become part of the consciousness, without time and matter, then we too become omniscient, omnipotent, and omnipresent, meaning that any possible outcome of any decision is already known collectively, so when we choose a life, we already know how that life will turn out. We open that life at page one and read until it's done."

"If that's true, then why would someone choose a life of pain or suffering? Why would you have chosen *your* life?"

"When you said that I should write a book, I asked you who would want to read a book about my life, and you said—"

"I would," she interjected.

She let out a sigh and smiled a thin but genuine smile.

"So what's with all the books? You didn't all of a sudden decide that you wanted to be a quantum physicist," she said.

I retrieved one of the books from the floor, moved around the coffee table, and sat next to her on the couch. I walked my fingers through the yellow leaves to the note titled *double-slit-experiment* and opened the book.

"The painting on my wall, the pause symbol, is what I painted after seeing a version of that experiment in meditation," I said, "They kept whispering about the duality of light."

She flicked her attention from the painting, to the book, and then back at me. "What is it?"

I explained the experiment to her, reading excerpts from my notes in the journal.

"You said they kept whispering about the duality of light; who are *they*?" she asked.

I shuffled around in my seat, set the books down on the coffee table, and said through a wince, "The light beings."

"So what does it mean?" she asked, without missing a beat.

A small laugh escaped as I shifted my position to face her. "You have no problem with magical light bulb people talking to me about quantum physics?"

INFINITY

She ignored my grin and asked, "If the light beings *are* real, then what does it all mean?"

I stared into her eyes as her question swam around inside my head. "I've been trying to figure that out."

"And?" Christine pressed.

"Maybe the soul is a wave or energy, reimagined as matter when observed," I said.

"Observed? Like when God is reading the book of your life?" she asked.

"It all sounds crazy when I say it out loud," I said.

"You're not crazy, the psychiatrist said so, remember?" Her lips flashed a smile, which quickly dissolved as her mouth practiced her next question.

"Do you honestly believe in the light beings or an afterlife?"

"I don't have a choice. I don't think there's anyone else in the world that *needs* to believe it more than I do," I said and met her wet stare.

"Yes there is," she replied.

The two syllable word blurred into focus on the billboard in my mind, along with the sub-header below, *after he dies*.

"I'm sorry."

"Don't be sorry," she said and leaned into me.

I put my arms around her, cradling her head in my hand as she wept.

Her voice was small, quivering, and muffled into my chest, as she hugged me tight and said, "Thank you."

CHAPTER 92

Comparable loss

Christine witnessed the episodic deterioration of her father with each reunion, the disease had progressed, and her father edged closer to being gone forever. Each time she returned, I witnessed the same, the deterioration of my friend, the accumulated toll of the disease, and the edging closer of a time when she too would be gone.

Within a year of receiving the phone call and news of her father's illness, Christine had closed the gallery, put her house up for sale, and had severed all ties, but one, to the city. As she made definite preparations for her indefinite absence, I did the same. The thought of losing Christine was devastating. I kept the sadness to myself, hidden under a thick veil of guilt over my selfish comparisons of loss, knowing that once she was gone, I would never see her again. She would devote all her time to her father *before he died* and to taking care of the remnants of her family *after he died*.

When the sale of Christine's house was finalized, I gave my one-month notice and packed up the studio. I gave my van as partial, monetarily insignificant, trade for an RV large enough to fit both Christine's remaining belongings and my own. The plan was for us to make the trip together, to spend as much time together as possible *before she was gone*, and *after she was gone*, I would continue on with Arthur.

INFINITY

***

I returned upstairs, having loaded the last of the boxes into the RV, and glanced around the bare studio.

"Are you going to miss this place?" Christine asked.

"I'm going to miss you more," I replied, then quickly added, "I know you have to go. You have to take care of your family, because that's who you are. It's one of the many reasons that I love you."

She smiled and hugged me, "I love you too."

"I'm going to walk Arthur before we leave; do you want to come with us?"

Christine nodded and the three of us left. We walked our usual route, and Arthur took a last sniff of everything, seemingly recording every smell and committing each to memory.

"I'm going to miss this," I said, looking out across the train tracks.

"Me too," Christine replied, both of us knowing that it was not the place that would be missed, but the lives we were leaving behind that would soon be only shared memories.

We finished our walk, arriving back at the RV, and I led Arthur in through the side door to the curl of thrift-store-coat bedding and his rawhide chew. After removing the key to the RV from the ring, I fed the studio keys through the letter slot and looked over at Christine. "You ready?"

"It needs a name," she said.

"What does?"

"The RV," she replied.

"Like what?" I asked through a grin.

"I don't know, how about Harvey?"

"Harvey the RV?" I let out a breathy chuckle, and we climbed in.

I pulled away from the curb slowly, unsure of the quality of my packing and stacking in the back, but other than a few minor shuffling sounds, and the rattle of what I guessed to be the chain linking the legs of my easel, everything seemed secure.

"It's okay, Arthur," Christine said softly, reaching back to pet him as he stood, turned in a circle, sat, then started the whole process again.

She directed me out of the city. "It's all highway driving for the next eight hours; let me know when you want to switch."

"Are you regretting not going by plane yet?"

"Not at all. I hate flying, and besides, I get to spend time with my two favorite people," she replied, smiling in my peripheral vision.

The rain started soon after we began the highway stretch, and I was relieved that the windshield wipers worked. "Let's see if the radio works," I said and fumbled with the volume dial for a second before Christine took over and found the power button. The radio powered on to white noise, and she scrolled through to the first clear station, playing *golden oldies*. We drove for hours in the rain, serenaded by Elle Fitzgerald, The Ink Spots, and Tracey Chapman, among others, some from several decades before I was born.

***

We stopped at a rest stop at a point that Christine said was about halfway. I refilled the gas tank while she went inside for *provisions*, and Arthur expanded his territory to include the local foliage. After replacing the pump-nozzle and gas cap, I joined Arthur out back and smoked a cigarette while we waited.

Christine handed one of the steaming paper cups to me. "Sorry that took so long. There was no coffee, and I had to wait for a fresh pot."

"It's okay. Arthur wanted to water the flowers anyway."

"I picked up a road map for you," she said, "So you won't get lost. After you drop me off, I mean."

"Thanks."

"So where are you going to go?" she asked.

"I don't know, we'll probably just wander around for a while, until we figure it out," I said.

"The lonely wanderer and his hobo husky," she said with a grin.

"Sounds like the title of a bad western," I said and returned a smile. "Should we get going?"

Christine gave a nod, and we walked back to the RV.

***

I had taken Christine up on her offer to drive the last stretch of our journey. After several hours meandering east on a winding road carved through thick forest, Christine slowed the RV and pulled to a stop at the side of the road.

"Everything alright?" I asked.

"We've been driving for nearly eight hours, and I almost wish there were another eight hours to go," she said and turned off the engine.

"We can sit for a while, if you're not ready."

"There's a trail through the forest, just a little farther down that my sister and I used to walk all the time," she said, "Do you want to take a walk?"

"Sure," I replied.

Christine led us along the roadside and through a gap in the brush that opened to a winding orange trail, snaking through thick forest. Arthur ran ahead, turning back every so often, to let us catch up.

"I used to love the smell of the forest after it rained," she said, breathing in with her head back and her eyes closed.

"It reminds me of the snake trail, from when I was a kid," I replied, "Only a lot bigger."

Christine began to snicker.

"What's so funny?" I asked.

"The lonely wanderer and his hobo husky in the snake trail adventure," she teased and continued to laugh.

"That definitely sounds like a bad western," I said.

"Or a series, like those old, choose-your-own-adventure books," she offered.

As we followed Arthur, we each offered increasingly ridiculous titles. "The lonely wanderer and his hobo husky in the great money train caper ... the gunslinger's arduous journey ... the beast of the dusty plains ... the mystery of the ghost horse ..."

"The return to Shepherd ranch," Christine said and slowed her pace.

I turned with a smirk, but she was no longer smiling. I wanted to tell her that it was going to be all right, but I knew, as well as she did, that it would have been a lie. I put my arms around her, and she sobbed into my shoulder.

I became aware of movement, somewhere in my periphery. I scanned the vertical stripe of trees and shadow in the middle distance, waiting for whatever had caught my attention to move again and reveal itself. A smile crept over my face, and I whispered to Christine for her to turn slowly and follow my finger. A second and third deer, larger than the first, emerged from the bushes, and a smile spread across Christine's face. They stood for a minute or so, looking our way, calm and still, save for the odd flick of an ear, before disappearing back into the forest.

When we returned to the RV, Christine asked if I would mind driving the rest of the way, saying that she was too anxious. As I drove, she stared out of the passenger window, appearing smaller each time I glanced over, perhaps recoiling into childhood memories replaying in her mind.

We passed through a small town, one road with a single stretch of stores on one side, a bar, liquor store, and gas station on the other. A couple miles beyond the town, Christine pointed to an open gate on the left hand side and told me to pull in. It took a couple attempts to pull into the driveway, and I almost took out the rusted mailbox at the corner as I did so.

INFINITY

We drove slowly along the gravel driveway toward the single-level, rancher-style house, completely wrapped in unpainted cedar, one half turned a greenish grey. I parked the RV in front of the uneven wraparound porch, next to the rotten stump of an old tree. The door opened and a woman stepped out.

"That's my sister, Rachel," Christine said.

"I imagined her with horns," I said and offered a thin smile. "You ready for this?"

"Not really," she replied, clunked open the door, and climbed out of the RV.

The sisters hugged briefly and went inside. I climbed out of the RV, walked around to let Arthur out, and then busied myself unloading the boxes, not wanting to intrude on what would surely be a tearful reunion.

I set the last box down, took a seat on the porch steps, and lit a cigarette. When Christine came back out onto the porch, her eyes were red from crying.

"You didn't have to move all of that on your own," she said.

"I don't mind. I like feeling useful."

"Thank you."

She sat down next to me on the step, and I put my arm around her. Arthur climbed the steps and pushed his nose between us, licking at Christine's face.

"Thank you too, Arthur," she said, ruffling his neck fur.

"He loves you; we both do," I said.

"I love you too," she replied softly.

"Are you going to be okay?"

She nodded, and after a short sigh, we stood and said our goodbyes.

As I pulled away, dust kicked up and spread in the air behind the RV, obscuring my view of Christine in the side mirror. I slowed as I neared the open gate and waited for the dust to settle, but when it finally cleared, she was gone.

CHAPTER 93

After she was gone

Arthur sat outside with his chew, and I went in to pay for the gas. I stood, turning the rack of keychain nametags, while the old woman searched behind the counter for my cigarette brand. I came across a Harvey keychain, which brought a smile to my face and Christine's smiling face to mind. I took the keychain and placed it on the counter next to the gas station equivalent of a ham and Swiss sandwich.

I turned the key and let the RV idle while I rummaged through the bag to find the keychain. I adjusted the rear view mirror, tilting it down to see Arthur, centered in the much emptier living space of the RV, and hung the nametag from the mirror's mounting stem.

"Harvey, the RV," I muttered.

I opened the map book and flicked through the pages. "Where do you want to go, Arthur? Looks like there is a big national park not too far from here. How does that sound?"

Arthur's tail drummed a soft beat against the floor, and I put the RV in gear.

It took just under three hours to get to the park, the last hour of which was spent wondering if I had missed the turn-off, as it had appeared much closer on the map. I followed the road signs and pulled into an empty gravel lot. "I think this is it; do you want to go for a walk?"

INFINITY

We conformed to signage directing visitors to various paths and trails, ignoring intermittent signage warning of fines for smokers and owners of unleashed dogs. I let Arthur lead the way, down into a gully, over and under twisted, moss-covered roots and thick, long-ago-fallen branches. A shallow rock-strewn stream sliced the vibrant green basin in half, and I chased Arthur downstream, slipping on, but cushioned by, the bed of spongy moss at the water's edge. The stream dropped away to a glistening lake below an outcrop of roots and rock, and I stood for an immeasurable time, trying to take it all in, before realizing that Arthur had somehow worked his way down and was chasing whatever wildlife resided in the long-grass field that stretched on for miles, fading into a distant blur of grey-blue hills.

Arthur tired as the sun began to set, and we found our way back to the RV under incredible pink and orange skies. After we had eaten, we retired to our beds. Lying on my side on the fold-down bed, I watched as Arthur continued to run in his sleep, wagging and whimpering over the myriad sounds of nocturnal wildlife, a welcome change from the mechanical symphony which had served as an unlikely lullaby for the previous five years.

CHAPTER 94

Catalyst

We made our way from one park to the next, stopping in between to pick up additional camping supplies, food, water, and necessities. I purchased a book about bush-craft and survival and several physics books to further my self-education. Harvey idled at every scenic viewpoint, while Arthur searched for a new, temporary oasis. Anywhere that Arthur took a liking to would be marked on the map with a red star and would be our new home until supplies ran low. While Arthur ran, chased, and explored, I sketched, read, or wrote in my journal. At the end of each day, I would lie on my back next to the fire and stare up at the clear night sky, unobscured by city light-and-smog pollution, and relax into deep meditation. The days belonged to Arthur, but the evenings belonged to me.

Of the seldom interactions with the light beings during meditation, few were describable in words. What I felt in their presence was emotional, love, acceptance, a sense of belonging, family. When they spoke in words, they echoed past interactions about time, matter, and light with slight variation; they said again that I was special, an important event, and that my story would serve as the catalyst for another, who would dissolve time, blend duality, and bring us all closer.

My continued study led me from wave particle duality and the creation of matter through conscious observation, to

INFINITY

theories of the zero point field, described as the vacuum state, a quantum state wherein waves and particles appear and disappear, fleeting into and out of existence. In my journal, I wrote that perhaps consciousness exists within the zero point field, connecting everything, serving as the conduit for fleeting messages between God and matter, and binding everything together as one; matter being the physical manifestation, the emotional expression of the consciousness. Thought being energy, and energy becoming matter, *we, like you, are but a thought*, we are a dream of the consciousness, the emotional expression of God.

As the months passed by and the nights grew colder, I would meditate before sleep in the back of the RV, falling seamlessly into vivid dreams that I would sometimes recreate in paint the next day. Of the dreams with reoccurring themes, one was of the phoenix of Greek mythology, fully engulfed in flames of every color, dissolving into blue energy and violet wisps of light, and another was of a snake devouring its own tail. The dreams were perhaps inspired by Panda's old stories, imagery ingrained since my early teen years: The phoenix rising from the flames, representing renewal or rebirth, and Ouroboros, the snake that devours its own tail, an everlasting cycle, representing wholeness, immortality, and infinity.

The winter was spent on the verge of epiphany, each hole in my understanding seemingly sewn shut with new threads of information, but with new understanding, new holes became visible at both the micro and macro scale.

CHAPTER 95

The return journey

Time rolled by, measurable only by the length of my hair and by the color of Arthur's fur. Another winter passed, a new journal was started, and my sketchbook was almost full, mostly pencil drawings of landscapes, each containing a version of Arthur, a flick book of my friend growing old. He began to slow, tire early, and spent more time by my side, listening to my theories about life, the universe, and God, feigning interest and comprehension with the lean of his head. During supply runs into town, he remained in the RV while I gathered the necessities and searched for his favorite chews.

Sometimes months would go by between supply runs and subsequently between human contact. The longer I was away from people, the stranger it seemed when trying to converse with a cashier or gas pump attendant; I felt more like a shadow lurking in life's periphery than a part of the human race. After so long with only Arthur to talk to, sporadic two-way conversations were obtuse and obtrusive and filled me with a strange paranoia that would follow me for days.

***

INFINITY

We began the return journey without a final destination, but with the intention of revisiting the red-star locations on the map, each one a familiar oasis, and each one had been our home for a time. We returned to lakes, rivers, waterfalls, and forests and watched the sun rise over rolling hills and set behind the ocean horizon, with Arthur curled up in my old coat, next to a fire on the beach. In the morning, I would relight the fire, boil water in an old can for instant coffee, and heat up a can of food for us to share before packing up and heading to the next red-star location on the map.

The map was splayed open on the passenger seat and the sketchpad open in my lap. I flicked through the makeshift photo album, smiling at the sketches of a seemingly much younger version of my old friend, while he slept in the back of the RV. On the first page of my sketchbook, he appeared as a small spec in the distance, then page by page, he moved from the background to the foreground, more defined, more detailed, remaining still for longer, long enough to capture his likeness.

I closed the book. "We're here, Arthur."

Arthur remained still. I opened the door, climbed down from the driver's seat, walked around the RV to the side door, and opened it. "Arthur, we're here, buddy, come on," I said softly, running my fingers through his grey fur. He opened his eyes, and I helped him out of the RV.

When we had first discovered the lake, Arthur had jumped in after the ducks, while I sat sketching the scene, laughing at his futile attempts to catch one. He had gotten back at me by shaking out his wet fur and spraying me, soaking my back with cold stinking water while I tried to shield my sketchpad.

I sat with my back against a tree at the lakeside, with the much older version of Arthur at my side, wagging his tail with what seemed like great effort. We watched the ducks swim in formation, a silent ripple spreading over the lake surface behind them. Arthur curled up with his head on my lap while I watched the sunlight strobe chaotically, hypnotically, flashing from a thousand blue silk creases in the surface topography of the dark water and through the delicate prismatic blur of dragonfly wings, as they hovered periodically at the water's edge. With my eyes closed and my head leaned back against the tree, the sun's penetrating light, glowing red behind my eyelids, dissolved behind the beginnings of a dream.

***

When I opened my eyes, the sun had moved behind a row of tall trees, obscuring both light and warmth. A cool breeze came off the water, directing Arthur's fur between my fingers.
"It's getting cold; do you want to go back?"
Arthur didn't wake.
"Arthur?"
I stared down at the gently swaying fur as his body remained still. I placed my hand in front of his nose, but no breath came out. My eyes filled with hot stinging tears, and my throat tightened around his name as I whispered it again, "Arthur?"

CHAPTER 96

Grave

I knelt, centered in a small clearing between three trees. Tears ran down my face, dripping onto the small camping shovel as I stabbed it into the dirt, clawed, scraped and scooped, widening and deepening the hole. The head of the shovel *clacked* and *rang*, bouncing off rocks buried in the soil, temporarily drowning out the involuntary sounds leaking from my throat with each staggered breath.

    I lifted Arthur gently, as though he would disintegrate, cradled in my shaking arms, and I carried him to the clearing. I stepped down into the four-foot ditch, slouched down with my friend held tight against my chest and wept into his fur, rocking back and forth.

    Under a triangle of pink sky, between the leaf canopy of three pine trees, I sobbed my final goodbye to Arthur and pushed the soil back into the hole. I pressed and smoothed over the top layer of dirt with my blistered hands, wiped my face, and moved to the trunk of one of the three surrounding trees. With my pocketknife, I carved Arthur's name deep into the bark, and circled it with a simple line version of a snake devouring its own tail, to serve as the headstone of my best friend's grave.

CHAPTER 97

Sentiment

I sat in the driver's seat of the RV for two days willing myself to turn the key between lighting and extinguishing cigarette after cigarette. I tapped one of the last three smokes from the last of three packs in two days and flicked the sketchpad back to the start. As I turned the pages, each new sketch inspired daydream memories of my time with Arthur. Smoke rose up from the cigarette hanging limply and stuck to my dry lips, stinging my already tear-filled eyes, and causing me to blink, releasing a tear that hit the page with a *pat*. I wiped my face and peered down through the blue tinted folds of smoke circling the cab. A wet wrinkled circle centered the sketch of Arthur swimming after the ducks, the same sketch that was wrinkled by his wet shaken fur the day the drawing was made, and drawn in the same place that he would draw his last breath.

    I leaned my pounding head back against the headrest and closed my eyes, filling my mind with color, painting over the images of Arthur, a new layer for every painful daydream or memory, first a red wash, then orange, yellow, all the way through to violet, white, and then nothing.

    When I opened my eyes, I was no longer in the RV. I was standing in the middle of a road, behind a child-size shadow, standing perpendicular to the curled up body of a lifeless child. Next to the child was a small red bike on its side with one of its training wheels slowly turning and pointed up at the sky. A man rushed to the child and dropped to his knees. As he pushed rhythmically on the child's small frame, the scene began to twist and melt away, revealing a shimmering, spinning vortex, like the open mouth of a serpent, seemingly comprised of fragmented prismatic light, and stretching out for what seemed like an eternity. The child-size shadow stepped into the serpent's mouth, and the scene dissolved to black.

As though opening a new set of eyes, the blackness opened to the interior of my old room in Panda's old house. A younger version of me sat on the bare mattress, slouched against the wall, staring back at me. I opened my mouth to speak, but no words came out, and as my mind raced to comprehend the scene, the boy on the mattress reached out to touch me. The room became dim, then bright again, but the scene was altered. The room was full of people. Where there had been a mattress, there was now a couch with the younger version of me sitting on it and still staring back at me. Sound cut in and out, as though played through speakers poorly wired. "This can't be real. I remember this," I said.

The people to either side leaned into my peripheral vision, craning their necks to glare up at me with shining eyes. The temperature of the room fell, permeating the skin of my back and neck. The boy on the couch fixed his eyes dead on mine and asked, "Who are you?"

I remembered the scene like it had happened yesterday. "I asked the same thing."

He reached out for me again, and the scene dissolved to white-noise static around his outstretched hand. A wash of grey-green colored the ground around the teenage version of me, now lying on his side at Simon's feet. I glanced around the densely populated cemetery. "It's not real," I said.

The winded boy on the ground echoed my words in a gasp, "It's not real?"

As the cemetery blurred in and out, my attention remained fixed on the boy.

"You're not real?" he asked.

"You can see me?" I managed, unsure if or how to respond.

"Yes, I can see you," he said, "Who are you?"

I brought my hand up to my face, feeling the grown-out facial hair and the long hair hanging to below my shoulders. *I'm him.* I looked all around trying to find the right words before the words were plucked from memory. "I'm your friend."

The graveyard grew dim, as the rows of people slowly dissolved to white noise, like a failing broadcast signal, double-exposed figures, fading one to the next, to the tall figure in the back, outlined with a haze of blond hair. All was enveloped by blackness, and silence. From the black, a blinding white light bled from an opening, a doorway. I approached the light as my vision adjusted to it. Beyond the doorway, a disheveled version of me lay squirming over broken glass and red-smeared tile. I looked on as he reached a hand out for the blood-smeared sink and struggled to his feet. Gripped tight in his other hand was a crumpled note, the note from Michael.

"Sorry," I said, recalling the word from Michael's message and how much it had hurt.

"Who are you? Are you me?" he slurred, his eyes seemingly gaining and losing focus as he staggered toward me.

I stepped back, away from the doorway, back into the darkness, and the light was gone.

My eyes reopened to a blurred rush of color. Pressure and pain surged through my body. I gasped for air, straightening up trying to push out against the space in front of me for more room to breathe. My heart began to pound fast and hard in my chest and in my ears over the sound of a blaring horn. I took several deep breaths and turned away from the blazing light, raising my arm to shield my eyes. The interior of the RV pulsed into focus, and I relaxed my arm off the horn. Reaching back behind the passenger seat, I fumbled for the lid of the cooler and retrieved a bottle from inside. I tipped the bottle with a shaking hand, pouring the lukewarm water over my dried lips, swallowing, sputtering, coughing, and gagging. I pulled at the door handle, pushing it all the way open with my

INFINITY

foot, and stumbled from the seat to the ground. On my knees in the dirt, I flailed my arm free from the thick, grey-fur-covered coat, slipped out of it, and made my way to the shade on the other side of the RV. After a couple minutes, I opened the side door to vent some of the heat, took another bottle of water from the cooler, and slouched back down in the dirt. I sat for a long while, trying to make sense of what had happened.

Once convinced that it was over and that I was okay, I climbed back into the driver's seat and turned the key. I pulled out of the parking lot and away from the lake, leaving not only my friend, but a part of myself behind.

CHAPTER 98

Fragmented

On my way to nowhere, I stopped at a gas station on the outskirts of town, refilled the tank of the RV, and replenished my supplies from the neighboring stores. I found a bookstore in town with a surprisingly large educational section and took my time browsing through the science/physics section.

One of the browsed books was an introduction to holography, which had been included in the bibliography of one of my other books as the source for basic holographic principles. The first chapter was about the creation of a hologram. *A laser is split into two beams, one directed at the recording medium and the other directed toward the object intended as the subject of the hologram. The laser light, reflected off the object, interferes with the laser light at the surface of the recording medium. When light is applied to the recorded hologram, the interference pattern captured at its surface diffracts the light and recreates the same light field that was produced by the original process, resulting in a virtual image of the object. Light from the object is captured at every point on the recording medium. If the hologram is shattered, every fragment will still contain the whole image.*

The word holography is derived from the Greek words, "holos," meaning, "whole," and, "grafe," meaning, "writing," or "drawing."

INFINITY

It was the last part of the first paragraph that had caught my attention in the bookstore. "... *every fragment will still contain the whole image.*"

Panda used to say that everything happens for a reason, no matter how small or insignificant an event may seem at the time, that it plays its part in the shaping of all events that follow. I had repeated the mantra, *everything happens for a reason*, for months after he died, and again after burying Arthur, but the reason for either event was never made clear, other than death being a part of life, a part that most of us have no control over.

While packing the acquired supplies into large plastic tubs in the back of the RV, I realized that I had absently purchased a bag of dry dog food for Arthur. I had found myself talking to him while driving, for minutes at a time before realizing, remembering that he was gone. Without him there, I was left with only my sketchbooks and journals to keep me company and time to dwell over the memories recorded within.

I read about the road trip with Christine, wondering if *before he dies* had become *after he died*, and if so, how her life must have changed. I had loved Christine and had often thought about the reasons we had not tried to keep in touch. The absence of telephone and permanent address aside, the fact was, neither of us would be the same people we had been. While shared memories would remain beautiful in our minds, reality would slowly degrade, replacing the characters played in memory with the updated version, making happy memories somehow impossible or synthetic.

The Christine in my memory was my friend, the owner of a gallery, and someone who appreciated the beauty and wonder in everything from simple conversation to paint arranged on a canvas. She was a kind, loving, beautiful person, filled with hope and optimism. I would never want to replace her with the inevitable update, the grieving daughter, unable to laugh or smile, and unable to portray her former self in my memories. I would not want to replace myself in her memories with a similarly degraded version, capable only of a single empathetic expression, complete with sympathetic head tilting and strained conversation about how she was holding up.

Like with painting, an artist makes the decision to stop at a certain point. It is at this point where the process has reached what he or she defines to be the peak of the bell curve, any less and it is unfinished, any more and he or she runs the risk of ruining the painting. Leonardo da Vinci said that, "Art is never finished, only abandoned."

Possibly to honor Christine's suggestion, or perhaps as a further exercise in self-reflection, I had begun the process of rewriting my journals. As I wrote, I thought of what the light beings had said, that my story would serve as the catalyst for another, who would dissolve time, blend duality, and bring us all closer.

Each day, I spent my time reading, making notes, writing, and rewriting, sitting at one of the red-star locations on the map. At night, I dreamed of old friends and listened to the echoes of conversation with the light beings, *A fragment of the whole, that contains the whole.*

In my notes, I wrote, perhaps consciousness is the original image, and that matter is the recording medium for the hologram. God created man in his/their own image; we are the hologram created by the image of God or consciousness, and we each not only contain the whole image of God, but are made of it. We are each, a fragment of the whole that contains the whole.

Observation of the wave collapses the wave into a particle; by conscious observation, matter is created from light, a dream manifested into reality. The subjects of the dream are unaware of the dream itself and are left questioning the nature and meaning of existence, and the motive of its creator. Not all subjects of the dream believe in the existence of a creator; some believe that the universe was created at the Big Bang, approximately 13.8 billion years ago, and all material in the universe began at a single point, the source. Perhaps, these are two different perspectives of the same theory.

INFINITY

The consciousness exists beyond time and matter, everything that can or will ever be, exists as a possibility, as infinite potential. Every possible outcome is predetermined, like the parallel destinies of Schrödinger's cat.

Perhaps, the Big Bang was the result of the consciousness becoming self-aware, the first collapse of energy, manifesting the beginnings of the universe, an expanding exercise in self-reflection, an attempt to experience itself subjectively; the God hologram being shattered into countless fragments, each one containing the whole image, and each given the task, or gift of self-reflection.

Everything happens for a reason, and perhaps the reason for life, is contrast. Without contrast, life would be indistinguishable. If all light were removed from a black-and-white image, it would result in a pure black image; conversely, if all shadow were removed, the result would be a pure white image. It is the contrast between light and shadow that reveals shape and form within the image. Life is the delineation of possibility, the contrast necessary to appreciate the shape and form, the God hologram fragmented to allow for subjective self-reflection, and appreciation for the beauty of the dream.

CHAPTER 99

Chrysalis

I arrived back in the city less than a month ago; the book is almost finished, and I have pared down my possessions to what I can fit into the olive-drab kit bag. I sold Harvey back to the dealer and took temporary residence in a hostel. A week ago, I pulled my savings from the bank, kept only what I need to outlast me, and dropped the rest at the feet of a cross-legged homeless boy who reminded me of someone I once knew.

This morning, I made a fire under the bridge that had once been my home and cooked up the last of my food, before adding my wallet to the flames. Like with painting, an artist makes the decision to stop at a certain point. It is at this point where the process has reached what he or she defines to be the peak of the bell curve, any less and it is unfinished, any more and he or she runs the risk of ruining the painting, of destroying its beauty and meaning.

I have only one more page of my book to write, which I will duplicate and keep in my pocket for the rest of my life.

CHAPTER 100

Epilogue

To whoever finds me and subsequently this note. I was seven years old the first time I died. I was twenty-seven years old at the time I wrote this note. Taped to the back of this page is the key to a post office box, located at the address written below. Inside the mailbox, you will find a collection of four books entitled "Infinity." These books contain the story of my life.

I apologize for giving away the ending, but as with every complete biography, the end is always the same. Life begins with birth and ends with death. I lived my life on the periphery of death, a ghost in transition, limbo, or purgatory. I hope to be reunited with all the friends I have lost in the place that will serve as the final destination for us all.

The story that I leave behind is not a story that was mine to write, but mine to read, to live, and learn. I present my life to you as an un-deciphered message, the catalyst for something greater. Death is not the end. I have been beyond death, and it is only a new beginning.

If you are reading anything but a hand-written copy of this book, then you were not the person that found it, but you may be the person that was meant to read it.

"Energy cannot be created or destroyed; it can only be changed from one form to another." - Albert Einstein

THE END